"SOUND … AND I WILL COME."

The Prince knew that he should ignore the sign, and flee the courtyard of this castle of evil while there was still time. Yet he could not stop himself from reaching up and ringing the bell. It gave off a most terrifying clanging that bounced from wall to wall, and the changeling horse cried out, "You shouldn't have *done* that!"

"What will happen?" gasped the Prince.

The first thing that happened was that a great black crack appeared down the whole length of the tower, and out of it billowed rusty-red smoke. It filled the court and turned the sky and the moon the color of blood, and it smelled of hot metal and burning oil.

The second thing that happened was that the tower split in half, and out of the middle a glittering, huge, terrible thing uncoiled itself. It was unmistakably the Dragon of Brass. . . .

TANITH LEE in DAW editions:

THE BIRTHGRAVE
VAZKOR, SON OF VAZKOR
QUEST FOR THE WHITE WITCH
DON'T BITE THE SUN
DRINKING SAPPHIRE WINE
THE STORM LORD
ANACKIRE
NIGHT'S MASTER
DEATH'S MASTER
DELUSION'S MASTER
DARK CASTLE, WHITE HORSE
VOLKHAVAAR
ELECTRIC FOREST
SABELLA
KILL THE DEAD
DAY BY NIGHT
LYCANTHIA
CYRION
SUNG IN SHADOW
THE SILVER METAL LOVER
RED AS BLOOD
TAMASTARA
THE GORGON
DAYS OF GRASS

Dark Castle, White Horse

Tanith Lee

DAW BOOKS, INC.
DONALD A. WOLLHEIM, PUBLISHER

1633 Broadway, New York, NY 10019

A DAW Book by arrangement with Macmillan Publishers Ltd.

Cover art by Ken W. Kelly.

DAW Collectors Book No. 665

First DAW Printing, March 1986

1 2 3 4 5 6 7 8 9

PRINTED IN U. S. A.

The Castle of Dark

Contents

PART ONE

1

Lilune: Dusk

Half an hour before, the sun had set, and the iron bell had rung in the bell-tower. Now, the girl who only got up at dusk, walked into the Hall of the Castle.

She was slight, but not tall. Her dark hair was so long it fell over her body like a sooty mantle. Eventually it reached the floor and spread out there, so that it swept up the dust behind her as she walked. She was extremely pale; though her eyes were very green.

Entering the huge Hall with its towering columns, the girl went to a window and looked out into the gloaming. She glanced at the evening star, a blazing drop in the west, then straight downward into the courtyard below.

One of the two old women was drawing up water from the well. The bucket creaked. The old woman sang crazily to herself in her crack-pot voice. The girl watched her. A black pigeon preened itself on the well-head.

The girl whispered something to the pigeon thirty feet below her. The pigeon stopped preening and seemed to be listening. The girl whispered again, her green eyes wide. It was a Calling she was trying on the pigeon, although she was supposed to be ignorant of such spells. The two old women locked the doors of the cellars where they practised their own witchery, but the girl was sharp-witted and sharp-eared. Many a midnight she had crept close and eavesdropped. She had a right to know, didn't she? She was sixteen, and tired of her strange shadowy lonely life. She whispered. The pigeon, with a clap of wings, suddenly bolted up into the evening sky. The girl shrank back so the old woman shouldn't see her, as the pigeon alighted in the window embrasure. The pigeon strutted and stared at the girl inquiringly. The girl was pleased with herself.

Below in the courtyard, the old woman shrilled suspiciously:

"Lilune? Lilune, my lamby. Is that you, my little owl?"

Lilune scowled and kept silent. The pigeon, released, flew away.

Then the other old woman spoke from among the columns of the Hall. She sounded just like the first old woman. They both looked the same, too; skinny, ancient, a-flap with tattered garments and tangled grey ringlets.

"Lilune, come at once and sup your drink before it loses its properties."

Lilune didn't like the drink on which she breakfasted. There were odd ingredients in it, which turned it black with a head of creamy foam. Sometimes the old women grated leaves on the surface, or flower petals, to tempt her.

"I'm not thirsty," said Lilune.

"But the lamb must have her drink, or she won't grow to be healthy and wise," clucked the second old woman.

"It won't be any use to me being healthy or wise," snapped Lilune. She wondered if this old woman had guessed she had Called the pigeon. Lilune decided to throw a fit of temper to distract her. "I want to go out!" she yelled. "Why can't I go out?"

"Later, little owl," soothed the crone. "When the moon rises. Then we'll go down to the lake and you shall look at the pebbles there, and the empty houses. But you must take your moonshade, for it's a full moon tonight."

Lilune clenched her fists in a real and desolate anger.

This was all she had ever known: the looming black Castle, the black woods that stretched away from it to the south and east, the swampy western marshes and the northern lake with its ruins, winter-frozen, or burning under a hot summer moon. And always these two old women hovering. Without ever having known anything else, Lilune nevertheless felt she was being cheated of something.

The second old woman plucked at Lilune's sleeve.

"Come and have your drinky, sweetheart. There's candied rose-leaves in it tonight."

Lilune suffered herself to be led to the table. It was pointless to resist. After all, she had Called the pigeon and the old women had not found out. She glanced at the hag's terrible, loving, mad face. Perhaps, Lilune abruptly thought, the Calling might be used to summon . . . other things?

2

Lir: The Harp

Lir came up the track into the village just as the moon was coming over the hills. It was a late summer moon, round and pale smoky gold. It coloured the tall grain in the fields, and the thatched cots. It coloured Lir's hair, which in any case was much of the moon's colour, and the light bronze box he carried on his back.

As Lir turned on to the village street, dogs, catching the footfall of a stranger, began barking. Almost immediately, four or five men were out on the street, eyeing him.

"What's your business?" one said to him.

"To pass through. Or to seek a night's lodging," said Lir. The men in the street reacted to his voice, for the voice of Lir had music in it.

"There's lodging," said a man. "What payment?"

"Whatever you require," said Lir.

"A day's work with us in the fields."

"If you wish," said Lir, easily.

The men laughed. Somebody said: "But what's that you carry on your back?"

"Only my harp."

The men laughed again and came to draw Lir into their midst.

"A minstrel, a song-maker. Come, no field-work for you. Shelter, a place to sleep, all you can eat. And the price is your songs."

"You may not care for my songs," said Lir modestly.

But the men only clapped him on the shoulder. They

took him up the street to the cut-stone house where the village's most important family lived.

Soon the doors stood open and the big room was crammed with men and women. They had roused their children from sleep and brought them, and the babies. The very old were brought, the sick, if they could manage it. For who did not know, even in these remote lands far north of the cities, the power of a song-maker?

They gave Lir a cup of ale, but he would take nothing else yet. It was his habit to play before he ate. He undid the bronze box and lifted out the harp. There was scarcely a sound in all the crowded room. They watched as he tuned the harp. It was made of a light blond wood, polished by use. The sound-box had a plate of brown bone, the pegs were bronze. The strings glinted like silver hair combed taut on the frame.

Presently, Lir began to make a song for the people in the cut-stone house, and the harp woke and came alive in his hands.

Lir never chose a song out of himself, the harp would choose it. Somehow, the thin bright notes of the harp would find the song, and when the moment was ripe, Lir would begin to sing it. Now, when the moment came, his voice rose effortless and sure. Sometimes it would be an old song, one he had learned from the wandering harpers he had heard as a child, or met with later on his own wanderings. Sometimes a new song, which created itself as it was sung. Sometimes it was a little of both. And sometimes, even Lir was uncertain, singing it, of the song's exact meaning. Yet always the song was the right one, for the harp made it.

Lir was a true harper. From the earliest, probably it had been so. Sooner than he could walk, he had sung. No doubt he sang nonsense then, but yet it was noticed. He was born one of many, the seventh son, and there were daughters too. Gladly, his parents apprenticed him to a roaming minstrel who was laid up through the winter in their village with a sore leg. And later, when a rich cousin died and money was available, they sent Lir off to learn in the Song-Makers' School in the town. The school taught many things: the arts of rhyming and shaping, of tricks and cunning and showmanship, for fingers and tongue alike. It taught etiquette, and how to flatter, and how to make it seem each verse you sang was fresh, devised only for him you sang it for that hour. From this school, and others like it, a minstrel might go and get himself a place at some castle court, even at some lord's house in a city. At sixteen, Lir with his beautiful voice, his skill and all the school had taught him, was fair set for such a place. He could have had pride and fame and wealth, but it was not to be.

One summer night, a minstrel came to the town.

It was a night when the moon was large and lasting, and a night-market was being held in the town square. By the sheep-pens and between the stalls and along the avenues where the red torches were stuck on poles, the minstrel strode. He was a wild-haired man with wild eyes. On his cloak were serpents of yellow thread, and on his back a box of yellow ivory. Any minstrel was generally popular. He would bring news, stories, good cheer, and welcome dreams to combat harsh reality. Perhaps his harping would ease the sick and the sad. Still, this was a town with a school of minstrels in it. Minstrels were a commonplace here. Yet the people stared at this one.

At the centre of the market place, he sat down cross-legged on a bale of straw. Opening his ivory box, he took out a harp, and set it in the crook of his arm. But he didn't play. He only sat, looking about him. Finally a girl cried from the market crowd: "Come, man. Let's have a tune we can dance to."

Then the minstrel cried back: "It isn't my night for dancing tunes, my girl. Nevertheless, this harp of mine is eager. I will tell you what. About my neck is a yellow gem. Let any man come up here and make a song with this harp of mine, and whoever pleases me the best, he shall have the gem."

This was new: a minstrel who paid others to do his business. But the jewel he had pulled from his neck looked to be a rare one. Pretty soon a lout came over and took the harp, and struck up a discordant jig. There was much laughter and abuse. Next, another man approached, with more talent. Several of the young men from the Minstrels' School were close at hand, walking about through the market. Eventually, one of these moved to take the harp. He played well, as if at a lord's feast. When he was done, he gazed at the minstrel with the gem-stone, to see if he had won it. But the man grinned and sent him away with a "Good enough, but not good enough for me."

After that, the young men of the school came thick and fast, vying with each other, joking and calling the wild-eyed minstrel an oaf when he dismissed them. "Doubtless this wanderer would play us all into Hell," they said. "Probably the Dark One himself, Hell's Prince, invites this old chap in to harp for him, after his supper of bats' brains."

"And maybe he does at that," said Wild-Eye, and the serpents rippled on his cloak. But the yellow jewel never left his grip.

A deal of music was made, all of it excellent now, and the crowd in the market-place was enjoying itself. The moon burned high and the torches burned low. Still, the yellow jewel had not changed hands.

For some while, Lir had been standing at the edge of the crowd, watching. The show entertained him, and strangely troubled him, too. He felt a wrongness. Certainly, he had no intentions of adding his own efforts to the contest. Those he considered superior to himself had failed with the exacting minstrel. Besides, Lir had a girl with him, a pretty girl, and summer nights are short.

It was just as Lir was getting ready to turn away that the minstrel called out to him.

"You, the fair-haired boy. You've been staring long enough. Now let us hear what *you* can do."

Lir felt the blood come up in his face, but he said: "It's not my night for harping either, sir. I'll sit the game out, with you."

The minstrel shook his head. He said: "Don't disappoint the harp. She chose you, not I."

Then a thing happened which was discussed at some length afterwards. For the harp was leaning by the minstrel's knee, and he never touched it that anyone saw, but it gave off a fierce twanging moan.

Lir discovered he had left his girl and was strolling across to the straw bale where the minstrel sat.

Lir had already learned to be sure of his trade in public, for the school taught that, too. In any case, with song or harp, he had never been shy. But he accepted the minstrel's harp with some caution. It seemed made entirely of bone; Lir had never handled the like of it. However, leaning on the bale, he prepared to tune the harp. The minstrel touched his shoulder. "No need," said the minstrel. "Only play."

"What will you have then?" Lir asked.

"Not what I will have, but what the harp will give."

Lir shrugged. He had a mind to sing one of the songs the school had introduced him to, a ballad of clever gibberish, to make the crowd laugh. But when his fingers met the strings, a vast fall of notes spilled from them, like water drops. He had not planned them, could not better them. And with a curious trembling of the heart, Lir let Wild-Eye's harp lead him. The song which rose was one he did not know, nor could he form it again, after. But it was very fine. It burst from him as leaves burst from the trees in spring, as marvellous and as natural. The music carried him away as if it had loaned him wings.

When the last chord died, only silence was left, and the moon overhead, like a visible white piece of the silence.

Lir realized the minstrel was attempting to retrieve his harp. The minstrel coaxed him, softly. "Leave go, she isn't yours. You must fashion a harp of your own. I will tell you how. Do you know the shrine at the cross-roads, half a mile from the town? I'll meet you there at midnight."

Lir was dazed, but he had the wit, or lack of it, to frown and ask: "Why?"

"Meet me, and see."

Then the minstrel had leapt off the bale. He bellowed about him in the big fluid voice only a trained singer could muster: "And now I will award the prize."

And striding to a member of the Minstrels' School who had played earlier, Wild-Eye hung the yellow gem about his neck.

The people in the square were astonished. They jeered. Even the fellow who had the prize was taken aback. Nobody there could blind himself to the fact that Lir had proved himself the prince of harpers. Lir should have had the prize.

Only Lir didn't care. He knew, with a giddy sort of drunken bewilderment, that the prize was not the jewel.

An hour later, standing at the cross-roads under the wooden shrine with the saint-statue in it, Lir began to wonder if he had gone mad. The moon was sinking over the roofs of the distant town. Just now it was poised behind the watch tower. Under that tower the pretty girl and Lir had parted company, and not in the most friendly manner. Lir thought of this and called himself a fool. Besides, did he need to be told how to construct a harp? Didn't he know? And were there not, anyway, sufficient harps already being made in the town for the young men at the school to pick from? Fool indeed. Then Wild-Eye appeared at the roadside, apparently from nowhere.

There was no traffic about so late, though the gates of the town had remained open for the market. The minstrel approached the shrine. He bowed to the saint, and put his finger to the saint's wooden foot, then licked the finger for luck.

"Well," said Lir impatiently. "Did you summon me here to make an ass of me?"

"No, but I will tell you how to be an ass, if you wish," said Wild-Eye. "Complete your days at your rhymers' school, then seek a place at some lord's court. Harp him for dinner and harp him to his bed. Praise his plain fat daughters for their beauty and his idiot sons for their sagacity. Coin phrases concerning the noble valour of his forefathers, who were land-thieves, pirates and cowardly back-stabbers. And when he throws you a purse of gold, catch it in your mouth as his hounds catch the meat he throws them."

Lir said noncommittally, "I don't deny there's truth in what you say. To be a court minstrel is to do all that. And worse, perhaps."

"Well," said Wild-Eye, "I think it a canny profession for those suited to it. But you are meant for another."

"Because your harp would let me play her?"

"Because all the gods, the old gods and the young, have made you a minstrel. Now I will instruct you in the fashioning of a harp. You will memorise what I say, and if you act on it, then you will have powers indeed. After that, you can select your own destiny. I shan't be near to see if you are wise or an ass."

Then Wild-Eye began to gabble. It was all in verse, the easier to be remembered, possibly, though maybe it was merely his jest. The gabbling was quite awful. The wild eyes rolled in their sockets, the hands clawed and gesticulated, the minstrel jerked from foot to foot as if he were possessed, or suffering a fit. Distracted, amused and unnerved, Lir never reckoned to recall a word. But he recalled every one of them, and some were terrible. He had guessed at once it was not simply a harp he would be making, but an instrument of magic.

When Wild-Eye concluded, Lir drew a breath and said carefully:

"Not for me, I think. It sounds dangerous, not to say unlawful. And I may botch the job."

The minstrel answered that with a string of foul words, yet without violence, more like a man spitting to clear his throat. Then he said, "Brother my brother, you may do it or not, as you please. But I warn you of this: If you do not, though you become the richest dog in the courts of the lords, your soul will ache like a rotten tooth."

Lir looked down at his feet, searching for a reply.

When he looked up again, the minstrel was twenty long strides away along the track. The serpents on his cloak thrashed as if they were alive, and the ivory harpbox shone in the last of the moon.

Lir trudged back to town feeling stupid and confused.

The next morning there was a mild uproar. The yellow gem the minstrel had awarded had turned into a shrivelled acorn in the night.

For seven days, Lir pretended nothing had changed. He received instruction at the Song-Makers' School; he put it into practice. He ate his meals. He slept. He patched up the quarrel with the girl and they kept their trysts in the dark green meadows where the poppies flamed black under the moon. But through the seven days Lir would catch himself chanting beneath his breath, the tumble of verses which had to do with the fashioning of a harp. And the school began to seem very shallow to him, almost unreal. Even his fellow students became unreal. Even his girl. He tried to reason with himself, to see his future as he always had seen it. He was lucky, and should be grateful. He would not cast this life from him like a handful of dust. He reminded himself of his parents and the hopes of glory they had pinned on him.

On the seventh night, he dreamed of roving the unknown countryside with nothing but the clothes he stood up in and one light burden on his back. And when he woke, he cursed himself for the sense of relief and freedom he had known in the dream.

On the eighth day he was useless. Nothing he was told would stay in his head.

That evening, the young man who had had the fortune to be awarded the shrivelled acorn, began to pursue Lir about the streets. The young man declared there had been a prize given after all, some secret thing Lir had got, which he had better hand over. At length, a fight ensued.

The morning of the ninth day, the Master of the Song-Makers' School had both youths before him, and berated them. Were they such numb-skulls, the Master ranted, that they would break their valuable harper's fingers on each other's jaw? They were a disgrace to the school.

The winner of the acorn hung his head and shut his black eyes. But Lir said painfully through a split lip: "Well, sir, I'm off anyway."

"Off where?" roared the Master.

But Lir could not say. Only that he was going.

Worse was the interview with his family. His father thundered, his mother and sisters sobbed, the new baby howled. His brothers would not speak to him, only *about* him, in his hearing. Such sacks of money spent on him, and now all he meant to be was a wandering rhymer, the offal of the road.

A day after that, Lir returned to the town. By noon he was working hard. Not in the Song-Makers' School, however. He had hired himself to a carpenter's yard.

He made the harp, one stage at a time, slowly.

It could only be done that way in any event. The wooden frame came of timber he selected, cut and carved for himself. He said what was needful to the wood as he worked it. He felt self-conscious, muttering the magics. Presently the thought of what he did came home to him, and his hair bristled instead. Once, the knife slipped and slashed his hand. Lir wondered at how he misused his hands—a harper usually did not risk them. But the wound healed clean. The strings of the harp, silky-wiry dried strands of gut, he stole. It seemed they must be stolen for the spell, but he performed a service for the man he would steal from before he did it—the spell did not prohibit that. The bronze pegs he forged while working two months in a bronze-smiths in a village in the hills.

The plate of bone for the sound-box was another matter altogether.

Thirteen miles from the town, there was a stretch of rank wood, and in the wood, an ancient burial mound where an elder people had buried their chiefs and lords. Wild-Eye must have known about the mound. At least, Lir hoped it was this mound Wild-Eye had had in mind. The doggerel verse was not specific. It merely stated that the bone used for the sound-box must once have belonged to a man.

Lir went to the place at the dark of the moon. Set in the middle of the lawless wood, the mound rose up like a sinister black shoulder. It had been opened and rifled of all its treasure hundreds of years earlier, but occasionally, there were still stories of someone excavating a tiny bit of gold or silver among the caved-in soil and the scattered bones.

Lir dug his way in at the fallen doorway. The smell of bruised vegetable earth was strong within. Lir put down his spade, struck a light and lit the small rush-candle he had brought. The narrow entrance widened into a big uneven hole of a chamber. As for bones, there was some choice. Lir let the candle swing over them. Which would be best? The doggerel didn't stipulate. Suddenly Lir felt acutely ashamed. These dead had been robbed of everything and now he was going to steal a part of their actual selves. Perhaps it didn't bother them, after so long. Or perhaps they would be glad to be out in the world again?

A shattered skull lay in the dirt. Of all the portions of a man, surely it would be most fitting for his brain's case to survive, the cup of intellect and reason. He thought of Wild-Eye's harp, all bone: which portions had gone to form *that*? He picked up the largest fragment of the skull and left the mound.

The skull fragment burnished up to a clear brown sheen like walnut. Shaped, filed and fitted with rivets to the sound-box, it was a pleasant thing to touch, smoother than the denser smoothness of the wooden frame. It was not that Lir would ever have dreaded the touch of dead bone. That superstition was not his. But the thought came to him that the skull liked its modern employment.

The harp was put together through an amber night when the harvest moon shone into the joiner's shed where currently he worked and had use of the floor for a sleeping couch. When it was finished, the moon had set and dawn was not much more than an hour away.

Lir sat with his back to the wall, looking at the harp.

What now?

For a lunatic enterprise, he had abandoned his career and prospects, and the good-will of family and friends. All this while—five months—he had gone from this trade to that. He had acquired smatterings of carpentry, joinery, smithing. His labour for various masters done, he had crouched nocturnally over the sections of the harp, chanting to them, like a witch at her cauldron. It seemed preposterous. Yet Lir had done it. He understood, though how he understood was something of a mystery to him, that he had done only what he must.

Finally, in the close dark between moon and sun, he took the harp to him.

He did not try for melody or pattern, They occurred. In a moment he was fingering an air he had heard but once, in his childhood. He had forgotten it, till now. Not that he sensed any particular magic in the shed with him. But he sensed a familiarity and ease, as if he had played this harp a thousand times before. He felt happiness, too. And rightness. The tune remade itself and became another.

When he stopped playing, light was showing under the door. He went out and saw the dawn star burning through a gooseberry sky. The joiner's wife was in the yard, pail in hand, on her way to milk the joiner's cow.

"You," she said, "you should be in the Song-Makers' School, not working as my man's dogsbody. Half the night I've had the earache, that terrible I couldn't sleep, and like knives when I came out into the yard. But I heard you at your music and I listened. I put my bad ear to the door, and the ache melted away out of me. It's a true harper you are, my boy."

"Thanks for that," said Lir. "Maybe I needed a sign, and you've given it me."

The joiner paid Lir for his service, seeing that Lir had been a good worker and was leaving them. Using these coins, Lir bargained for a bronze box for the harp, a week later at a fair. By then, he was already travelling, wandering.

When the nights grew colder and the rains of autumn began to blow with the red leaves along the hills, Lir briefly faltered inside himself. For he knew he was crazy, abroad with not two coins to rattle together and tomorrow's bed and meal uncertain. Still, even when the frost sheathed the grasses, and he glimpsed two grey lions slinking through them after prey; even when the pools froze and the villages were remote from each other and the snow came, even then Lir wandered with his harp across the land. He did not turn back to his former life. Did not think to. Never would.

3

Lilune: The Lake-Shore

They walked sedately along the shore beside the lake, Lilune and the two hags. The two hags would not let her run; they liked to keep an eye on her at all times. They had made her bring the moonshade, a big, heavily-fringed black umbrella. Lilune held the moonshade over her head, keeping off the rays of the round golden moon.

The enormous lake spread like a polished shield, utterly motionless. Frogs croaked from the marshes, the forest trees periodically rasped their dry leaves together. There was no other sound. Lilune kicked a pebble down the shore, but the turf blunted its noise. Lilune stopped and picked up another pebble. She threw it furiously into the lake. The lake's perfect surface broke for a single instant, two or three rings floated away, and then the water re-formed flawlessly.

"In a book yesterday," Lilune announced, "I read of a fearful beast that lived at the bottom of a bottomless lake and rose up at full moon to devour men."

"You musn't read books unless we see them beforehand," said the old woman on Lilune's left. "I'm sure we have never seen that one. Where did you find it? You must give it to Granny as soon as we're home."

The old woman on Lilune's right said:

"It makes no sense to say that something lives at the bottom of a bottomless lake. If it's bottomless, there is no bottom to be lived on."

Tears of rage stood in Lilune's eyes. She blinked them away.

"I want to look at the empty houses," said Lilune.

The houses stood about a mile east of the Castle, on the long downward slope between the woods and the lake. The houses were built of timber and the same sort of stone the Castle itself was built of. Some had little windows of the cloudy, greenish glass which the Castle also had, here and there, instead of shutters. The houses had courtyards, and herb gardens run to seed. Beyond them, around the curve of the lake, were huddles of smaller dwellings, cots whose wattle roofs and whose doors had fallen in. By a well with black mud in it was a tree struck by lightning. It had been struck seven times in all, once on Lilune's birthnight.

Although the old women didn't argue with Lilune about going to the houses, and even encouraged her to visit them when she was extra sullen, Lilune knew they didn't really care for the spot.

"Why are the houses empty?" Lilune asked as the first group of walls came in sight. It was a stock question. The answer was a stock answer.

"The people have gone away."

"Why?"

"They were afraid of this place."

"Why didn't we go away?"

"We were not afraid."

"Why not?"

"Because we are brave."

Lilune couldn't remember ever having seen any people except the two old women. She had never even seen herself, because there were no mirrors in the Castle. Once, when she had noticed the old women became reflected in some of the darker furniture as they passed, Lilune had attempted to catch her own reflection, but all she ever glimpsed was a blurred, pale-ish wisp.

Lilune did not know if she had ever had a mother or father. She did not know that a mother and a father were necessary to birth. But then, she didn't know much about anything. Occasionally, she managed to steal a book from the room full of books, parchments, spiders' webs, mould, which was called the Library and was kept locked, as the cellars were. Ivy grew everywhere over the walls of the keep, and right up to the Library window. Lilune had learned to climb through the ivy to the window and get in. But the shutters wouldn't always open, and she hated the climb, was afraid of falling, being hurt.

Lilune entered the courtyard of the first empty house. She examined the paving, the rather small house door. She asked a new question.

"Why are we brave?"

The old women reacted predictably. One said:

"The moon is too strong. It's time we went back."

Lilune lifted the moonshade high in the air and threw it across the courtyard. As her head went up, she saw a face staring at her from a crack of window just above the door.

Lilune was surprised. It was the only really surprising thing that had ever happened to her. So she simply stood transfixed and gaping. The old women had no difficulty in recognising her emotion and following her gaze to the window.

Immediately the two of them rushed at Lilune. Each seized one of her arms.

"Come away," they rasped. "Away at once!"

The face vanished from the window.

Lilune struggled grimly. The old women clung to her and hissed.

Suddenly, the man whose face had been at the window came out of the doorway into the courtyard.

He was ragged and dirty. Lilune judged he looked nearly as elderly as the old women. He was the first human stranger Lilune had ever seen. He smiled ingratiatingly at them, as if the bizarre struggling in which they were engaged was quite normal.

"I don't mean any harm," said the man. "Only a poor pedlar—" he tapped a pack he had dragged out with him. "Lost my way in the forest. Looking for a town hereabouts. Thought I'd rest up the night, go on tomorrow—

meant no harm." Then a crafty smile replaced the sickly one. "Like a bit of ribbon? A bracelet? See—" He bent to the pack and jerked it. He pulled out a string of beads and shook them at Lilune. "For you, missy? Or some garnets to set off your white skin." Red glass danced between his hands.

Lilune was fascinated. Only the biting grip of the talons in her arms kept her from going nearer to the pedlar.

The hags sizzled. From Lilune's left, one said:

"Don't you know you shouldn't be here, pedlar?"

The other hag said:

"Swindler that you are, you don't deserve death by the lake."

"Eh?" asked the pedlar. He was nervous again.

"Death," said the old women together.

Something apparently made the man turn his head then. He glanced away from them, through the courtyard gate, up the slope to the distant loom of the Castle.

"I never saw that," said the pedlar. "The moon wasn't up. But it's just an old castle by a lake . . . . ."

"Run," said the old women, "*run for your life*!"

"Now see here," said the pedlar, backing away. His eyes met Lilune's. He surprised her again, for his look was full of terrified entreaty. Without warning he grabbed up his pack and fled with it, dodging by them, out of the yard.

"Fool!" spat the second old woman.

Lilune shuddered. She felt afraid, and didn't know why. The pedlar had been afraid too. He had seemed to plead for her help.

The old women, taking advantage of Lilune's confusion, started to haul her from the courtyard and along the shore. Already, the fleeing pedlar was out of sight.

"What frightened him?" Lilune gasped.

"Ssh. Don't trouble about it."

Lilune desperately craned her neck, trying to see the man. She didn't have any name she could shout after him, so could not shout. Something about the Castle had horrified him. And what the hags said.

"What did you mean?" Lilune said. "When you told the man he would die and he must run away?"

The hags, of course, did not answer.

They hurried her along the shore. They had forgotten to retrieve the moonshade.

Lilune began to cry. Her hands were cold. In the midst of crying, she thought: Perhaps I Called the man here, with the spell. I Called the pigeon, I wanted to Call some other—thing—and the man arrived. Lilune seemed to have become two people. One wept in miserable panic, the other thought very coolly: Yes, I *did* Call him by the spell. I'm certain. When I'm alone I must Call again. Call and Call. See who comes next time.

4

Lir: Northward

A rover, sheltering rarely in the same place for more than one or two nights at a time, Lir had acquired a knack of sleep like a cat's—swift, light, alert. Also his sleep was crowded by dreams, the vivid wild dreams of a poet. Occasionally, these dreams would wake him.

Seated in the cut-stone house in the village, he had bought a meal and a bed with his songs. The villagers were generous and appreciative. After he had eaten, he had sung on for them, till at length he had played himself out. He and the harp could give no more. Intuitively, his audience had sensed as much, and made no protest, though they gazed at the harp wistfully. Still haunted by the music he had poured out for them, they stole from the house and wandered homewards in the light of the setting moon. When they were gone, a pallet was brought for Lir to a broad nook at one side of the room. He lay down and slipped into the shallow, multi-coloured waters of his sleep.

The dream which woke him was this. He heard the harp humming, as if there were some tremor in the stone floor which disturbed it. And gazing at the harp in the dream, he saw it no longer had strings. Instead, the frame held a picture.

The picture was mainly blackness, shadow. Yet through the shadows blundered a small human figure. Despite its smallness, for the picture was altogether not large, Lir got the impression that the running figure was spurred by fear. It was that of a man, neither young nor very old, clutching some kind of bundle in his arms. His white face was continually looking back over his shoulder. If anything pursued, however, Lir could not make out.

Lir woke, not alarmed, but tense.

In the dark, the room was virtually invisible. But he could just glimpse the harp standing beside his head inside the nook, as if familiarity gave him a power of sight the darkness would not. Lir sat up and took the harp. He touched the strings. He had been on the minstrels' road a year, or thereabouts. During that year, he had periodically dreamed things connected with the harp. These things generally turned out to have something to do with reality. For example, he had once dreamed the harp was strung with silver, and the next day a man had given him silver coins when Lir played. Another time he dreamed flames were flickering through the frame of the harp where the strings should be, and then cold ashes. Three mornings later, he came to a village which had been gutted in a fire. There seemed no particular reason why the harp should anticipate certain events and not others, nor why the presentation should be so fanciful, extravagant even. Nor could Lir have put such premonitions to any use, had he considered the matter with usefulness in mind. In fact, he did not consider it. It was merely another facet of the harp and its magic, magic to which he felt oddly accustomed, with which he had been peculiarly at peace, from the first.

However, this picture in the harp seemed more than normally obscure and definitely foreboding. Lir was not exactly troubled by it, but it had dashed sleep from him. After a minute he rose and went to the door of the cutstone house, unbolted it, and stepped outside.

It was cool, the sky umber. Dawn was approaching from a distance, as yet just a feel of waiting in the air.

Something said into Lir's ear: *This way*.

The voice—which was not a voice, more like a popping in the ear or the drum sound of blood after running—did not startle Lir. It was too intimate, too soft. He turned to see who had spoken, but there was no one; the street was empty. He hadn't really expected to see anyone. Then it came again.

This way. This way.

"Which way is that?" Lir asked, also softly, but aloud.

This way.

Lir discovered himself turning slowly leftwards, from the east to the north . . .

Here, said the voice which was not a voice.

"Why?" Lir asked. He did not speak now, only thought the question.

This way, said the voice.

"Northwards?"

This way, said the voice, fading, dissolving.

Lir looked into the north. There was nothing special there he could recognise. Close to the village was a carpet of wheat, further off, some trees, then low hills, sky.

Magic, the elemental thing he himself had come to possess through the harp, had made him sensitive to another's magic. For a second. It was passed now.

The dawn star was rising. Somewhere a dog whined in its yard. The sun walked up the slope under the eastern fields.

Lir blinked, and in the blink had a sudden mental image of the sun's golden face, cruel and snarling and maned by rays. And with an arrow shot through its forehead.

Breakfast was apples and ale and a chunk of bread. The master of the cut-stone house gave Lir a bag of coins, a good fee, for the village was prosperous. Someone asked if Lir would be back in the spring. The cows would be calving then, and sweet music would aid them. Lir had had similar requests before. Once he had sat in a reeking barn and harped a little horse into the world. If the music had helped or not he could not be sure, though the farmer was sure and gave him a gold piece. Perhaps the harp had true magic even for the beasts. Certainly, seeing the foal struggle valiantly out into the light, Lir had been moved, but the harp had played a summoning rhythmic dance that had nothing to do with his awe.

"Maybe," said Lir now, "in the spring I'll be this way."

"And where till then?" another prompted him.

"What lies north of here?" Lir inquired. Then he was curious, for he had not planned to go north, but east, following the late Summer across the land.

The villagers told him as much as they had ever learned. Few villages lay northward, no towns they had heard of. Four or five days' journey north there were forests. The forests were dense and the land poor land for farming. Lir caught a slight unease behind the talk. The villagers seemed to express, without words, that instinctive attraction to the north, that magnetic pull which sorcerously draws men, birds and animals, just as it draws the iron lodestones of ships: the attraction which makes men wary, avoiding the north as the lodestone cannot. In the old songs it was always in the north that the dragons were, and the monsters without name.

An hour after, travelling along the eastern track which led from the village, Lir saw flock after flock of birds flying northward. He saw no birds fly in any other direction. Later, a cart crossed the track. A man with a load of timber hopefully invited Lir to ride with him to the next village in exchange for a song. Lir seldom refused those who begged his music. He got into the cart, which was going north.

Sure enough, in five days, Lir came to the edge of the forests.

For three days there hadn't been a village, or, at least, none he had sighted. On the fourth day he spotted a farm-house, but it was derelict. A roofless, hollow watch tower overlooked a slender river. The stone bridge across the river had a toll-gate, but it was down, and no one about. The other side of the river, poppies burned like fires. Presently, the outposts of the huge woods appeared, the tall trees heavy with foliage, their trunks girded by ivy.

Waking on the fifth morning, Lir saw a lion in its mellow summer coat, strolling in and out of a woodland shadow a quarter of a mile down the slope. But the lion was sleek with food, no positive danger. Once the leaves fell, its pelt would change through honey to grey, and it would pad southwards and eastwards, and become a threat to man and his herds. Even so it was an old and tried lore of the woodsman that no lion attacked a sleeping or static thing, not beast or man. Who knew the manners of lions would be safe enough, whatever the season.

The forest was moist, green, dark. It was not chilled by shade, it filtered the sun inwards and imprisoned it. It was hot, and noisy with miniature life. Here and there streams bubbled through clefts of moss and fern and boulder. There was food in plenty, as there had been all over the land, rogue apple trees, damson and pear, fish in the waters, roots and vines that gave evidence of cultivation, now abandoned, but haphazardly productive. Not bad farming land at all, merely thick-treed.

Lir had been prepared to meet with outlaws, robbers, various flotsam cast up from the towns. A minstrel, with his poverty and talent, usually went unharmed. Lir had harped in a robbers' camp before now. In this tumble of country, though, he realized he was meeting no one, and once in the forest, he could see no mark of men.

Of the spell which had Called him, if it were a spell, he had had no reminders. To begin with, he had accepted the omens and his own curiosity, and continued north in amused obedience to them. Now, the terrain itself put a spell on him, for it was beautiful. He sat long hours in drowned glades, beneath the umbra of trees, unlocking music from the harp. When the woods absorbed him, he came to feel he was the only human in the whole of the landscape: enchanted, disoriented, free.

Then, on the the seventh night of the journey, he dreamed of the running man again.

The forest altered by night, became another forest, sticky with shadows, creaking and rustling, dank and coal-coloured. In the dream, the man ran through the forest, and it was the forest which was so black and which formed the shadows of the dream. The man clutched his bundle, as before, but soon he threw it down—in order, presumably, to go faster. This dream-picture was life-size and not framed by the harp. Lir could see the man in detail. He looked like a pedlar, middle-aged, sly, dirty. Terrified.

Shortly the man ran right across Lir's vision and away. Then Lir saw something moving through the blackness after the pedlar, although he couldn't see what it was. It was as if a portion of the shadow itself had come alive and was flowing forward, wriggling, twisting, flowing again. . . . And then it seemed to unravel. The pedlar's discarded pack lay on the ground, and the—thing, whatever it was or was not—spilled over the pack and gradually evaporated like a sort of smoke. Lir perceived that the dark forest of the dream was lightening. When he opened his eyes, the real forest was also paling with sunrise.

This time, Lir *was* troubled. Dream or not, he experienced a violent relief that the pedlar had apparently escaped. And relief was followed by a distinct reluctance to go on with his exploratory careless quest. He had not actually intended to search out the source of what he had heard Calling that morning in the village. Or had he? Had he been persuaded, unknowing, to search for it?

Lir got to his feet, and as he did so, became aware of a long hollow sloping away down through the trees on his left. And from the hollow's farthest end a bluish fume was rising. Not mist. It was the unmistakable smoke of cooking fires; he could faintly smell them over the forest's tangled scents. Strange he had not been conscious of the nearness of his fellow men the night before. Now he felt impelled to go towards them, and simultaneously, he hesitated. It was almost too perfect. Five days without a trace of humanity and suddenly, in his moment of doubt, cooking smoke. As if this place had been deliberately chosen and put here to allay the doubts of travellers. But there was nothing sinister in the smoke. And sunlight soaked through the forest.

Ten minutes later, Lir, having descended via the hollow, emerged in a clearing. A glistening stream threaded it, a scatter of thatched dwellings rose on the bank. Some woman was toasting wheat cakes on a hot griddle, unseen but making the air glorious. A cow was lowing to be milked from a shed.

It was the kind of village Lir had thought to find all along the way, and had not. There was nothing remotely eerie about it.

As he stood there, a couple of girls came from a house with pots to fill at the stream. They didn't seem afraid when they saw Lir, only shy. One went for her father, who in turn fetched the chief-man of the village.

The villagers were very friendly to Lir. He was used to hospitality in part-payment for songs, but the odd thing was that these people—who invited him into the chief-man's house, gave him food, admired him—never mentioned the harp he carried. As if they had never seen a travelling harper. Or if they had, had forgotten.

Then the chief-man said to Lir—not a question; a statement: "You will be going north."

Lir set down his cup.

"Is there no other way to go in this land?"

"Well, for sure there are villages round about. But the town is northward."

"The town?"

"The old town by the lake. A wonderful place, they say."

"Who says?"

"Well, I've never been there, young man. But in my grandfather's time, there was much coming and going."

The chief-man fell to describing the delights of the lake-side town, the taverns, the exotic market, the tower with its iron bell. Lir suspected the man was lying about the town, and could not fathom why he should. Perhaps it was all the pride they had here, to boast of the splendours of the north. And still no one mentioned the harp. The chief-man's wife packed food for Lir's journey onwards through the forest, but they wanted no recompense. Except, it appeared, his promise that he would visit the town.

And they obviously desired that he should press on northwards as soon as he might. Lir concluded he must oblige them. Even if he changed his mind a mile down the track and retreated south once he was from their view.

The sun was well up when he stepped out of the house. One of the shy village girls stood gazing at him. He said to her: "And have you never gone to the town?"

"Oh, no!" she cried, as if such an idea were blasphemous. "But it's a fine one. And the Castle there is the finest of all—"

Something nonsensical happened then.

The chief-man burst forward and struck the girl. She didn't cry, but shrank down and cowered. Everyone else stared at Lir. Their faces were rigid with a dreadful misgiving.

"The girl's stupid," said the chief-man to Lir. "There's no Castle in the old town. Just the bell-tower, a few crumbling walls."

Lir crossed over to the girl and lifted her to her feet. She wouldn't look at him, hanging her head as if in shame. Clearly she had sinned in some way by mentioning the Castle. Lir recognised he could not rectify the matter, other than by demonstrating his lack of offence or alarm. He thanked them therefore for their care of him, and assured them he would make for the lake and the town, saying there that the village had sent him. This appeared to please them extremely. He went off into the forest lit by the glint of their smiles. Somehow he guessed, without turning, that their smiles went out the instant his back was to them.

He had determined to turn south. But his curiosity had, if anything, grown more intense. Was there a town? If so, a thriving town, as recounted, or a ruin? What did the mysterious Castle contain? A ghost? Were there witches there? Lir really didn't believe any of this. Magic had come to him so naturally and cleanly through the harp, he had never properly credited any other sort. Graves and grim uncanny situations had always left him unmoved. As for the dream, its troubling effect had dissolved in the morning forest's green sunshine. It seemed unimportant.

He went on, northwards.

The forest began to break up that day, then reformed. This secondary woodland was different. Older. The thick-boled, arching trees massed close together. The sun was practically invisible, yet still it was not cool. The undergrowth steamed and vapours curled through the trunks. Even at noon these were matted, sombre woods; at night so black Lir built a fire between two stones only that he might see about himself. At dawn, the light drizzled in unwillingly. Birds sang, but they had a mournful isolated sound.

A witch wood, Lir thought wryly. He breakfasted on some of the food the chief-man's wife had packed for him.

He hadn't been walking for half an hour when he came across a bundle lying in the undergrowth. It was a pedlar's pack. No doubt of it.

Lir stopped. He knelt and turned the pack over. One of the straps was broken. A necklace of red glass spilled from the pack, like a trickle of blood.

The dream was true: the relay of an occurrence in the near past. Here the pedlar had discarded the pack and escaped his danger. Here the formless apparition had flowed, and faded in the pallor of sunrise. Lir was not afraid, but he was unnerved. It would be easy to retreat, go southward on a changed route to avoid the village. In a day or less he would be back in the younger acres of the forest, next in the warm meadows.

Lir sat down, his shoulders against the trunk of one of the towering trees. He took the harp from the bronze box and brushed his fingers over the strings.

The music which came was sad and meandering. It slid itself into an antique ballad. Lir sang, his voice piercing the sulky shade and quiet as the sun could or would not. But the song brought no cheer. It told of a maiden weaving black thread on a shadow-loom, bound to the loom by the iron chains about her waist.

When the song was done, Lir sat immobile under the tree. A bird in the woods made a noise like drops of water constantly dripping on a frozen pool, drip after drip.

Lir could sense it now, the voice like the throb of his pulse, threading his veins, almost unheard:

This way. . . . This way. . . .

I have a choice, he told himself. I think I have a choice. But if I turn aside, I'll always wonder what I turned aside from.

He got up and strode towards the spell.

5

Lilune: The Cellar Door

Lilune crept down the stairway, shielding the flickering rush-candle with one hand. The stair, which led to the cellars, was of shiny stone caked with rat and bat droppings. Lilune could hear the bats rustling overhead and the rats twittering in their crannies, agitated by her feeble light. But her sharp ears were primed for other noises and her sharp eyes for traps.

It was midnight, and a while ago Lilune had noticed the two old women were no longer watching her. The moon was waning, and on such nights they frequently sought the cellars of the Castle, where they practised their magics. Whenever she could, Lilune spied on these activities, but sometimes the old women put too many precautionary safeguards in the way. Tonight they had apparently not bothered. Of course, Lilune was still supposed to be sick. Lilune had helped foster this idea. She had been ill, ever since she had seen the man in the ruin and he had run away. The two hags had fussed, bringing clammy cloths full of herbs to lay on her head, making occult passes over her. The shutters had been closed against the moonlight. Perhaps because of that, occasionally Lilune had imagined she was in the woods. Several nights elapsed.

The odd thing was that although she had been feverish, although she had sobbed, shivered and tossed, a part of Lilune's brain had stayed lucid. All the time she was awake, that part had gone on and on working, repeating the spell of Calling. It was as if her life depended on the spell, and her entire will had concentrated on that single effort, leaving the rest of her body to fend for itself. Only when she slept, hot short night-sleeps, did her will relax. She had no dreams. She never dreamed.

Tonight, however, was the ninth since the pedlar had run away. Tonight Lilune was completely better. But she had pretended to be listless and weak. The old women had let her have two books. Lilune said she just wanted to stay in bed and read them. In fact, she thought the books were extraordinarily boring—"safe" books the hags had selected for her. One was about the rearing and feeding of sheep. The second was a treatise on the ancestry of the common worm. As soon as the hags were gone, Lilune sprang from her bed.

At the foot of the stairway was the door which led into the cellars. Lilune checked. A cobweb was stretched across the bottom stair. Obviously, it was spelled. If she broke it, the hags would be warned of her approach. Lilune stepped over the cobweb, and pressed her ear to the thinnest door panel.

"Are you sure?" one hag was asking the other.

"I am. Poor lamby. She had hardly the strength to raise the goblet to her lips. She won't follow us."

"Maybe," said the first hag. "But sometimes it comes to me, perhaps she is fooling us. Or trying to. She's cunning, the nasty darling. And the pedlar—what are we to make of that? No one has ventured here in ten years."

"Do you think she's learned the spell of Calling?"

"Too possibly."

"What shall we do?"

A long pause. Lilune held her breath.

Then one of the hags behind the cellar door said: "I do believe she's got too clever for us. We shall have to chain her. Just as they warned us. Chain her with iron and bind her later with spells."

"Oh!" wailed the other hag. "Poor lamby. Poor tricksy precious."

Lilune, her eyes wide, trembling with terror, backed up the steps away from the cellar door—*and broke the cobweb*.

6

Lir: The Castle

The woods swept up the land, then poured over. You could see quite a way from the crest of the hill. The trees ran on eastwards. Westwards, they blended into a gluey cauldron of marshes. Ahead, a dark blue lake under a dark blue sky shone like a sapphire. Along the lakeshore there were ruins, hovels and wooden houses, the raw outline of narrow streets just visible through overgrowth.

Between the forest and the lake-shore, on Lir's right hand, was a rocky upthrust, bare of trees. Perched on the rock was a Castle.

The sight of the Castle struck inside him like a solitary chord.

It was black. Even by day, black. Like a raven perched there on its rock. Contrary to the woods-village's story, it was not ruined. Built, in the manner of all castles, to be the palace-fortress-treasurehouse of its lords, it had lasted where the town had not. Its many towers crowded against the backdrop of trees and sky. Those towers looked as if they could never fall. Despite that, there was something about the Castle, an emptiness, a visual silence. And Lir knew quite well that the only thing left was to climb the rock and enter the Castle, if entry there was.

Nothing seemed to be Calling Lir now. Which was logical enough, for he had arrived.

It was noon when he reached the huge southern gateway of the Castle. Massive doors of timber—black timber—

blocked the gate. It looked impenetrable. But ivy was growing up one bastion of the gate, and across the doors. In the ivy was concealed a little porter's door, and Lir, going close, discovered it. When he touched the porter's door, it swung lankly. He went through into the bailey court.

On the west side were constructions of timber and stone, stables, a kitchen; all had evidently fallen into disuse. Various watch towers stabbed up from the walls, to which stairs led from the bailey, but the stairs were clothed by weeds. Weeds pushed through into the court. The bell-tower was set in the northern wall, near to a north gate that made the vast south gate into a dwarf. Lir could see a bell pendant in the open skull of the tower.

Built into the juncture of the north and east walls stood a square castle keep. It seemed to have been made of ivy, rather than stone.

In the blistering sun, the Castle sweated, a black-green sweat.

Nothing moved. There was no wind, even to comb the ivy.

Close by the south wall of the keep was a patch of turf. Three cypresses dominated it, branches linked like dancers' arms, among the rank grass. Between the cypresses, something, catching the sun, winked.

Lir went over. He parted the grasses. The cypress shadow pooled like ink, and from the middle of the ink there glared back at him an enormous brassy face.

It was an image of the sun, done like a man's head, but the head of a cruel madman in the midst of raging. Gilded rays spoked and writhed off from the face. Pointed teeth champed in the open mouth, and the eyes were holes that aped blindness. In the forehead of the sun-face was a wooden plaque, much scored and indented. The surface of the face had also been scored and scratched. Lir suddenly realised what the plaque was: a target. And he remembered then that he had mentally pictured a likeness of this object, that dawn when he first heard the Calling. The sun, with an arrow shot through its forehead.

He crossed the grass and went up the shallow steps to the keep's south door. He was slightly startled to find the door locked from within. It occurred to him that he had been reckoning the Castle was vacant. At least, humanly vacant. The Calling had surely begun here, but Lir guessed he had come to terms with the spell by thinking of it as something quite abstract and formless: not even a ghost, more a remnant of will-power left clinging to the walls, as the creeper clung to them.

And now he'd have to think again, because doors locked from within meant mortal occupancy. People lived here. People who feared the sun so much they hid from it, and shot arrows into its effigy.

Lir wondered about what went on at this moment inside the keep. No smoke rose up, no noises were audible.

A turret pointed from the corner where the keep joined the outer east wall. The turret was attached to a tower that stood inside the keep. It was about fifty feet above him, but mantled to its peak in ivy. As a child, he had scaled many trees that were taller.

He climbed off from the steps and up the tough skeins of ivy to the broad embrasure of a slim window. The casement was of cloudy glass. It was also open.

That he was entering as a thief would enter, uninvited, devious, did not distract Lir. Only later did the suspicious ease of his entry become unpleasantly obvious to him: its dishonest undertone, its hint of witchy enticement over which he had no control.

The interior of the turret was musty and gloomy. It was a particular gloom, a particular mustiness. Lir recognised it from the Minstrels' School, the dust and smell of books and parchments. The turret itself was bare, but led down by a short stairway into the upper chamber of the round tower. This was the library of the Castle. Or it had been. On the shelves, the old books, bound in vellum and leather, leaned on each other. But here and there moss was growing on their spines. Where parchments stood rolled in brown jars, spiders spun perpetually. The wide hearth was veiled by cobwebs. Lir, from habit, inspected a volume or two, but flakes of leather came off in his hands. He abandoned the library, went through its door, descended another stair into a lower room which was worse. Once, it might have been an armoury. No longer. A few pairs of rusty swords hung crossed on the wall. The odour of mould and dust was depressing. The door which would lead out into the keep was locked and key-less.

Lir returned to the library and tried the window. The shutters, bolted from within, gave grudgingly.

He could see immediately how the ivy, which had constantly re-woven itself over the window, had equally constantly been broken by someone who had climbed in on this side of the keep. Lir stared down the length of the tower. The creeper had been torn right the way to the courtyard. About three feet from the window was a length of soot-black ribbon embroidered with gold thread. The sort of ribbon a rich girl would tie about her waist.

Chancing the damaged ivy, Lir swung down it. He dropped off, light as a cat despite the harp-box, into the inner courtyard of the keep. The ribbon fluttered to the ground beside him. Something about it appealed to Lir: the evidence of an unknown girl living here who wore such finery. He wound it round his wrist, glancing about him.

The Hall of the Castle had its west wall in common with the west wall of the keep. One more tower loomed before it. The door of the Hall stood patently ajar.

The Hall was very ancient, very impressive.

Columns of granite upheld the roof. The floor was paved, with only one layer of dust, and with broom tracks to show it had been previously swept. A handful of withered rushes decorated it, weeks dead.

Windows let in light along the west wall. They looked over into the outer bailey, at the derelict bakery and a well. On the north wall of the Hall was hung a carpet of a beautiful dull red, but its tapestry scene had retreated into smudges. Under the carpet was a dais with a great wooden table. The table had been polished and gleamed vividly amid the filth. There was a single carved chair to go with it.

Lir had no inclination to sit in this chair. He seated himself in preference on the floor of the dais. He was hungry, and taking the last crust from the pack the chiefman's wife had given him, he ate it. He considered the well he had seen through the western windows in the bailey court. There was sweet water in the well, perhaps, and he could draw it up and drink. But the Hall was drowsy-hot. Glazed shafts of sun were already starting to come in at the western windows as the sun declined from the zenith. The shadows were soft, almost furry; they crouched beneath the columns like bears.

Lir took the harp from its box. He touched the strings. At once the whole of the Hall appeared to quiver, ripple like a disturbed pond.

Suddenly he was asleep and dreaming.

There was a girl, motionless in one of the shafts of sunlight—but it wasn't sunlight anymore, it was the glow of a harvest moon. The girl wore a dress of a weird tarnished bone-yellow silk that had been white twenty years ago, a dress that must be older than the girl herself. The under-sleeves of the dress were black linen embroidered with gold; they looked more recent, as did the black, gold-embroidered ribbon around the girl's extremely narrow waist. The girl's hair was black, too, and her brows. Her eyes were the sharp unlikely green of smashed window glass. She was so pale otherwise that these brows and eyes seemed to have been painted on her face, which itself might have been cut out of parchment.

"You're late," said the girl, in an imperious voice, to Lir. "You have no business to be so late."

"Did *you* witch me here then?" Lir asked lazily, half asleep even in the dream.

"Who else? And now you will take me from the Castle and I shall see the world."

"And what payment do I get for this service?" Lir asked interestedly.

With great condescension, the girl replied:

"I will pay you in trouble and terror."

Lir woke. The Hall, of course, was empty. But the sun-shafts had deepened and lengthened. He thought he had only dozed the space of three or four minutes. But apparently it had been the intense slumber of an hour, or more.

He stood, leaving the harp to lean against its box on the dais. He crossed to one of the windows and gazed down at the well in the bailey. Already the dream was receding. He wondered what it had portended, if it were true or false. The ribbon he had wound about his wrist had been in contact with the harp as he slept. Possibly it was a true dream. A warning.

A flock of pigeons was circling the afternoon sky. Sometimes it moved out towards the lake, then back again, widening the circle but never quite deserting the towers of the Castle. Lir considered whether the pigeons might be in some fashion attracted to the Castle, tethered to it, unable completely to get away. Next he considered whether he, like the pigeons, were also tethered. Despite the dream, the warning, he felt no urge to vacate the Castle. Instead, he was instinctively waiting for the sun to set and the emergence of the dayfearing inhabitants.

What will happen if I make off, after all?

He set his hands on the window-ledge. In another moment, he was descending by means of the useful ivy, into the bailey court. He paused by the well, decided against trying it, walked across the bailey, returning to the south gate through which he had entered.

A quarter of an hour later, Lir was striding down the rock away from the Castle. Half an hour later, he was climbing towards the upland forest.

Nothing howled after him. No supernatural leash tightened on his limbs, no barriers blocked his path. He found the whole thing abruptly funny, and laughed aloud as the woods closed round him.

An hour later, he became aware of an error, a mistake. Like a sleep-walker, waking in unfamiliar territory, Lir hesitated, striving to get his bearings. What was the matter? It was a question of weight—yes, that was it.

With a ghastly lurch of shock, Lir grasped what was wrong. He had done something which was preposterous. It was the act of a man who had lost his mind, or whose mind had been clouded by witchcraft. Certainly, he had stridden from the Castle free as air. But he had forgotten the harp, leaning on its box in the murky columned Hall.

The harp was a part of him. It was as if he had left his right hand, or a fragment of his soul behind him.

Lir ran between the trees. There was a sickness under his ribs. When he could no longer run, he staggered, and after a little while, began to run again.

Panic had got hold of him. He mistook his direction and doubled his journey and his anguish.

When he came out of the woods for the second time and saw the black Castle, raven-like on its rock between trees and lake, the sun was a golden blaze three fingers' span above the horizon. Lir plunged up the rock and through the porter's door in the south gate, and froze.

Even from the gate, he could see that now the entrance to the keep, formerly locked against him, stood wide. It was an hour to sunset, but *someone* was awake.

Lir glanced about. Nothing.

On impulse, he ignored the open door, sprinted frantically across the bailey and leapt again for the ivy, this time of the keep's west wall, and the hall windows that pierced it. He was fifteen feet above ground when the quavering, crooning voice immobilised him.

"Sweetheart, where are you going? Come down to Granny, bad lamby."

"Such hair," said one old woman to the second. "Like candlelight on fine gilding."

The second old woman snapped: "Hair's hair. And death is death. And cats climb walls. What are you after, catty?"

Lir said casually, "There was a village in the forest. They advised me to visit you."

The old women started. They were identical, two eldritch twins.

"Then the village is yet bound?" they asked each other.

Lir wasn't afraid of them, but they would have made anyone wary. And his heart still rattled from their voices which had arrested him half way up the wall. He had sprung down into the bailey and confronted them.

"You must go at once," said the old women in chorus. "Away!"

Lir didn't move. "Why?"

"Because there's evil by night."

Lir frowned. Experimenting, he said:

"A black vapour, which moves like a worm through the wood?"

The old women clutched each other, and hissed at him malevolently.

Lir was conscious that their resistance to his staying made him want to stay. And all the while, the ache went on inside him, the ache to get to the harp.

"I was here earlier and left something behind. Let me fetch it, and I'll be on my way."

"What thing?"

"I am a minstrel. It was my harp I left."

"A harper," they breathed. Even they responded to his trade. They muttered together. Finally, they permitted him to re-enter the keep and next the Hall, though they followed him, giving off crackling noises like burning fat.

The harp leaned where he had set it down.

Lir raised it, finding he was trembling and that gradually the trembling eased as he held the harp.

The two hags stared at him.

"Play!" one screeched.

"Play! A tune—"

"Didn't you tell me to go?" Lir inquired mildly. He wanted to question them about a black-haired girl, but guessed the sort of lunatic answer he'd get.

The women pleaded, jabbering: the sun wouldn't set for almost an hour, it was as safe as it would ever be. They'd watch out for him, create a spell to guard him. But he must play, just one song. He saw they were starved and the harp was food to them.

Lir skimmed a chord.

Immediately, he was aware of something flawed, something not right. The harp was replying to his fingers as it had always done, leading him, guiding him. Its magic enfolded him, he was borne away by it. But the magic was not as it had been. It was—

Lir attempted to reason. He attempted to lift his hand from the strings, but found he kept on playing. Through heavy-lidded eyes he peered about. The Hall was soaked in a muddy amber light, and he was floating on the currents of the light; his head reeled and his fingers darted on the strings, while the bit of skull on the sound-box groaned and hummed.

Oh, I understand, Lir thought dementedly. I'm not playing the harp myself. It's the Hall which is playing it through me, the Castle itself. The Castle is all will, directed at the magic of the harp, forming a different magic. This magic is a vat of dark beer and I'm drowning in it.

He noticed the two old women then. They had sunk down in a small heap on the dust. Their eyes were shut and their poor withered mouths gaped toothlessly.

Lir played on. He couldn't stop. He didn't care. He thought: I should be afraid of this. I should fight it. But he wasn't afraid and he did not fight. The music that spurled from the harp was turgid and endless. He yawned and his eyelids blindfolded him as they closed. The joints of his fingers cracked as they rushed about the harp.

It was the discordant clanging of an iron bell that roused him.

He was on his feet, but the harp was hanging in his hands and he was no longer playing. He put the harp on the floor, gingerly.

The Hall was bathed in a new colour—dusk. Lir walked to one of the windows. In the west, three hot clouds were all that remained of the sunset. The sky was turning bluer, and stars brightening. The bell boomed on. Lir asked himself who rang it, or if it was bewitched too, and rang of itself to mark the safe beginning of the night.

He watched the cool sky and breathed the cool breeze of evening, trying to clear his head.

The bell had stopped.

Five seconds after it had stopped, screaming replaced it.

Lir jumped aside from the window. The two old women lay motionless. No, the screaming was nothing of theirs. It came from beyond the Hall, away across the courtyard—and up in the air.

Lir raced through the Hall, down the steps, over the courtyard. He was heading for the tower that rose southwards of the Hall.

There was a door in the tower's base. Lir threw himself against it and it gave way. Just inside, a key hung on a hook. He grabbed the key and dashed up a stone stair. He realized all this, too, was connected with the muddy magic the Castle had doused him in, but there was no leisure to worry about it.

The screams had given way to moans.

He reached a dim landing. There was a door with a ring-handle that turned instantly in his clasp. The door, in any event, had a flimsy look. He was bewildered as to why he had been made to pick up the key.

Beyond the door was a murky area out of which the moaning had come. But the moaning had drifted into silence. Lir stood still, key in hand, as his eyes adjusted to the gloom.

The barest illumination was given by a slot of western window that held a slot of sky and one cold star. Enormous thick shutters had fallen back on either side. Beneath the window was a large, dark mound. A bed. A most bizarre bed.

Black curtains overhung it, but these had folded aside. The frame of the bed was wood, and soared up into a tall carved head-board. A head-board, actually, that was as tall as the bed was long.

On the bed, something stirred. There was a rustle, and then a highly ominous *clank*.

Lir blinked, and there formed before him a whitish blur of face that appeared to be disembodied and drifting. It was the face of the parchment girl.

"You're late," said the girl. "You have no business to be so late."

Fully conscious of the repetition, Lir responded with: "Did *you* witch me here then?"

"Who else? And now you will take me from the Castle and I shall see the world."

"And what payment do I get for this service?" Lir said carefully, as he had in the dream.

"Payment!" the girl cried. The clanking sound increased. "None. You must do it because I require it of you. Because I demand it!"

7

Lilune: Lir

She had retreated in fright up the cellar steps, severed the spelled cobweb—and the hags had rushed out upon her.

What followed was disagreeable.

Words had been shrilled, definitely magic. Something had smoothed itself across Lilune's mouth and nostrils, moist, scented. . . . That was all she remembered, till she woke, as always, on the bed, at the ringing of the bell.

Initially, she had simply been scandalised. Though the two old women had always thwarted her at every opportunity, she had never been attacked by them before. But presently she recalled the threat of bindings and chains. Just then the bell ceased and the shutters of the window and the drapes of the bed burst open, of their own accord, as they always did. Lilune sprang up in the bed—and iron jangled at her wrists and waist. Undeniably, she had been chained, as threatened. The irons stretched to vast bolts in the floor, with very little slack. She could stand upright on the bed and manage a couple of paces along it, but no more. She wrenched at the chains, and learned their implacable strength. And she began screaming.

She thought she screamed for hours. She stopped only because her throat pained her. After that she moaned in fury and alarm for what seemed many more hours. Then the door crashed wide.

The man who came through the door she could make out perfectly, for her night-vision was well developed. She had seen only two men, but this second man was so unlike the pedlar that she might have supposed him to belong to another species. She knew she had Called him, of course, as she had Called the pedlar. But he was a great improvement on the pedlar. She became arrogant at that, partly because she was nervous at her predicament.

The brief conversation which ensued astonished Lilune. She was used to seeing others, whether helping or hindering, as mere extensions of herself. This man, whose hair was the colour of the summer moon, was apparently a real person, just as she was.

There was a silence, broken by the racket of the chains.

"Who did this to you?" the young man said at last.

"The two old women."

"Why? Because you've taken up witching, too?"

Lilune laughed proudly. "I spelled *you*, didn't I?"

"Yes, I believe you did. But it's the Castle, as much as you. The Castle Called me. And now it wants me to do what you say, let you out into the world. I can feel the Castle wanting that, the wanting dripping down the walls of it, like its sweat."

Lilune shivered. The young man showed her the key he had brought.

"Is that for the chains?" she asked.

He came over. The key was for the chains.

Lilune flexed her wrists. "Well," she said, "let's get away."

The young man studied her.

"You're free. You can go where you please."

Lilune understood he meant she could go on her own. It frightened her. She had never been alone. She had never been more that a mile from the Castle, and always escorted.

"No," she cried, "you must go with me. I'll make you go with me."

"Can you?" he inquired. He seemed curious rather than intimidated.

She was somewhat fearful of him. Yet it was a new sort of fear. He interested her. And besides, he was her only hope. Here was the turning point in her life, and it turned upon his readiness to aid her, obey her.

"I can make you do whatever I say," she whispered.

"I don't think so," he said. "But I'll see you on your road. Perhaps I'm obliged to do that much."

She walked after him. At the door she glanced back with a grimace of insecurity and joy at leaving the room. They descended the stair, and went into the courtyard. She clutched his arm.

"The old women—"

"Charmed asleep, I think. No danger, at any rate."

"Oh, you're wrong. We must hurry."

"I have to get my harp from your Hall."

"No!" she shouted.

"Yes. I am a harper and the harp is my livelihood."

He strode away from her towards the Hall. Lilune hugged her own arms in hysterical impatience. The sky was indigo. The waning moon lay curled in the east. She ran through the keep, towards the south gate of the bailey, and hovered in the bailey gate, waiting for him.

He was her future.

8

Lir: Lilune

Lir had been slightly surprised that the girl was not wearing what she had worn in the dream. Presumably that garment had had to do with the waist ribbon. This was a gown of dull dark red, like the tapestry in the Hall, and at her waist was a thin gold chain. He could envisage the two old women dressing her like a doll in these antique fineries. When she moved about, he had become aware of her unnatural quantities of hair flooding the bed behind her.

He was sorry for her, but he didn't like her. The insane hags had locked her into chains, striving to keep her their property forever. He had to rescue her. And yet he couldn't shake off the knowledge that he didn't relish her company. No matter. The first village or town could foster her. Probably they had owed fealty to her Castle in former days. He pondered over what might have happened to her kindred. He did not interrogate her. It was scarcely the time for it.

In the Hall, he paused beside the heap of hags. He could see they were alive—and hear. Both snored. But the magic: the Castle was pulsing with it. It was becoming hard to breathe the intensity of the atmosphere. The desire to put much distance between himself and these sweating black stones, was growing by the minute.

He lifted the harp, replaced it in the box, and settled the box between his shoulders. The light burden soothed him, seeming to balance his own weight. He went out again, into the court. The girl had vanished. Then he saw her through the door of the keep. She was at the south gate.

Go, the Castle was soundlessly, insubstantially murmuring.

Was that all it was: the will of the Castle that she go free of it?

When he reached her, her teeth were chattering, if with excitement or distress he could not tell. But she smiled, a fierce, brave smile. Beyond the gate, the ground mist was rising.

"*Now—*" the girl said.

She sprang from the Castle gate and flew down the rock, and her hair flapped behind her like a raven's wing.

PART TWO

The Journey Through the Woods

They were unable to move any further.

It was due to the mist, which had risen like smoke from the dank, warm woods, and solidified to become an impenetrable night fog.

Not much showed through. Not the waning moon, not the stars, not even the sky. Each tree was visible at a distance of two feet. And choked by the wet odour of fog, Lir had missed a similar odour. A stench of decay and the dull throb of frogs checked him. He realized he was advancing blindly into the western marsh, and the girl with him. He retraced their steps painstakingly to a huge mossy cypress they had just passed. The girl's face was taut and angry.

"It's the old women," she spat furiously, "making spells to trap me."

They had been walking for an hour and a half before the fog closed their path, going southward into the forest. The girl had said little, but she had simmered. Her rescue, which to Lir was an unanticipated task, was to her an adventure beyond any adventure ever undertaken. She was out in the world. At first, she dived on ahead of Lir. But she had no inkling of direction. Presently, she dropped back and strode beside him. Then, unused to prolonged walking, she began to slacken. Finally she stopped.

"I must rest," she said. "You will wait for me."

Lir complied, frankly amused by her domineering tone.

She sat on the ground and said broodingly: "My hair catches on all the roots."

"You should have cut your hair," Lir said.

She looked appalled, almost terrified.

"No—I musn't ever cut my hair."

"Plait it, then," he said.

But she didn't know how to. She ordered him to do it.

Lir could plait a woman's hair perfectly well. A succession of sisters and girl friends had left him familiar with many routines of feminine life. So he took up the black waterfall and worked on it. Somehow though, he didn't like touching it. It was soft hair, and fine enough: beautiful, probably miraculous, for it must be near six feet in length. But it was very electric; it crackled between his fingers. When it was plaited, he wound it up into a complex knot and tied the long black and gold waist-ribbon about it. It was lucky for her he'd kept the ribbon. Even so, the extraordinary bundle of hair dangled below her shoulders.

"That will do," said Lilune.

He couldn't be bothered to teach her good manners. He was intending to leave her at the village in the woods, the village that had been eager for him to visit her town and her "ruined" Castle.

The mist was already thicker, filling the gaps in the trees. They went on, but inside fifteen minutes the woods had clotted into a pale-black void. Ten minutes more, and the sounds of the marsh had warned Lir to retreat to the foot of the cypress. He had to admit he was unsure of their precise position. Perhaps they were actually into the marsh, for the noises of it seemed all around. And was the fog a spell? His memory of the two old women disinclined him to believe this. Yet maybe they had hidden powers, despite their obvious senility and craziness. If he credited the power of the Castle, why not theirs?

"What are you going to do?" Lilune demanded.

"There's little I can do. We'd be wise to stay where we are with the marsh in the vicinity."

"No, that's not good enough," she cried.

"Well, you're the witch," he said. "You dispel the fog, and we'll move on."

Lilune scowled. Her magic was limited to that one spell she had overheard at the cellar door. She had never thought she would need any others.

"I can't," she said reluctantly.

"That's settled then. Be patient. I doubt if those elderly ladies can track us down in this weather, even *if* they conjured it up." Without considering, he added, "We'll sit tight till morning. The sun will burn off the fog as it usually does."

"The sun," Lilune said. "Morning."

He suddenly recalled the gilded sun-target in the bailey court, the quiet of the noon Castle, his supposition that the inhabitants feared daylight. Even though the hags had been active in the hour before sunset, the girl had not. He looked at the girl. She didn't appear upset, only pensive.

"I'd forgotten about that," she said.

"The sun? Why are you afraid of it?"

"I'm not. I've never seen it, only in pictures. It's like a lion's head, snarling, with a great mane of fire. Isn't it?"

"Something like that."

"I don't think I'm afraid of it," she said.

"You musn't be," he said. He felt very sorry for her again.

She was apprehensive. She was out in the world, now, and there would be no shuttered room or closed bed available when the sun rose. What would happen? But this young man would see it was all right. She would make him see it was. Somehow.

He asked her name then, and gave her his in exchange. It was a friendly gesture on his part. But they didn't speak again. They wrapped his cloak about them to keep out the fog, and sat, leaning against the cypress tree. Not the first time for Lir, such tree-leaning, with a girl under his cloak. But the circumstances had been different, and the outcome. For they had never been girls like this one.

Lir slept. Lilune watched wide-eyed. She was not bored. She was in the world.

* * *

She had not reckoned it possible she could sleep or even drowse, but she had. When she woke, she was aware at once there was an alteration. The woods had a new flavour, a new smell. Birds rustled and chimed high overhead. Then the colour began.

It started with a greyness in the mist, a greyness in the stems of the trees that grew visible through the mist. Slowly, foliage and blades of grass flickered out of nothing. Water drops glinted like opals. The mist was thinning, sinking into the ground or fading into the air. And suddenly a rose-pink fire flared up behind the trees and turned the wood pink, a pink that reddened into gold.

Lilune got to her feet. She walked away from the cypress, into a mossy avenue between the trunks. She flung her arms around herself, as if trying to contain herself against this onslaught. Everything was burnished and gilded now, and out of the gilding fresh colours were seeping, as if layer after layer of colour were rising to the surface. And the wood became golden green.

Lilune started to cry. Then she started to dance. It was a stately, courtly dance the two hags had taught her. It wasn't right, but it would have to do.

Lir woke up and saw the girl dancing with a stilted grace under the trees. She caught sight of him, and still dancing, she cried: "Look! Look!" Not meaning that he should look at her, but at the morning forest. He was touched by her wonder. Obviously, she truly never had seen a dawn before in her life. Why was that faintly chilling?

"I told you there was nothing to be afraid of," he said.

But less than an hour after, he learned he had been wrong.

There was no breakfast, but she seemed not to care. Lir himself was used enough to travelling on an empty stomach. They set off southward, skirting away from the marsh that could now be glimpsed as dull glimmerings beyond the western slopes. With no mist to hinder them the going was easy. It promised to be another hot day, and he hoped to make decent headway before the girl had to rest. She wasn't accustomed to the sun or the day's heat, but the roof of leaves would act as a sunshade, and it was cool as yet.

She had fallen into step a couple of paces behind him, lagging because she was so taken up with staring at everything about her.

Presently he glanced over his shoulder and thought she was in tears. But she said, venomously, as if it were his fault: "My eyes are watering."

"Let me see." But she wouldn't.

"It's the sunlight," she grated, pushing him from her.

It was. She kept on doggedly, scraping at her streaming eyes with her hands, her sleeves, straggles of her hair. But then her eyelids swelled and began to seem bruised. She could barely see, and sat on the ground and beat her fists on it.

"You're not used to the sun. Let me bind your eyes," Lir said.

"We must get further away from the old women," she shouted at him. "How can I walk properly if you bind my eyes?"

"I'll lead you."

"No. You'll carry me."

"All right." Certainly, she wouldn't weigh much. The heaviest thing about her would be her hair. Very gently, he bound her eyes with a strip of her underskirt which she tore off and gave him. He picked her up and she weighed even less than he had allowed for. It was like carrying a life-size ragdoll.

They went on another hour like this. And although she was not heavy, the extra burden began to tire him. But when he set her down she said immediately, "There's no time to rest here." And when he paid no attention, she screamed: "We must get on!"

It was not temper, but defiance. Not only her eyes were affected now. Her mouth was dry and cracked, and her startlingly white skin was flushed and peeling. It occurred to Lir that, in spite of her tantrums, she was courageous. She was ranting, but not whining.

"I think," Lir said quietly, "that we'd best find or invent some sort of shelter. You can't survive this mild sun under the trees. Noon, or open ground—"

"I *can* survive it," she said.

But she could not, and knew it. He left her in the shade, and went off in desperation, unhopefully searching for an area of deeper shade.

When he returned, she was huddled to the earth. Her eyelids had glued together and the skin of her hands looked boiled.

"There's a hollow tree," he said. He lifted her with extreme caution. Through her garments, her flesh burned him.

"I'm frightened," she whimpered, no longer brave.

The hollow tree wasn't very far. He put her inside it, and with his woodsman's knife cut armfuls of brush to seal the entrance. He hung his cloak across. Then he sat down against the cloak-hung opening, his body one final barrier between her and the morning. Of course, he could tell it was more than simply being unused to sunlight that was affecting her. No wonder she, or one of her mysterious kindred, had shot arrows into an image of the sun.

He opened the harp box he had placed on the grass. He wanted the harp to play coolness for her, and darkness. He wanted the harp to mix day into night.

The harp seemed reluctant, resisting him. It was like rowing against a strong current. The witchcraft in the Castle had damaged the ability of the harp in some subtle wretched way—or was it he, the minstrel, who had been flawed?

Then the tide turned under his hands. Music flowed like water. Lir felt his tensions leaving him. The harp carried him, as it always had, and the song was a midnight river. . . .

When the music had passed, he sat unmoving before the hollow tree. Muffled by the trunk and the brush and the cloak, he heard the girl say: "It's all right now."

"Good."

Lir set himself unwillingly to doze the day away. Fog or no fog, they would have to travel by night.

It had taken Lir roughly a day and a half to reach the Castle from the village in the forest. With the girl, and forced to proceed in darkness, he calculated the journey could take twice as long. Additionally, there was the problem of sheltering her from sunrise to set. He considered leaving her, making on alone, procuring a pony—had there been ponies in the village?—or other form of transport, coming back for her. But he did not rate her intelligence particularly highly. She might wander from the tree. Lose herself. And though he had seen neither boar nor lions this far north in the forest, that was no guarantee they were absent. And she surely could not deal with lions, this daft girl.

Despite her earlier cries, he didn't think the old women would pursue her. He almost wished they would. Though he doubted he could let her be borne off again to their chains.

In the late afternoon, he allowed himself a brief exploring trip and filled his water-flask at a rock pool. He brought some berries and edible leaves to the hollow tree.

He had heard no further sound from inside the trunk, beyond that first statement of assurance. The sun went out and the gloaming gathered, and with no warning Lilune sprang from among the smashing brush like a wild-cat. She looked better, her skin still reddened but whole, her eyes unswollen and clear. She stared round, accepted a drink from the flask, declining the berries and leaves.

"Eat something," he said. " We should try to cover a reasonable distance tonight."

"I never eat anything," said Lilune. "The old women made me a drink. It was black with a creamy head. They put petals on it."

Perturbed, Lir said bleakly: "The water will have to do then." He unhooked his cloak from the smashed brush. "Lilune," he said, "are all your kin-folk dead?"

"Kinfolk?" she asked blankly.

"Your father, mother," he elaborated.

"I have none. There are only the two old women."

"You mean your parents died when you were very young."

"I mean I have no parents. *Had* none."

Stupidly, the hair rose on his neck when she proclaimed this.

"Never mind," he said. "I expect there'll be some woman in the village glad enough to care for you."

She shrugged. Already, bathed in the intensifying dark, her skin was paler.

There was a mist, but no fog. Without travelling precisely at a gallop, their speed was fair. Periodically, they rested, but the girl's walking pace had improved. The thought of dawn nagged at Lir. Lilune gave the impression of having forgotten about the sun.

In the hour before dawn, they came on another hollow tree. Lir, grateful for this luck, called a halt. In any case, the girl was exhausted.

When he began to shore up the opening of the tree, Lilune told him, in her usual imperious manner, to wait.

"I must at least watch the beginning," she said.

When the glow and colour started to flood the woods, she peered from the tree, happy and excited. He found her tiresome, heart-breaking. Once the light had grown steady, and the woods green, he patched up the entrance to her refuge, and sat down again before it, resignedly, to wait.

There were no man-made tracks or paths in that part of the forest. Lir had plotted their southern direction purely by the position of the sunset, the moss on the trees' northern faces. Deliberately, too, he had let their way tend slightly to the west. He sensed, with the instinct of the wanderer, that this would be a shorter route between Castle and village. On their third night, he recognised a particular crippled tree he had noticed on his northern trek. His sense of short-cut had paid off. Lilune and he were a deal nearer the village than he would have believed possible.

And perversely, tonight, the girl flagged. She demanded to rest each hour, and for longer at every stop.

About the black second hour of the morning, they came on a thread of wrinkling, singing stream. Lir was positive this was an extension of the stream that had run by the village.

"A couple of hour's steady walking might see us there," he suggested to her. But she had sat down on a rock, absorbed by the stream, showing no intention of hurrying.

"I'm tired," she said.

"Well, I can carry you."

She blinked at him in cold disdain.

"I will tell you when I require it." More sensibly, she added, "Besides, I slow you when you carry me. I doubt if we'd gain much."

He permitted her five minutes by the stream. When he said she must walk on, she did so without protest.

They seemed to move quite fast thereafter, following the stream. But three hours later, the black sky changed to a pallid one, and the village was not in sight.

Lilune was afraid at the lightening sky. Her fear took her by surprise. There was so much to be aware of she could forget the sun by night. She was also confused, for the beauty of the dawn thrilled her, even as she dreaded the coming of the sun. She wanted to cry when the sky lightened, mainly with disappointment in her limitations.

She was vague as to why Lir was determined on reaching the village. But it must be for her benefit. In order that she might observe more strange, real people and things.

The trees were thinning even as the light broadened.

Lir checked. He pointed.

"There. Smoke. It's the village, about a mile off."

Lilune could not see the smoke. Her eyes were already smarting.

He untied his cloak from its lodge on the harp-box, and

wrapped it over her head and shoulders. Then he grasped her hand and pulled her along, half running.

The door of the chief-man's house opened. The chief-man himself stared out. When he glimpsed Lir, the man's face tightened.

"What do you want?"

Gone, evidently, was the friendliness of the former reception.

"I'm sorry to trouble you," Lir said, "but I have to ask your help."

"You should go north," the chief-man mumbled, with weird irrelevance.

"In fact I have been to the north, and visited the town you recommended."

The chief-man shrank. He looked frightened.

"Get off," he growled. "We've no more we can spare you. Get off!"

"Gladly. But I have a girl with me, and she's sick."

"What girl?"

"A girl from the north—"

The door would have slammed shut, but Lir caught it midway and thrust it aside again, sending the chief-man staggering. Lir was angry. He swore at the chief-man, who swore at him. Physical blows seemed likely, when all at once the man's expression melted into total submission. His gaze was on a point beyond Lir's shoulder.

Lir turned. He had left Lilune in the trees at the edge of the clearing, but she had abandoned their shade, crossed the narrow stream and come up the short track into the village. She was the most pitiful of figures, crouched in the cloak, softly moaning, near-blinded and weeping. The chief-man sank to his knees. "Lady," he said, "be honoured."

The alteration was startling, but not unreasonable. Lilune's folk would have ruled this land from the Castle, in earlier years.

"All right," Lir said, "you honour her. Now let her in."

"Welcome to my home," whispered the man.

Lir guided Lilune through the door. Other people had

appeared on the track outside. Their faces were white, abject. No one spoke.

Lilune drifted into the darkest corner of the room and knotted herself together with the shadow. A smaller chamber led off to the side. The chief-man went into it. Lir heard him muttering, and caught the words "she" and "the chest". A woman's voice announced itself in short breathy grunts. Just then, the chief-man's son thrust in through the outer door. He looked incredulous.

"She can't stay here—" he began shouting.

From the side-chamber the chief-man shouted back: "Hold your noise!"

The chief-man's wife slunk from the side-chamber. She cast at Lir one awful wavering glance, brimming with accusation and distress. Curtseying to Lilune's muffled, knotted shape, the woman said: "Lady, please to come with me."

Lilune got up and trailed the woman into the side-chamber. Lir brought up the rear.

The chamber was a windowless cupboard of a bedroom. It was littered with clothes, blankets and other items which had been thrown out of a big chest standing against the wall alongside the bed. It was the kind of chest most prosperous households would have, a fine ancient thing of black carved wood.

What added a singularly macabre quality to the scene was that everyone appeared to comprehend, wordlessly, just what was necessary. Lilune moved to the chest, and stepped over its rim and folded herself deeply inside it. The chief-man let the lid down to cover her. There was something else, too. As the tall, carved lid was shutting, Lir received a mental picture of Lilune's draped bed in the Castle: the tall, carved head-board. It occurred to him that the head-board had not been a head-board, but also a lid, which Lilune had drawn down to cover herself, or which had magically drawn itself down, as she slept through the hours of day-light.

The man and his wife came from the side-chamber, drawing a thick curtain across the doorway.

"Thank you," Lir said. He said it lamely. He felt thanks had no role to play in what went on here. The chief-man and his woman stared at him. The son stared at him. And behind the son, the outer door was filling with villagers who also stared. "What is it?" Lir asked.

Scornfully, the chief-man's wife rasped: "Don't you *know*?"

"I know only this. I found the girl in a Castle you told me was a ruin and was not. She can't bear the sun. I trusted I might leave her in your fostering."

The woman chuckled bitterly.

"One hundred years past, they made a pact with us, with the village, the folk at Dark. 'Keep faith with us, and you'll be spared,' they said. What price their oath?"

"I—" Lir began.

"You," she grated. "Her *creature*, her *slave*. They always have one or two, to serve them at Dark."

"Will you take *my* oath I don't understand what you mean?"

The woman narrowed her eyes.

"Perhaps I will. Husband," she dug the chief-man contemptuously with her elbow. "Tell him."

"No," said the man.

"I must if you will not," she said.

She pushed out of the house, swiping the staring crowd aside. Lir went after her, and the villagers, including the woman's husband and son, plodded after Lir. Something very odd had gripped the village. It no longer functioned as a village. Milk was souring in its pails in the sun. Three or four goats were prancing, tetherless and unherded, into the woods. Untended washing lay scattered over the stones of the stream.

The chief-man's woman seated herself on a tree stump at the water's edge. The rest of the village gathered, and seated itself about her, as if she were a story-teller, or a harper, even, and the crowd had abandoned its work to be entertained.

"The Castle," the woman said. The crowd quivered. Almost a minute elapsed. "The dark Castle, the Castle of

Dark. It is an evil spot. Evil is built into the stones of it. It is not only the Castle. It is the ground where it stands. The very ground is evil, the soil, the rock, the trees that grow there. Before any men lived in the world, as we know men, there was evil in that place."

Lir, minstrel trained, noted at once that this was a tale, a narrative ballad handed down, generation to generation. But a *true* tale?

"Those who dwell in the place may be tainted with its evil," the woman resumed. "Not everyone. But some, always some. One by one, tainted. A hundred years ago there was such a one. He bound this village. He said he would spare us, and his descendants would spare us, but if any travellers came here, we must send them to Dark, send them to *him*. It was a pact. The village kept it. 'Go north,' they said to the travellers; they said: 'Visit the fine town by the lake.' And the village was spared. But after that evil one was gone, there were none. Not for forty years. The town prospered. Then another was born. There was the sign. The lightning struck the tree. The town was quickly deserted. The mother herself, when she beheld her child scorched by the sun, fled the Castle. They say she left two guardians—to preserve the child. To keep it *in*. We knew. Sixteen years ago, on the night the lightning struck. We had our own signs, signs that the evil one who bound us left for us. And when a lone traveller came, we sent him north. There were only three. The first died in the forest; it was spring, and a lion was roaming. The second was a pedlar. The third was a young man with gold-fair hair. And he has returned and she has come with him, the new evil one from the Castle of Dark."

The woman was silent.

Leaves and birds were audible in the words, and the goats maa-ed far off and the stream sang. No other noise.

Lir touched the woman's arm gently.

"What is the nature of this evil?"

The woman caught her breath. She leaned forward and said in his ear: "Black Soul."

"I'm sorry, but that means nothing to me."

"It will," she said. She looked as if she disliked him and pitied him, too. The same combination he had felt for Lilune.

"What do you intend?" Lir asked.

"We could kill her," the woman said. "You *can* kill them. The other was killed."

Lir took her arm and held it hard.

"No, you won't do that."

The woman stared at him with contempt.

"She's enslaved you."

"Enslaved be damned. You won't murder a harmless girl for a superstition. Not while I'm with her."

"No."

"It amounts to this," the chief-man said, unexpectedly putting on his authority again. "We'll keep the pact. You must get her away from the village before sunset."

"How can I? The sun—"

"It's all right," the man said. "You can carry her in the chest, and there's a cart will bear the chest. And the village has a bull strong enough to tow the cart. It'll be our gift to you. To ensure us safety. We'll aid you, if you keep your side of it."

Lir hesitated. The "gift" would be a huge loss to the village—a cart, a bull—he was nervous of their generosity. But what alternative did he have?

"Yes, I agree. When I reach the next village, I'll try to get your property back to you."

The chief-man started to demur, but his wife broke in, saying that would be appreciated. Then she screamed at a boy in the crowd to run after the escaped goats. The village whirled into activity.

The stubborn bull trudged up the ascent.

It was late in the morning. They had been going nearly three hours: the bull dragging the cart with the chest in it, the man driving the bull, Lir walking at the rear of the cart with the chief-man and his son. The villagers showed no sign of wanting to turn back.

Lir wondered if they had decided to escort him personally to another village. They were not making directly south, but south-west, up a steep, hilly, overgrown cart track through the woods.

Lir was tired after his night's journey. The girl, he thought, would be fast asleep in her black box. There was no conversation with the three men. Then he began to hear a fresh sound over the trundling of the cart. It was the rush of a river.

Soon the top of the ascent was in view. The trees parted and they emerged in yellow sunlight on the brink of a steep slope strewn with boulders. Below, through a rocky gully, a fast-running river plummeted on south-westward.

The man driving the bull halted the beast.

'Old road goes south from here," the chief-man said to Lir. Lir scanned south along the angle of the slope. As he was doing that, a numbing brightness went off inside his skull.

Perhaps twenty seconds after, he discovered he was lying on the slope. His brain throbbed, and none of his limbs seemed to be working. He could see, but smearily, as if his eyes had been coated with grease.

The chief-man's son, who had struck Lir from behind, was assisting his father and the bull-drover. They were raising the chest from the cart.

Lir yelled, but no yell came out. He tried to crawl along the slope towards the three men, but nothing happened. So he lay there and watched as they lifted the chest high over the river-gully and presently let the chest go.

There was a moment's stillness, then a grinding, distant splash. The chief-man's son was already hefting a boulder to sling down on the chest.

Lir closed his eyes, and fell into a pit a million feet deep.

PART THREE

9

Lilune: White Water

The river, high enough even in the summer's dryness to cushion the impact of the chest, was also too swift to sink it. In a moment the current was dashing the chest along on its own south-western race. The slung boulder missed the target, only causing the chest to rock a little. Then the chest was out of range.

The river had quite some way to go. A journey of twists and turns, of lathery descents and shallow swirling pools. At the end of the journey was a waterfall that leapt over a cliff, eighty feet into the estuary below.

Trained by the ringing of a bell for sixteen years to wake with the dusk, no longer needing the bell, Lilune woke. Initially, she thought herself in the lidded bed at the Castle. But as she was heaving off the lid, she recalled everything that had happened, and that she was in a chest in the village. Then the lid toppled up. Twilight gushed in, and water.

Jolted in its river-borne flight, the chest bucked and spun. Lilune, sitting bolt-upright within, grasped the wooden sides, and gazed about her.

She was utterly shocked. Disorientated, she did not feel terror for nearly a minute. After that, terror caught her up. She shrieked for Lir, though able to apprehend that there was no one about. Only the river, explosively flinging itself and the chest forward. And instinctively, she was aware of the river's urgency, the sense of a goal. The water ran so swiftly it seemed to boil. It was white as milk.

She at once concluded that Lir was to blame. He had betrayed her, persuaded the villagers to do this to her. If he had not specifically engineered the plan, he had obviously agreed. They had meant her to drown, or to be smashed to pieces. She had never suffered such fearsome treachery. Although she was frightened, life surged through her.

Overhead, pale stars ran to keep up with the race of the river. Banks, hills, swooping arcs of trees shot by.

Terror became exhilaration.

Now tall stones jutted from the stream-bed, but were unable to check the river, unable even to retain the chest. As if enchanted, the chest was swept between the stones on ropes of white water.

Then, across the tumult and the encroaching dark, Lilune became conscious of an absurdity. The spurling torrent ended in mid-air.

Astounded, curious, Lilune craned from her unorthodox boat. She was craning when this boat jumped up and tilted into foam-frothed space and crashed down amidst the waterfall.

Instinctively she grasped at the lid of the chest. It thudded to, trapping her inside a toppling square black nightmare. She was flung from side to side, even as the chest was flung. Slim spurts of water jetted through its joins and carvings. She screamed, but the cascade of the waterfall boomed, drowning all sounds but its own.

About sixty feet down, the chest struck a rock. It was a light, glancing blow, but it catapulted the chest out of the body of the fall, so that it missed the whirlpool at the column's foot. The water beyond was almost level, smoothing as it ebbed out into the mouth of the vast estuary. Here the chest landed, and, improbably, floated. Or appeared to. For as it circled in this flattened expanse, no longer pushed forward by the driving urge of the river, it seemed to grow sensitive to its own weight in relation to the depths below. Gradually, the corners of the chest dipped. A fraction at a time, it was deciding to sink.

Lilune could not understand what had happened. She was simply struggling to release herself from her floundering prison. Fluid swashed about the interior of the chest, but the external pressure of the waterfall had been relieved. The lid flew open with such force that it unbalanced the chest. Lilune tipped out upon the lid, the chest turned turtle, and she sank into the estuary.

Lilune could not swim, but, like any drowning thing, she frantically thrashed towards the surface. Her own buoyancy raised her, and a gigantic parasol of rapidly unplaiting hair. As her head broke from the water, the upended chest bumped gently into her arms. Enough air had been trapped inside it so that it had not sunk, but bobbed resiliently.

She was not thankful or amazed at her luck. Luck seemed only what she should anticipate. It didn't after all matter that Lir had failed her. The world itself would care for her, as the two old women had done. Despite this assurance, she wished Lir were with her. As she climbed aboard the chest, she wished he had been there. The thought that he had let them cast her into the river hurt her. But she was unused to this sort of hurt, and did not understand what she felt.

The warm night dried her hair and her garments surely and quickly. The sky was moonless, but the stars burned their steady fires, tinting the water of the estuary. Southward, another light edged the horizon. The soft breeze that blew from the south held a tang of salt and smoke. There was just sufficient tidal rhythm in the estuary to carry the chest, with Lilune seated on it, toward the salt, the smoke and the light.

Three miles away, the estuary yawned out into the sea. But two miles inland, a great walled town massed on the estuary's eastern bank. Lilune was already gazing at the town, not completely realizing what it was. The only town she had ever seen had been her own, an empty ruin.

Presently she noticed that the smoothed water, no longer

white with speed, was white with flowers. Sodden, broken, they unravelled before the chest. Some previous incoming tide had carried them here. Now they were drifting back to the south with Lilune.

Soon the light, red and volatile, stained all down the water towards her. Smoke turned the stars blue.

She could make out the source of the light, which was not only the town.

Ahead, the water was covered by a host of craft. They were being rowed by many oars, sedately, to and fro. Prow and stern of each vessel was ablaze with torches. And the breeze was bringing snatches of laughter, shouting and the twang of music.

The upended chest rode leisurely on the current towards those fiery barges. And Lilune gaped at their splendour. Dazzled, delighted, she passed into their midst.

Singly, or in groups, the occupants of the pleasure-barges became aware of a phantasmagorical figure caught by their lights. A girl seated on a floating casket, framed by hair that spread for a yard or more over the water.

Lilune regarded the people. The people regarded Lilune.

10

Lir: Down-River

Lir came to, disturbed at something that was worrying him, unable to think what it was. There was the ache in his head, but there'd be a reason for that. Too much sun, or too good ale.

He crawled to his knees, hearing the plash of water below, wanting to get to it. He had been on his knees three seconds, when suddenly he threw up. After his head cleared, he felt better.

Then he remembered.

He slipped and slithered a way to the river, drank, and bathed his face. The water was faintly warm. The sun tilted in it, past the zenith. Lir stared down, seeking for the splintered chest, a submerged face and floating hair. Despite the glare of the sun and the brisk movement of the water, he could see cloudy shapes of rocks on the floor of the river. None of them looked like the chest. Or Lilune.

No trace remained of the villagers either, except cartwheel ruts, going away. There was little point in returning to the village. It would achieve nothing. And they might kill him this time.

In fact, he was confident he'd have known if Lilune had drowned here. The sensitivity to such things which the harp had sharpened in him, and which he now took for granted, would have told him. It was quite possible the rapid current had whirled the chest along with it. If he meant to find the girl, all he had to do was follow the current down-river.

At the prospect, he was overcome by fatigue and a nauseous, weak hunger. He sat on the bank. He didn't want to follow down-river, didn't want to search for the girl. He wanted to sleep. To wake up and have someone bring him hot oat-cakes, friendship, chatter. He wished he were a child again, among the tumble of brothers and sisters in his parents' smoky little cot.

He slept, and the sun burned down the sky and on to his face. When he roused, the sun was setting. His weakness had vanished, and his wishings with it. He got up, whistling glumly, and walked south-west along the bank.

An hour later there was a pear-tree grown in the bank, leaning over to him, offering hard young sweet pears. Two hours after that, further up the bank, he glimpsed badgers playing madly under the stars. He noticed he had automatically elected to go on travelling by night.

He confronted the fact that he would have to go on until he found the girl. It wasn't compassion any more, or irritated responsibility. The village had been prepared to drown her, they were so afraid. And yes, the Castle of Dark had had an aura, a will that refused to be denied. He had to get to the girl because he, also, was beginning to believe that something had come away with her from the Castle. Not wickedness, superstition, a black but invisible thing riding on her shoulder, like a plague germ, like death. . . . No. Lir rejected the hysteria of the village. But *something*: a breath of the will of the Castle. The influence which made her vulnerable to sunlight, indifferent to food; made her attract assistance on one hand, murder on the other.

And it was easier to realize this since he was no longer in her company. Look at her, and you saw merely a girl, odd, thin, foolish and unworldly—spoiled. But alone, he remembered the crackle of her hair when he plaited it, the lid on her bed in the Castle. And yes. He remembered the pedlar's pack in the forest and the dream of the pedlar's fear, and the flowing, wriggling, twisting darkness that had pursued him.

Lir did not cover much ground that night and lay down to sleep again long before it was over. He woke about noon. He returned to the natural habit of journeying with the sun. That day he had to climb away from the river, for the banks became sheer. The umbrellas of willows aided his passage over the slope. He kept a sharp eye for the chest. He could perceive the current made swifter progress than a man who must negotiate the ups and downs of the land.

The forest was receding as the river sustained its southwestern angle. The terrain broke up into tree-fringed ridges, pointed hills. It was difficult to keep exactly parallel to the river. Eventually Lir resigned himself to losing sight of it from time to time. The water-course cut like a knife through a landscape which itself meandered. He did not reckon Lilune had come ashore at any place, this far. Nor did he think the chest had been wrecked in the river. He would have to trust to that.

Signs of civilisation were the next disruption.

On the third morning, there were valleys golden with wheat, meadows white with sheep, inclines scattered with villages to the east of him. Presently, a village in his path. And here they recognised a harper, fed him and begged for songs. He lost another day that way. Nearly two days, and the night between them. He knew he should have got on. Somehow, he did not.

It was almost as if, at last, something was trying to turn him aside from refinding the girl. The something which had lured him to her in the beginning?

Then there was another village, and he practically ran through it. For, questioning a child on the outskirts, he had heard how the river, tending back southward to the sea, ended in an eighty-foot waterfall.

11

Lilune: The Court

Lilune watched the candles glimmer and dance. They reminded her of very bright moonlight.

She was pleased with the candles. She was pleased with the dish of sweetmeats, which she didn't eat, but played with, lining them up in rows and heaping them up in towers. She was pleased with the goblet with the red drink in it. She liked the people, too. They were very nice to her. They gave her whatever she said she wanted. They treated her as if she was special, fascinating, and simultaneously they treated her with a kind of reverence.

She had been right; she had not had to rely on Lir.

Just the same, she was sorry he couldn't see her now, in her mint-green dress edged with cloth-of-gold. With her hair plaited into two floor-sweeping plaits with gold bees fastened into them. It was a shame he couldn't. And he should have seen the young men bowing to her as well. They called her the Lady Lilune.

Not that there hadn't been a few discordant notes. But she wouldn't bother to think about these. They didn't matter. The surly townsfolk, for example, didn't matter, did they? Some of them had been on the barges in the estuary when she arrived, and they hadn't mattered then.

The men who rowed the barges had been plainly unnerved by her appearance in their midst—some took one hand from the oars to make signs against bad luck. But the passengers in the barges, their magnificent clothes and their jewellery glittering in the torchlight, passed from staring to exclamations and waving. Then the largest vessel of all came gliding up. It had thirty oars, a fringed canopy and minstrels playing harps, tabors and pipes. At the stern was a gilded chair. In the chair sat a young man. He was not like Lir, but dark and pale as Lilune herself. He had a long lean sallow face and long white hands so thick with rings his fingers never touched each other on the insides. He sat and looked at Lilune, and then he smiled and called out to her.

"Regal and floating lady. Will you join us?"

Lilune nodded. She was just as intrigued with these people as they with her.

The dark and pale young man gave an order. Three of his companions took a couple of oars and poled the chest into the side of the barge. Then they reached for Lilune and swung her off and into the barge. Lilune heard a woman exclaim how much hair the castaway had. Lilune was glad the gold chain glinted at her waist, though she had no other jewels.

"And now," said Dark-and-Pale as Lilune was conducted up two little steps in the barge to his chair. "Who are you and where do you come from and why do you travel in such a—such a *notable* fashion?"

Lilune answered his arrogant gaze with her own arrogant gaze.

"I am Lilune," said Lilune. "And who are you?"

Dark-and-Pale laughed. Not a real laugh.

"I am the Duke of this region. That town over there happens to be mine. And this stretch of water."

"Oh, yes," said Lilune, interested but not impressed.

"I think you, too, are an aristocrat, Lady Lilune," said the Duke, making the best of things. "But how did you come to be jolting down the estuary on a wooden box?"

An instinct checked Lilune. She did not know what it was, but she obeyed it. She widened her eyes. Softly, she said: "I don't remember."

Nearby, a second woman gasped, and said: " My lord, I do believe she's been cast adrift by some evil person.

Obviously she is noble and young and fragile. The shock has caused her to forget."

"Well, she's a pretty toy," said Dark-and-Pale. "Let's say the river has given me a present on this night of my birthday. I agree she's of genteel birth. She shall live at my court till her wits return. I'll be her guardian. How about that, Lady Lilune?" he added.

"Maybe," said Lilune cautiously.

The Duke laughed. It was no more a laugh than the other, but it was louder. "Do you hear?" he inquired generally. "The saucy miss. Certainly she's high-born, to insult me as she does." He leaned forward and peered into Lilune's face. His eyes were hard, both clever and stupid together. "I think you are a witch," said the Duke.

Everyone laughed. All the laughter was like the Duke's laughter. Not real, but loud.

The barges began to row for the eastern bank of the estuary.

Duke Dark-and-Pale asked Lilune questions, which she either did not reply to or else replied to in ways that might have startled him. He could have been trying to catch her out, but he always smiled or laughed.

"And where were you born?" he demanded playfully.

"I wasn't born."

"Ah! You hatched from a raven's egg, possibly? But then who educated and reared you? The raven?"

"Two old women."

"And did the old women throw you into the estuary?"

Silence.

"Yes, she's a witch," said the Duke. "But the rest of you must be very polite to her. It's my new game. It might be amusing."

Someone whispered to another: "And if she doesn't amuse him, he'll probably throw her back in the estuary."

The Duke did not seem to hear this, though he smiled yet again.

Lilune really didn't hear. She was, in any event, totally certain by now of her knack for survival.

Steps led up from the black water to a wharf. Two

torches burned at the head of the steps. The barges were moored, and everyone idled ashore. The Duke had quickly become bored with the nocturnal boating organised to mark the evening of his birthday. Lilune had provided a diversion. Now the band of minstrels marched into a broad street which led from the wharf, and stood there playing energetically. There were also soldiers and attendents to escort the Duke through the town, and many strange carriages roofed with hoops to support canopies that had been dragged off in the summer night.

The Duke presented Lilune to a group of nervous women, who then shared their hoop-carriage with her.

They bounced up the broad street, with the minstrels marching before. There was a fish-market off to the right, but here stone houses rose with the street, and soon the stony walls of a castle loomed over the houses.

The castle was not like the Castle of Dark.

There were torches blazing on the gate, and high on the walls. Two watchtowers ascended above the gate, and there were soldiers there, stamping and saluting, as the procession went through the timbered doors. The keep was built on a platform. Its single inner tower commanded a view of the estuary far below. Though smaller, the buildings were all in repair and light pierced every window.

They went into the Hall, and Lilune saw how the candles glimmered, at least a hundred of them. The Hall was so bright, hung everywhere with tapestries. Rushes and sweet herbs were crushed on the floor. Only one window had glass, but the glass was stained, blue and red.

And there were so many people, so much movement.

Lilune sank down on the cushioned bench the women guided her to. She was overcome, but she had no fear.

"No, no, not there," the Duke called. "I want her to sit by me."

Lilune was taken on to the dais and seated beside the chair of Dark-and-Pale. Servants were bringing food. It was a banquet.

"What will you eat?"

"I never eat," said Lilune.

He smirked, and had servitors heap her plate. Lilune built a pastry castle but, softened by gravy, it collapsed. Roast pigeons, re-clad in their feathers, shocked her.

"For sure, then, she doesn't eat," said the Duke. "Bring some milk for the baby, with honey in it."

Lilune drank the milk. The taste was strange. After the milk, she had some wine. Frequently the Duke turned to her. "What do you think of this?" he would ask, indicating an object or activity. Lilune occasionally told him what she thought. Her answers were often absurd. But sometimes the unknown instinct would check her and she would remain quiet. "Witch-baby," said the Duke.

Everyone but the Duke treated Lilune with vast courtesy. They seemed charmed by all she said and did.

"Tomorrow noon we shall go hunting," said the Duke. "You shall ride with me."

"No," said Lilune. "The sun makes me ill."

The Duke took it as a matter of course.

"Very well. We'll hunt at night. A moonless night, but never mind. You shall make a spell to call the deer to us."

Lilune's eyes grew round. Did this man guess the Calling spell was the one magic she could perform? Again something prompted her to denial. "But I can't work spells."

"How you disappoint me. Then we must wait for the night of the new moon. Which is in five or six nights, is it?" The Duke queried this with a steward at his elbow.

The word "hunt" did not appeal to Lilune. She was uncertain why not. She saw the steward looking at her as the oarsmen in the barges had done. Was he afraid of her? She thrust out her goblet to him. "More wine." He filled the goblet.

The Duke laughed.

Lilune wondered why he laughed so much when the laughter wasn't laughter. She wondered what would happen next.

The eating and drinking—and the laughter—went on for ages, and Lilune found it dull. Large sleek dogs came nosing between the tables for scraps. Lilune was uneasy about the dogs. The minstrels sang songs about feasts and hunts and how wise a Duke had to be and always was. Nobody took much notice. Lilune tried to visualise Lir harping in this Hall, and couldn't. It was nearly midnight.

Duke Dark-and-Pale was discussing horses with two nobles and had not asked Lilune anything for quite a while.

Abruptly he swung round to her and chucked her under the chin. It was instinct once more which told her that he did not like to do this. Could it be that Dark-and-Pale feared her, too?

"Our raven-chick can't sleep in the Ladies' Bower," said the Duke. "It's awash with sunlight all day. We must find a darker, gloomier spot for the witchy miss."

"The cellars, my lord?" ventured one of the nobles.

"Oh, too damp for the lady," said the other, chidingly.

"I think," said the Duke. Everybody hung on his words. "I think the Northern Turret," said the Duke. "There are no windows anymore. My father bricked them both up years ago. It was my father's private chamber," the Duke added to Lilune. "He disliked draughts. A snug eyrie, and black as the pits of Hell."

Then the Duke gripped Lilune ceremoniously by the arm, though he quickly let her arm go when they were out of the Hall. All the people in the Hall, apart from the servants, followed the Duke as he conducted Lilune up the staircases of the big tower. In the upper storey was a pair of carved doors—the Duke's own apartment. A passage ran on, with a tiny stairway at its end. A sconce with candles burned in the wall to light the stair. At the top, the Duke opened a door and showed Lilune into the Northern Turret.

Obviously, he had decided on the Turret earlier, even before Lilune had mentioned avoiding the sun, for someone had been up ahead of them to light the candles in the room. Tapestries veiled the stone-work, and there was a great woven rug on the floor. On a burnished table were jars of parchments, ink, quills, a few impressive newly-bound books. Against one wall was a narrow curtained bed.

Lilune responded to the room. She hurried to finger the books. They were whole, without mildew. She saw a title: *The Romance of the Blue Knight*. In the tapestries, beautiful women picked flowers by rivers and spotted lions flew through the air and helmed warriors slew dragons. Even the curtains of the bed had pictures embroidered on them. Even the rug. In such a room, you could never be alone.

"She likes it," said the Duke.

The ladies of the court sighed and clapped.

Lilune glanced at the door and beheld the enormous lock, without a key.

"I want the key to this door," she stated.

Duke Dark-and-Pale bowed. Mockingly he said:

"Whatever the lady wants. Naturally, she shall have the key."

In the end, they went away, and with the iron key the Duke had presented to her, she secured the door. After that, she searched the chamber for any chink behind the tapestries. There were hair-line cracks in the stone, no more.

Till the morning, she sat at the table and read. The books were the best she had ever seen, and they, too, were full of coloured pictures. She sensed the dawn, even though no light came in, and she heard the birdsong. She got into the narrow bed, and drew the curtains tight. Gloatingly, she fell asleep.

Next evening, they brought her bread, sweets, pears and wine. She drank the rose-scented water they left her to wash in, and washed in the wine, for novelty. Three of the ladies entered with their own waiting-women. They gave Lilune a spectacular green dress, and the women plaited her hair.

When she went down to the Hall, remembering how dull she had found the prolonged eating, Lilune carried a book with her.

"Look at this mannerless madam," said the Duke, but he did not take the book from her.

Later there was a pageant, with people dressed up as unicorns and horses, and young men as knights riding on their shoulders. They pretended to fight with wooden swords. The young man who had won came and kneeled before Lilune. The Duke gave her a gilt chaplet to put on the victor's head. Everyone paid her a lot of attention. When she grew tired of it, she got to her feet and went up to the Turret, locking herself in to read. No one moved to stop her.

The following night, four young nobles attempted to teach Lilune chess. Lilune was bad at the game, but the chess figures appealed to her. She stole them, to play with in the Turret. The people at the court didn't interest her so much any more, though she liked their treatment of her. The Duke she did not like, although she didn't properly understand she didn't like him, as she rarely thought of him.

The third night, he gave her a pair of white kid riding gloves.

"Can you ride?" he asked.

"No."

"I must instruct you."

So the fourth night, Duke Dark-and-Pale and his court went riding through the town. Lilune was appalled at being put on the horse. She felt a mile from the ground, and also dreadfully uncomfortable.

"I don't like it," said Lilune. "I shan't ride hunting."

"Very well," said the Duke. "Perhaps you will accompany the hunt in a carriage."

Lilune had forgotten that the idea of a hunt had seemed displeasing to her. It was lovely that everyone fell in with her wishes, kept tempting her, soothing her. She yawned.

They returned through the town, with Lilune riding pillion behind one of the noblemen. In the market there were several townsfolk milling to and fro about a huge lighted tavern. These folk saluted the Duke. They had unfriendly, respectful, red faces that became less friendly than ever and paler, as Lilune herself went by.

At one end of the market-place was a gallows. An old man was sitting under it, uncaring, muttering to himself. He paid little attention to the Duke, just bobbing his head a bit lower. But his watery eyes ran over Lilune and the uncaring glaze slid off them. He tottered up and shuffled away.

"You must excuse these oafs, lady," said the noble who had Lilune on his horse. "Anything different, and they gawp."

Further on, a shadow in an alley spat. Perhaps the man was only clearing his throat, but the noble offered to go back and thrash him. Lilune let the noble dismount and search the alley; the man had run off.

Lilune knew herself safe surrounded by the court. Even though the Duke trotted his horse back to her and said it was her witch-eye scared his town, still, she knew herself safe.

She wondered what Lir would have done if someone had spat at her in his company. But then, he had let the villagers try to kill her. . . .

The Duke gave her a silver pomander on a gold chain. He flinched when their hands touched.

One of the candles in the Turret chamber blew out suddenly.

Lilune turned to it, puzzled. There was no draught in the Turret that could blow out a candle. Then another candle gusted out just as suddenly, and Lilune felt cold air. She had been too absorbed to feel it before, in her reverie of pomanders, townsfolk, nobles, horses. But where could the draught be coming from?

There was only one area—the door. Lilune went to the door. She set her hand on its panels. And it creaked. It was ajar.

Lilune had not left the room since she lay down in the bed this morning. Nor had anyone come knocking on this, the fifth of her nights at the castle. Which meant that somebody had entered while she slept. Somebody who, although he had given her the key to the Northern Turret, had kept another key of his own.

Lilune drew a long outraged breath. It was more than petulant anger. The instinct, which had begun to warn her to do this, avoid that, now clamoured with alarm.

She ran from the Turret, down the stair and down other stairs. She ran into the Hall. Duke Dark-and-Pale was strolling with six courtiers. A groom was feeding the dogs titbits from a tray the Duke held. Other courtiers drifted about in their always-aimless, loud-laughing way.

"You!" Lilune screamed across the Hall at Dark-and-Pale.

Instantly his head jerked up. He fixed her with his eyes. She saw many contradictory things in those clever foolish eyes. She saw he was frightened of her and did not want to recognise or reveal his fear. She saw he had challenged his fear—and her—by spying on her in the Turret and leaving the door open as proof of his spying. And she could see, too, he was sweating.

"Well, my Lady Witch?" he murmured.

Lilune experienced an odd combination herself of fright and power.

"You must give me the other key!" she demanded, walking towards the Duke.

Each of the dogs started to growl and their hackles lifted.

"No," said the Duke.

Abruptly, the sense of power left her. As the candles had blown out suddenly in the draught, so her trust in the security of the court was blown out in her.

The Duke, sweating, snapped his fingers at a minstrel. "Play the song now."

The minstrel, quavering, not glancing at Lilune, commenced an ancient ballad that told of a maiden chained to a loom by iron fetters. The Duke smiled. His hospitality had covered his own apprehension of Lilune from the start. And now he had seen her sleeping the daytime sleep like death, the sleep from which there was no waking until dusk fell.

Lilune flung about and fled. Back up the stairways, and up the small stair to the Turret. She slammed the door, and dragged the heavy table to block it.

She sat down against one of the table legs and shivered.

Soon, she didn't remember Lir had let the villagers throw her into the river. She wanted Lir to be in the Castle, to rescue her.

After a long, long time, she heard a dog snarling outside, and Dark-and-Pale spoke softly to her through the panels. "New moon tomorrow, but no hunting for you, I hazard. What will you do, Witchy? You can't do anything."

"Yes I can," she whispered fiercely.

But she didn't know what, nor did he hear her.

Her worst terror was that when she slept the next day, they might force an entry to the Turret. What would they do to her? Leave her in the bailey court perhaps, to the sun's mercy. They would need to do nothing else.

She tried to construct a plan of escape, but there were soldiers throughout the castle, who would capture her if the Duke ordered it. Did they guard the Turret door? And there was no way from the Turret, saving the door. Only the hair-line cracks in the stone.

Finally, she crept behind the curtains of the bed and stretched out there.

The candles burned low and smouldered and died.

Although it was night still, feverishly, Lilune dozed.

In the end, beyond her own muffling and beyond the walls, she heard a cock crow. It was, to Lilune, as if the crowing cock passed a death sentence upon her.

And then, struggle as she would to keep awake, to be ready to fight and claw and shriek when the door was smashed and the soldiers burst in, she could not. Horribly, sleep dragged her down. And down. It was the old training of her Castle—the bell which woke her, the closed shutters and the dark by day which lulled her to sleep.

She should never have lain here. She should have saved the candles and relit them. It was no use now.

And down.

She slept.

12

Lir: The Walled Town

The descent from the sunset cliff had been treacherous. East of the waterfall, the ground collapsed in a series of enormous subsidences to the plain of the estuary below. A giant could have negotiated the subsidences with no trouble. A man had to climb with agility and care. A third of the way down, Lir had paused to scan the whirlpool into which the waterfall plunged as it hit the estuary. He had paused on the headland, too, scanning, searching. Anything that crashed into the whirlpool would be shattered and engulfed, later cast up again, and, if the tide were strong enough, drawn on toward the three-mile-distant sea. Nothing was visible in the water, near or far. But Lir had lingered those two days—or more—in the village which asked him for songs. He couldn't be sure now if lack of wreckage meant Lilune had survived the fall, or if her broken body had merely been washed out on the tide.

It would be easier if she had died. He saw that. It would mean that whatever dark thing had accompanied her had perished with her. Or at least lost its power to work through her any more.

But he could not think of her only in that vein. She was a human being. He didn't like her, yet, considering the chance of her helpless death, something grieved inside him. Because she was younger than he, and had never properly lived.

Sunset had practically faded when he got off the rocks on to the plain. He had been told of a walled town a mile south of the fall, and had dimly spotted it from the cliff-top through the peach-yellow air. A wide-flung outpost of the forest had swept in from the east towards the town. As the dark intensified on the flat plain, Lir caught the gleam of the town's lights.

They would have shut the gates by this hour. Maybe if he walked to the town and yelled, they would let him in. Maybe not. It seemed on the whole more simple to spend the night here and go on tomorrow.

He lay down against the rocks where the brush was thickest and the grass deep. He lay down still wondering if the girl were dead.

He slept and dreamed Lilune was watching him through the strings of the harp. Her face had no expression, but just in front of her face was a shifting transparent shadowy something, like a gauze scarf.

Lir woke at dawn. He intended to rise immediately, but fell asleep again. That time he did not wake till almost noon. He had been tired, but the sleep seemed unnaturally prolonged. Even then, he could have gone on sleeping. He thought of his previous idea of the magic, now holding him off as once it had lured him on. The water in the estuary was too salt to drink, but there was a pool close by. He ate the two apples the last village had given him, but saved the bread.

He started off towards the town. He had been walking a minute or so before he understood himself. He knew—not supposed, not theorised, but *knew*— Lilune was alive and she was in the walled town. And whatever darkness had come from the Castle with her was in the town at her side. Lir did not question or doubt this knowledge. It was absolute.

He no longer scanned the smooth surface of the estuary for broken shards or skeins of hair. He picked up speed.

Soon there was a road that came in from the woods and led southward to the town walls. Then there were the walls themselves, the gates with their watch towers. Inside, a line of roofs ascended a hill. A castle topped the hill.

The town gates stood wide. It was a quarter past noon. A couple of men in leather jerkins, with iron skull-caps and swords, lounged on the walk above the gate.

"Halt. Who goes there?" the shorter of the two bawled as Lir approached.

The other wiped his face with his hand. "It's a harper."

"Is it? A harper? What's he want?"

"To harp for the Duke, likely."

The short man bounded down the inside stair from the walk, hurtled through the gate and barred Lir's way.

"Duke doesn't want a harper. He's got harpers. Six of them. All fools. Doesn't want a seventh fool. See?"

"I see you're in my way," said Lir. "Are you telling me I can't enter the town?" "One's sufficient."

"Am I telling him that?" Shorty asked the tall man. The tall man shrugged, uninterested either in his companion's antics or in Lir. "Well," went on Shorty, "what if I am?"

"I'm a free man," said Lir. "Not a felon. Free, a traveller. What grounds have you for keeping me out?"

"Told you," explained Shorty. "Too many harpers. And other things," he added.

"Other things?"

"Witches," said Shorty. He made a luck sign over himself.

"Six harpers," said Lir. "How many witches?"

"Just one," said Shorty. "One's sufficient."

"Shut your mouth," said the tall man.

"Well, this roving harper ought to hear what kind of a town he's trying to get into. You ever tangled with witches, son?"

"No," said Lir, thinking, though, that he probably had.

Shorty sidled nearer. He had decided to like Lir, to warn him, set him straight. "How do you judge a witch?" asked Shorty, putting his arm over Lir's neck. "She floats on water, doesn't she? Well, this one did that, floated down the estuary five nights back. The Duke was out boating. It was his birthday. And the witch floats right in among the barges. And she puts the Duke under her spell. Which is surprising, 'cos he's not that sort of a Duke, if you take my drift."

"Shut your mouth," said the tall man again. But he had turned his back to Shorty, gazing off in the other direction, at the estuary, pretending to ignore them. Shorty ignored him.

"And ever since, the Duke's been doing as the witch says. Riding through the town when decent folk are in their beds, and taking her, too, all dressed in finery. And tonight he's to take her hunting. By the light of the new moon. Now it's not natural, is it, I ask you? To go hunting *at night*?"

"This witch," said Lir. "What's she like?"

"Like a witch should be," said Shorty with grim satisfaction. "Black hair in two black plaits that nearly brush the ground even when she's on a horse. And a white face. And greeny eyes."

"You saw her?"

"Didn't I."

"And what has she done to make you think her a witch? Beyond her floating, of course?"

"Ask in the town," said Shorty, shortly. The tall man had produced an earthenware beer jar and was unstoppering it with much gesticulation. "Got to wet my whistle," said Shorty to Lir. "Get off with you. Can't stand here jabbering."

"I can go into the town then?"

"It's on your own head."

Lir walked round the town. He behaved nonchalantly, but watched everything that went on, as any stranger might. There were a great many people, all busy at their trades, with merely the occasional, mainly unfriendly, glance for him. Altogether it was not a friendly town. Nor one that welcomed a wandering harper. They had harpers of their own, or their Duke had. Lir had come across other towns like it in the past. Usually the overlord, Duke or petty princeling or whatever he was, would be to blame, exacting high taxes, not bothering with the welfare of those he governed. And the folk soured. They needed money to pay their tax and money to give themselves some of the things the overlord had. They forgot the sweet meadows and the clean woods outside the walls. The countryside meant grain and herds, and a river meant fish. And if the sky meant anything, it meant a cruel God who took no notice of their pains and chastised them if they sinned. Generally, Lir kept away from towns. He wouldn't have stayed two hours in this one, if it hadn't been for "the witch".

There was a fish-market adjoining the wharf, and a tavern on the east side of the market. On the north side was a gallows. Lir went into the tavern and sat down. Patently, nobody wanted a song. He paid a copper piece for a mug of watered ale, and sat drinking it slowly. He listened to the talk around him. The tavern was full of men making a late dinner. They had coins but not much conversation. They spoke in surly complaints and boasts.

Lir finished his ale, and reluctantly bought another.

"I nearly didn't come into town," he remarked mildly to the boy who served him. "Somebody said you were plagued by a witch."

The boy nodded. "So it is. A witch at the castle."

Lir was aware the talk all about had got louder. As if they had caught his words and wanted to smother them.

"But how do you know she is a witch?"

"It's at night," said the boy. His face flushed. Someone was sparing attention for him—he was important. "My old mum, she says it's at night we'll witness it. Lock the doors, she says. And stay under the covers."

The tavern-keeper came over and clouted the boy so hard he began falling. Lir grabbed him before he landed on the filthy floor and steadied him back upright.

"You paid for ale, not chat," said the tavern-keeper.

"Neither did I pay to watch you ill-treat this child," said Lir.

"Fancy airs," said the tavern-keeper, but he slouched off. The boy was one thing, a fight with Lir another. Lir slipped the boy a coin and went out. The boy ran out after him.

"Where will you sleep? Get indoors before moonrise, my old mum says."

"Don't worry," said Lir.

He started up the broad slanting street of stone houses that led to the castle.

Guards patrolled the ramparts over the castle gate, their mètal caps and swords bright in the afternoon sun. Three stood below in the gate-mouth. The timbered doors were fast shut.

Lir could imagine no other way in.

He sat on the step of one of the stone houses. Presently a porter came out and ordered him to be off.

"I am a harper, looking for a night's engagement."

The porter slammed the heavy door.

The guards in the gate had taken note. One nudged another. They laughed.

Lir took the harp-box off his shoulder. He lifted out the harp and tuned it. Then he began to stroll leisurely up and down the street, to the castle gate and back, playing the fastest, slickest tune he could get the harp to give him. And a quicksilver song came too. The guards stopped sneering and grinned instead, stamping in rhythm. Lir ended the song near the gate. He leaned on the castle wall to retune the harp.

"You there," a guard called.

"I?" Lir was surprised.

"Yes, you. I never heard a harper as good as you."

"Oh, but your Duke has six harpers," said Lir.

" Six jack-asses. They bray. They have songs to please the nobles. Sickly rubbish. Give me a proper song like that one you sang. A fine tune and a fine solid beat to it. And sharp words. Do you have another?"

"About thirty songs like that one."

"Sing them," commanded the guard.

"No, no," said a second guard. "Let him come in at supper-time, into the barracks in the Dexter Tower. What do you say, Harper? There's food and beer for you, and maybe payment, if the sergeant likes your songs."

"Just as he tells you," said the third guard. He pulled a

careful face. "The Duke is very clever. He's going hunting by moonlight tonight, when normally only the Dark One goes hunting. There'll be none at home save us mice. And our beer and venison. What do you say?"

"Done," said Lir.

13

Lilune: Moonlight

Lilune, who never dreamed, was dreaming. It was not a nightmare. Not yet. It had nothing to do with the bursting in of the Duke's soldiers through a smashed door, or the lion-faced sun burning her. Somehow, asleep, she was convinced no one had, or would, smash the door. They were too nervous of her. She was not precisely certain why they were nervous. Yet somehow it was as it should be. And liberated from her own fear, she was dreaming of how the only exit from the Northern Turret was through the hair-line cracks in the stone. And of how smoke or vapour could pass through them. And she could see the smoke seeping away through the cracks. Outside, the day was over. Stars were glowing like water drops on mauve enamel sky. The thin baby moon hovered, as if waiting anxiously for her.

She was glad to find it. She was up in the air, much higher than when she had been placed on the horse. The sky would have seemed unbearably vast without the moon for company.

Then Duke Dark-and-Pale rode out of the castle gate far beneath her, and all the court after him. The court followed the Duke always, as if they were a herd of sheep and he the shepherd. Tonight, he was taking the sheep hunting. Lilune should have been with him, among the horses and the pack of ferocious, sleek dogs. But she *was* with him, wasn't she?

She sank through the air. She was a foot or so above his head now. But he wouldn't spy her. Never.

Dark-and-Pale was not himself. She could see this very clearly. His false smile seemed to have been carved on his face so he should not accidentally lose it. His eyes twitched, his ringed hands fidgeted on the reins. He had gone on with the freak of hunting by moonlight because, he said, it pleased him to be different. But it was because of Lilune he was hunting by moonlight, and it was Lilune he was aware of, though he couldn't, as she supposed, glimpse her.

The hunting party rode through the town and left it by the north gate. They proceeded along the road that led into the woods.

This area of the woods was the Duke's. His wardens patrolled it, and kept tally of the game. For tonight, they had traced the slot and spoor of a great stag. The wardens had identified the covert and the feeding ground of the stag. Next, they had marked off a course for it to run, closing escape-ways with nets and "scarers", to keep the stag moving on a fixed trail. Once selected for death in this manner, few beasts had the opportunity to get away. The Duke reckoned on excellent hunting in his woods. But night-time was another matter. The wardens had shaken their heads.

The woods closed round the hunt.

Men were racing ahead on foot; presently, they raced back. They had located the fresh spoor of the stag. About ten of the dogs were released and went surging off between the trunks. The hunting party hesitated a moment, kindling torches against the gloom. Shouts and roars of pointless laughter went up with the smoke. They spurred the horses to a gallop after the dogs.

There was a glade, freckled by thin moonlight, and deep in grass. In the glade, the stag had been feeding with three or four hinds about him. As the hunt bore in on them, they fled. In that second, Lilune felt the terror of the deer in the glade. As if she were one of them.

The great stag, separating himself from the hinds, erupted

through a covert. He swerved towards a black cave of trees, but a net strung with jangling bells across the path—one of the "scarers"—sent him frenziedly aside and on.

Lilune knew he would die. He would be forced around the course, the dogs baying, the hunting court baying too, with their silly laughter. He would plunge on until he was done. He would fall at last, exhausted, shuddering, with a bone-dry mouth, and the huntmaster would slit his throat.

She seemed to be in the brain of the stag. She screamed with his silent anguish. She felt the sweat boil from him, and the huge heart pounding. She knew everything he did not; she knew how he would be killed.

But with him, she learned what it was to be hunted.

She wanted to wake up now. She struggled. It was a nightmare after all.

The stag careered about to regard what pursued him. Then leapt on. Red-eyed dogs were jumping in red torchlight.

Through the stag's staring eye-balls, she saw the moon rip by overhead, goring the darkness with vicious horns.

The stag tried to escape the course again. Again a flapping raucous barrier thrust him aside.

He had miles further to go, but did not know it, to get to the dry mouth and the slitting blade. Each mile would be a little worse.

Lilune screamed and screamed, and the scream seemed to grind her down until she was no more than a scream, which went on and on.

14

Lir: The Night-Beast

In the guard-barracks, hot and yellow with torchlight, the soldiers of the Duke were roaring with laughter, banging their beer cups on the table and yelling for more songs. Lir had just given them a riddle-ballad. As always, the harp had added to the song, and new riddles had come springing to his mind and lips. It was undoubtedly both astute and funny, and the Duke's guards liked it. Tough and dangerous men, they had grown affectionate and genial. They'd got their own harper to entertain them, exactly like the Duke.

The sergeant had already awarded Lir a silver piece. That was for a sentimental ode of the backlands. But the mawkish words had somehow twisted themselves about, becoming beautifully simple and moving. The sergeant had wiped his nose on his sleeve and said gruffly: "I swear I never heard the song so nicely done."

During all this, Lir was two people. One who ate and drank, played tunes on a harp, devised riddles and jokes. The other who waited, tense and restrained, thinking only of a black-haired girl and where she was to be found.

She had not been with the hunt, that was sure.

Lir had observed the hunt riding out, from a vantage point near the castle gate. He had noted the Duke, not much older than himself, and the frivolous court trailing after. They appeared to be galloping to get away from something, rather than to go chasing it. It was dusk, but star-bright and torch-lit besides, as they came under the castle walls. Lir watched methodically, seeking Lilune's small but distinctive figure. And she was not with them. In the east, the scrap of moon had sat on top of the Duke's woods. The moon had filled Lir with apprehension. It had a look—as if it were calling, summoning. . . . Then one of the guards had conspiratorially shouted down to Lir, and he had slipped inside the gate.

"Give us the ballad," a man bellowed now, "of *The Three Dragons*."

There was a chorus of agreement and dissent.

Before Lir could himself speak, the door shot open, and a guard came in hastily from outside.

"What are you doing in here?" the sergeant barked at the newcomer. "No slacking! Someone has to stand his duty at our Duke's gate, and you're it. You and your mate. It's no good whining to me. We threw the dice for it, fair and square, and you and your mate lost. Perhaps our harper will stay for tomorrow and you'll have a turn for a song, and Lank there will be out on the wall, or Blue-Nose."

The two men named Lank and Blue-Nose groaned ceremonially. But the guard in the doorway shook his head.

"No, sergeant, it's not that."

"What then? You spotted an army coming up the road?" Everyone jeered. Lank winked at Lir. "Or battle-galleys in the estuary, maybe?"

"No, sergeant. I can't swear to what I *did* see. But I saw something. And it was in the town. And I'd say, sergeant, it was an unwanted sort of a thing."

The guards guffawed, but the sergeant waved them down.

"Come on then, lad. Do your best. What was it like?"

"Like nothing—well, no. Like a big sort of dog, really. Though it didn't move like a dog. Like a woodscat more than a dog. But it was a deal bigger than either."

"A lion, could it be?" the sergeant asked.

" Well—it might . . ."

"Did your mate see it?"

"Yes, he did."

"And *where* did you see it?"

"Inside the town walls, like I said, where the street runs up from the north end towards the castle. Kind of slinking along it was, but not really slinking. Kind of—*slithering*."

There was a sudden uneasy silence. The guards glanced at each other, took up their sword-belts and one by one got to their feet. They filed after the sergeant, through the door on to the walk that led from the Dexter Tower across the top of the castle gate. Lir went out with them.

The mate of the first guard was by the parapet, leaning over. He turned back to them with an unmistakable relief.

"It's down there, sergeant. Where Sly Alley runs round behind the castle from the market. I watched it go, but now I can't place it."

"And what do *you* think it is?" the sergeant inquired.

The second guard swallowed.

"It's nothing I ever saw in my life."

The soldiers stood, looking over the town towards the virtually invisible unlit alley and its surrounding houses. Only the crackle of the wall-torches sounded. The night was hot, and motionless.

Then from the midst of the night, rose a single, splitting, raw and ghastly shriek. Just one. One was enough.

"Our God defend us!" rasped the sergeant. Then, snapping alert: "You, you, you and you! Take your gear, and out there on the double."

The soldiers bounded down the wall-stair. One snatched a torch. The porter's door in the gate was already being opened. They sped through it and around the wall eastwards, Lir running in their midst.

There were no more shrieks, which was sinister rather than reassuring.

They ran between blank house walls into Sly Alley.

The woman was lying about half way along it. The torch picked her out at once, though it was pitch-black in the alley. She was alone.

The soldier with the torch stood over the woman, while another lifted her against his knee with unexpected kindness.

"She's not dead."

"Probably tipsy and toppled down."

"No, she's not drunk either."

The woman's mouth was open, and she breathed slackly through it. After a minute she opened her eyes, too.

"I was . . . looking . . . for my man," she muttered. "I came out to look . . ."

"And then what!" asked the soldier who supported her.

"Don't know," said the woman, but her eyes flickered nervously round the faces bent above her.

"Yes you do, mother," said the soldier with the torch.

"Was it a lion?" the third soldier asked.

Lir walked between the soldiers. He crouched down where he could face the woman. He took her hand and said, "Tell the truth to me."

The woman started to cry.

"No, no," Lir said gently, brushing the tears off her cheeks. "You're safe now. But you must tell me."

"It was all black," said the woman, gazing at Lir. "It was skinny and all black. It came wriggling into the alley on the ground and I thought it was smoke. There's a fire somewhere, I thought. I must raise an alarm. And then it straightened up. It had two long hands, so long they were, and they were reaching for me. And there were two lights in it like two holes with the moon shining through. And I screamed. But it touched me. It touched my head. And I felt all my strength going. As if it pulled my strength out of me like thread, unravelling it like yarn, and pulling it out. And I couldn't speak or cry out any more. And then I forget."

The woman tried to stand, but she couldn't.

Two soldiers supported her into her house, and presently stepped out again.

"Will she live?" one said to Lir.

"If we were too quick for it—" he broke off, and realized he was shaking from head to foot.

The soldiers crowded in the alley about the torch.

"What *was* it?" one said.

The soldier with the torch said, as if he had something bitter in his mouth: "The Duke's witch. What else?"

Fifteen streets off to the north there came a dim shout, and an urgent drumming that swelled louder.

"His lordship returning," the torch-soldier said. "He seems in a hurry."

The soldiers tramped back to the castle wall, and halted on the east slope as the hunt dashed into view. The hoofs smote sparks on the rough street. The horses were foaming and the dogs crazy. The court was not much better. The gates were swinging wide. The Duke clattered through into the bailey court and dropped from his horse. He was glaring about him, as if searching for foes.

The steward approached down the platform steps of the keep.

"Is all well, my lord?"

"No! Not well."

Grooms were hastening to the horses and kennelboys to the dogs. It became obvious that the Duke was the most agitated of all. And the court, as ever, was blindly following his example. His nobles clustered round him. He thrust them aside. He virtually ran away into the keep, and the court ran after him in evident horror of being left behind.

The four soldiers and Lir had re-entered the gate in the wake of the hunt. The sergeant had descended from the rampart and was talking to one of the Masters of Hounds.

"No kill?" the sergeant asked, cautiously.

"None."

"What's up, then?"

"His lordship's half slaughtered the horses, and my dogs, too, I shouldn't wonder. He let the stag go, ordered us off. Said he saw a phantom, a black phantom, riding on the stag's back."

"Excuse me, sergeant," said the torch-soldier, sidling closer, "but might I ask the Master if anyone else saw it?"

"Well," said the Master. He shrugged, but his eyes flickered slightly. "There was something. It was one of the 'scarers', I reckoned, torn loose and fallen on the beast. There were two little shiny things in it—the bells. It was dark as death. That's what comes of hunting by night. Can't see what is or isn't. But his lordship swears the witch has raised a fiend to vex him. And he's rushed home to catch her in the act."

"Hey, the harper!" the sergeant exclaimed.

Lir was sprinting across the bailey towards the platform steps and the keep. He mounted the steps three or four at a leap. The door of the Hall stood open across the inner court. Two guards discussing matters whipped around as Lir passed them. They bolted after him.

Lir was rushing on without plan.

He beat the guards to the door and was inside. He stopped at last when he beheld the Duke seated in his gilded chair. The Duke was drinking wine in gulps. Demonstrably, he had not been able to make himself seek Lilune, unfortified. But in that instant, he registered Lir.

The court gasped, and drew back from Lir as if from a leper. The Duke gazed at him with malevolence through a mask of fear.

"What's this?"

The guards skidded in and both grabbed Lir by the shoulders.

"Your pardon, my lord. Only a mad harper."

The Duke laughed his unreal laugh. But the laugh was softer, and it trembled.

"Mad harper, are you? I've got a mad witch in my castle. She practices against me. Possibly the mad harper can spell her with his music and bind her." It was a feeble sickly jest.

Lir responded by lying steadily.

"Yes, my lord. I can bind her. That's why I'm here."

"You know her, then," said the Duke.

He had changed his garments, and changed his demeanour with them. He wasn't in a panic any more, though his eyes twitched. He had brought Lir into his private chamber. There were five guards outside, and ten more on the stair up to the Northern Turret. He had told Lir the witch was in the Turret, that she had barricaded the door and that therefore her only way out must be through sorcery. But the moon was setting. Perhaps she got her power from the moon, like her name. Perhaps she wouldn't try any further tricks tonight.

"Why does your lordship suppose I know her?"

"Because you declare you can bind her."

"That doesn't mean I know *her*, my lord. Just my trade."

"Oh, a liar," said the Duke, scornfully. "You do know her. Of course you do, transparent youth. You want to save your sweetheart. We hang witches here. Does she come from the north?"

"Yes, my lord." Lir considered he should give in.

"They usually do," said the Duke.

"A Castle by a lake," said Lir. "It is the Castle that's to blame, not the girl."

"We can't hang a castle," said the Duke.

"If you hang her," said Lir, gambling on the Duke's superstition, "her phantom may continue to haunt you, vengefully. It would be better if I bound her and took her safely away."

"Take her where?"

Lir was uncertain, was not thinking much further than every next sentence.

"Back to her Castle. She was bound there harmlessly for many years."

The Duke smiled a pale and hateful smile.

"You love her. She's spelled you."

Lir resisted the impulse to deny this. He only said, "You'll be safer, my lord, if you leave her to me."

"A threat? A word from my royal mouth and the men outside the door will enter and cut your head from your body."

"Then you would have *my* vengeful ghost to haunt you as well, my lord."

"You *are* quick, are you not? Quick and insolent. All right. I leave it to you. You know the way. My men will break down the Turret door if you require it."

Through the unshuttered window, the sky remained dark. It would be a couple of hours yet till dawn. But the moon had set, and there had been no other disturbance in the town.

As Lir went along the passage from the Duke's apartment, he heard the doors being barred on the inside. The guards did not meet Lir's eye. When the Duke had left to change his garments, before Lir was commanded up to him, they had brought the harp in from the barracks, and dumping it near Lir in the almost-empty Hall, they had each spat, to show how they currently esteemed him. He was in with the witch. *Spit-spat*. This depressed Lir, but he dismissed it.

He went up to the top of the Turret stair. The guards retreated to the bottom. Through the barricaded door, no stirring was audible.

Lir leaned on the door, asking himself why he was involved in this macabre foolishness. He wasn't afraid. It wasn't that which had sent him shaking in the alley. It was aversion, outraged commonsense, but not fear. And he wasn't afraid of Lilune, though the thing which had come about through her disgusted and angered him. But partly, despite all proof, he didn't completely believe in it.

The guards were ridiculously retreating along the passage, inch by inch.

"Lilune," Lir said to the door.

He surmised she was asleep, tranced. She might wake at sunrise. It had seemed natural to her, although the sun was her enemy. Or she would wake at sunset, before the trance or the power or whatever it was, robbed her again of her own will. He would make her let him in when she woke. He couldn't think how, but he would.

He sat down by the door.

The guards had vanished from sight. Plainly, everyone would avoid this area while they were able. A bit of candle in a sconce fluttered lamely on the wall.

He had to sleep sometime. He closed his eyes, his back against the Turret door.

Lir woke because the castle was collapsing, with an unspeakable thunder, round his head.

"What is it?" he stupidly inquired.

He became aware it was not the castle, but the timber

door of the Turret, at which a gang of soldiers was heaving a wooden post. Their aim was made more difficult by the incline of the stairs and the restricted space. Frequently, the post thunked on the stone walls. The lock of the door seemed already to have broken, but the barricade within was taking some shifting.

The sergeant leant over Lir.

"Pretty mess you're in," he said. He did not seem as unliking as his men. "Duke's hysterical. He says you're a warlock in league with his witch. You shouldn't have slept past sunrise, my lad. Guess what we've got orders to do?"

"Cut off my head," guessed Lir.

"Not exactly. We're to throw you in the Turret with the witch and shut the pair of you in from the outside. That way, Dukey says, if you're innocent she'll slay you and save him the bother of hanging you for impertinence. If you're guilty, he's got you penned together. I don't know what he plans, that being the case. But I lay odds it'll be no fun. Either for you, or the maid.

"Thanks for your news. Not that it's much help to me."

"No, not much help."

Lir remembered he had gone to sleep leaning against the door which was being battered. Someone must have hauled him down the stair. The harp-box sat at his side.

"I've got my orders," said the sergeant.

"Though you don't care for them."

"That's it. Are you afraid to be shut up in there with the witch?"

"No."

"Good."

The barricade surrendered suddenly. The soldiers and their post sprawled forward into the chamber.

Lir thought the racket must have roused the girl, but the men in the room were righting themselves, and cursing agitatedly. There was no hint of Lilune.

Carrying the harp-box, he walked up the stair, and got past the soldiers.

It was day in the world, but the windowless chamber was benighted. Stumps were all that remained of the candles. There was enough dull light, however, shed from the doorway, that he could locate the wrecked table that had been the barricade. Beyond, against the wall, heavy curtains concealed a bed.

She was lying on the bed, hidden but present.

He recollected how the chest had plummeted into the river and she had never cried out. He recollected her static soundlessness in the hollow trees of the forest. Once she slept by day, she did not wake.

"Here," said the sergeant. He put three fatty white candles on the piece of table that was still upright. "Do you have a tinder?"

"Yes." The soldiers had withdrawn on to the stair again, lugging their post. They did not look at Lir. Lir didn't exist for the soldiers any more. "You'd better have your silver back," Lir said. "If your Duke plans to murder me, I'll have no need of it."

The sergeant did not answer. He went through the door, and the door was pushed closed. Lir heard a fresh barricade being erected on the other side.

He struck flint and tinder, lit one of the candles and fastened it in a sconce.

There had been books on the table, and parchments, which had fallen to the floor when the table cracked in half. The soldiers had trampled on the books and parchments.

Lir seated himself in the solitary tall chair. He didn't credit any of this. He didn't credit the predicament he was in.

When Lilune woke, he would have to prevent her falling into the second sleep, the night-sleep. The nightsleep which loosed the night-beast . . . but it was all nonsense. Even if it were true, it was idiocy and he an idiot to be part of it.

He should admit he *had* been spelled. Though the—Power—had wanted to keep him away just recently. That brief thick sleep which the soldiers had interrupted. Hadn't he been *intended* to save the girl? And did it mean that, although she appeared to be in danger, she was not, for the power itself could protect her at last? Was it becoming that strong?

He had so far slept one hour in eighteen, but he didn't sleep in the Turret. He watched the flickering candle.

He began to suspect the girl actually wouldn't come-to at sunset. She might slip directly from the day-trance to the sorcerous night-trance.

Lir went to the door and spoke through it. He had heard vague noises come and go outside: the soldiers on guard, swopping shifts, murmuring.

"What time is it?" Lir asked the unseen soldiers.

No reply.

"Will you warn me when it's sunset?"

No reply.

"I've got your sergeant's silver coin, and some copper. All the coins for the warning."

A pause. Then a voice:

"No one here will help you, warlock."

"If I were a warlock, I could easily divine when the sun set," Lir said reasonably. "Doesn't that strike you?"

But nobody replied again.

Lir crossed to the wall of the Turret farthest from the bed and pulled aside the tapestry. He investigated the hair-line cracks. Selecting the crack also farthest from the bed, Lir started to scratch at it with his woodsman's knife. The soldiers had not bothered with this knife, and no surprise. It was a handy blade, but cheap. It buckled slightly as it laboured against the stone. The sound of the scraping set Lir's teeth on edge.

It wasn't much of a hope, but there was nothing else to do.

When the first candle smeared out, Lir lit a second.

There was one left.

Outside, all noise had ceased. The soldiers had doubtless retreated off down the stair, as previously.

Lir had an intuition that as soon as the sun set and dusk commenced to gather, the Duke would revert to panic.

The Turret had not protected him from the witch's games before, had it? Lir tried not to speculate on what the Duke might want to do to his captives. For practitioners of the Black Arts he could choose burning, hanging, drowning. Or worse.

Lir chisled at the stone. It would take a month to make a perceptible impression on it. He had a few hours. Work harder, then.

Lir was leaning against the wall. Both his arms ached searingly. The ache spread over his shoulders, up his neck, into his skull. Fine stone-dust powdered the floor. The hair-line crack looked no wider. The knife had just snapped off from its haft.

The second candle was ebbing. With no proper method of telling, Lir sensed the sun was going down over the estuary. But he had been picturing that constantly. Maybe there were hours yet. Maybe it was already midnight.

Quiet, but very distinct, a sigh drifted to him through the curtains of the bed.

Lir froze. Even the pain in his arms froze, went out.

He had not looked beyond the curtains, not once. Now, he forced himself to go towards them, to take hold of them and draw them aside. It truly wasn't fear. It was merely that he knew the moment was coming when all disbelief must be suspended. The moment when he would confront the impossible.

But inside the curtains, on the bed, there was only Lilune.

The last of the candle offered a muddy light, but it was enough to catch her pallor, her wide eyes. She seemed stunned to find Lir there with her. Her white face was all nervous question.

"You?" she said. "Are you here to kill me?"

"No."

"I was afraid of—something. I screamed, but I couldn't wake up." She seemed bewildered. "But I'm so tired. I can't wake up. I can't."

"You have to try," he said.

Suddenly her expression was wiped from her face. Her lids dropped shut.

He shook her roughly, but she was already gone. She hung limply from his hands and her two plaits poured on to the floor. She appeared dead, and he couldn't see her breathing. He let her slip on to the pillows.

The candle had slunk lower in the wall sconce. There was hardly any light in the chamber. But the deepest gloom had fixed in the shadow of the curtains, creating a sort of cloud above the unconscious girl.

Involuntarily, Lir took a step backwards, and did not understand why. His eyes had not interpreted the message as his instinct had done. Then the darkness began to alter its shape.

It was as if smoke, or mist, were rising from Lilune. Not from her garments. Not even from the surface of her skin. But out of her nostrils, her mouth, her pores. And as the smoke, or the mist, rose, it turned blacker, and more black. Initially, it made a broad, curled-over thing, which had the semblance of a crouching animal. But gradually the substance elongated, straightened, stretched into the air. It was so black now that the blackness glowed on the shadow. It swayed up over the prone figure of the girl like a malificent flower, and its slender stalk was fastened in her heart. It had achieved a discernable form.

It was like Lilune herself. Nearly like her. It had a rippling stuff about it that suggested the mane of hair, unbound. But it had no lower limbs, only the snake-like stalk on which it grew from Lilune's body. Its arms—if arms they were—were raised, menacing, questing. And in the black oval of its face were no features, until two slots began to shine there, two horrible, luminous, colourless shines. . . .

It seemed to stare at Lir. A great while it stared at him. And it weighed him, his use to it, living or dead. And gradually, it released him from that relentless, eyeless stare, preferring his living use. It melted down over the bed and across the floor like a spilling of black candlewax. It spilled to the barricaded door, and hesitated momentarily, and at length soaked through the door and was gone.

PART FOUR

The Witch Hunt

Lir listened for a full minute, and heard no sound, no outcry, from the passage. That could mean anything. That the Duke had called off the guards, or stationed them further away. That they had stationed themselves further away. That the—the *thing*, able to sift through a door, had thereafter sifted through a wall, going by another route in order to avoid the soldiers. It could mean, of course, that it had reached the soldiers and slain them. In its own unique, vile way: drawing their strength, their life, into itself.

The minute was over. Lir ran to the door. He beat on it and yelled: "Let me OUT!"

The silence went on.

Lir was already constructing his escape before he grasped what he was at. It was simple. perhaps he had unconsciously reasoned it hours before. The stone castle, the stone Turret draped with heavy tapestries, the door and barricade of wood, the summer heat and dryness—the lighted candle.

He slung the harp-box on his back. With a violence that eased his nerves he ripped the curtains from the bed. Not stopping to glance at her, he wound the girl in these coverings, wound her up like a bundle of washing. He felt a brief loathing, touching her, though she was blameless, could not prevent—but no matter. There was no leisure to think. He slung her, as he had slung the harp, over his back. And next he dragged the tapestries from the walls and made a washing bundle of himself. Finding a puddle of rose-scented water in a ewer, he dipped the edge of his cloak in that and bound it over his nose and mouth. He lit the final candle from the sputtering flame of the earlier one. He gave the candle flame the door to lick.

It was slow, beginning. When the flame got a hold on the timber, it was quick.

Blooms of smoke blotted out the room. But as the panels burned through, Lir could see the flame running on over the shafts of wood they had wedged against the door to block it.

Even now, there was no reaction in the passage.

Lir cast the ewer at the flaming door. The ewer crashed directly through the charred timber. Lir cast himself after it.

For a second he was in an inferno. Fire surrounded him. Fire breathed on him greedily. And the wooden obstacle resisted the impact of his weight, the blows of his tapestry-bandaged fist. And then the panels gave.

Kicking flaming tinder away before him, choking and blinded, he burst forward and half-stumbled, half-jumped the length of the whole short stair. He was on fire and had carried the fire with him. He fought to free himself and the girl from the blazing wrappings. In a whirl of sparks, he emerged, hissing and spitting like a scorched cat. The fiery embroideries went flying, falling in crackling heaps against the stone walls. Lir discovered himself mildly singed but otherwise unharmed. Lilune over his shoulder was less damaged than he.

The fire would burn itself out in the enclosed stone passage and the Turret, though smoke would coil through tiny crevices into chambers below, giving its own signal. Certainly, there were no soldiers at hand to deal with either fire or fugitives.

Nor was there any other thing close by.

Away along the passage was the door to the Duke's apartment. That door was also unguarded, like the other.

Lir had a single conviction. He had determined that the thing, the "Black Soul", as the villagers in the woods had called it, could not survive without Lilune's physical body to harbour it. That being the case, it must at all times be aware of the sheltering body, must never stray too far from it. And if Lilune's body itself were moved, as Lir was now moving it, the Black Soul must surely become aware of that, too. It wasn't a particularly comforting theory, but it made sense. And in a way, it gave Lir some control over the thing. If he could get Lilune far from the castle and the town, the Black Soul would desert the area to follow her—and Lir. Lir accepted that the thing had gained influence over him before, but then he had been unprepared. He would have to resist.

He was negotiating the passage at a steady lope. As the passage curved, approaching the lower stairway, it brightened. He rounded the curve and at the stair-head, immobile in the light of the wall torches, were the sergeant of the guard and seven men.

The sergeant gaped at Lir. Lir returned the gape. Each stood rooted, but the sergeant's sword, and those of the soldiers, black-iron and business-like, were grasped ready. Then the sergeant shook himself and grated:

"Your good luck, lad, we waited to see what'd come around the corner before we bonked it. What's that smoke?"

"The Turret's on fire."

"You and you!" barked the sergeant. Two soldiers dodged past Lir and up the passage.

"Suppose you let me go free," Lir said.

"Lad," said the sergeant, "I don't have to agree with what our Duke says, to do it for him. And he says bring you and the wench out to the market-place. All you've done is spare me and these boys the trouble of unbarring your door." There was sympathy in the sergeant's face, but no intention of weakening.

"Tell me," said Lir, "did Death brush by you on the stair?"

The sergeant blinked. Behind him, his men jerked agitatedly.

"What do you mean by Death?"

"I mean the phantom that's loosed when the sun sets.

The thing your men and I almost met yesternight. The thing I can rid you of. But only if you allow me, and the girl, to get away."

"Calmly," said the sergeant to his men, not bothering to glance back at them, knowing their agitation without glancing. "Talk like that won't save you, Harper."

"Save me from what?"

The sergeant grimaced. "Whatever our Duke has in mind."

Lir relapsed in a nearly speechless frustration. To come this far and be trapped. And as they wasted the precious minutes here, Death did indeed roam at will.

The sergeant took Lir's arm in an unmistakable captor's grip. He told one of the guards to remove the girl from Lir's shoulder and carry her. Reluctantly, the man obeyed.

They trudged down the stairways of the castle.

The fish-market was crammed with soldiers. That explained the absence of a watch outside the Turret room. The Duke had plainly wanted the majority of his guard about him, for his maximum protection. There were, however, no townspeople evident. The tavern was shut and unlighted.

The young moon was already high over the market. This, and the torches flaring in men's fists, lit up many items, but only one item that Lir saw. The gallows.

Lir's body seemed to hollow out. He seemed to have no blood left and no bones, just a cold sand blowing about inside him.

The Duke appeared, ten soldiers with drawn swords at either side.

"Don't you like it?" the Duke asked, waving at the gallows.

"This is your justice, is it?" Lir got out. He was vaguely surprised that his voice, harper-trained, did not betray his horror.

"Justice for witch and warlock."

Lir tried to think of something to do. Could think of nothing. Literally nothing. He found his eyes were fixed on the sergeant. But the sergeant's face was rigid with a dreadful pity for Lir. The pity a man felt only for someone he could not, under any circumstances, aid.

The soldier carrying Lilune suddenly set off towards the gallows.

The girl hung limp, unknowing. Her peculiar plaits, decorated with little gold insects, trailed over the man's back and along the street. The men who marched behind took fastidious care not to tred on them.

And now Lir was being marched in the same direction. The Duke, incongruously, marched in step, though there were three intervening guards separating them.

"Perhaps you'd like to give us a song, before you go," said the Duke. He was still panicky. But he was obviously enjoying this. It was presumably beginning to reassure him that he had the upper hand.

Torches had been stuck into formerly empty cages on the house walls. As they passed beneath these torches, a wave of red light broke over them. And between the torches, a wave of dark. And abruptly, Lir became aware that a bit of the darkness always ran over into the torch-light, a dab of light always glowed in the dark. Two dabs of light.

It was there, in the shadow under the walls. It maintained a constant distance from them, but as they went forward, kept pace with them, trailing them, like a hungry, wary dog. Lir alone, apparently, had seen and recognised It. If he gave an alarm, would that be of use? Would it buy time for Lilune and himself? Likely not.

Why did the thing hang back? Was it the torch-glare it was avoiding, or the vast numbers of men? It had not been fond of fire-born light, attacking in the black alley, rising in the Turret in the last feeble splutter of the candle. Though It had no aversion to the moon. As for the soldiers, It was insubstantial, therefore not easily hurt. And the scare Its appearance would produce . . . it occurred to Lir that he was supposing the thing had a brain to deduce these facts. More likely It was elemental, instinctive: mindless. He comprehended then that It had merely approached in terror, to witness the destruction of Its shelter, Its actual life: Lilune. There was no rescue It could attempt.

They had reached the gallows.

The scene was one of utter finality. A wooden cart was drawn up ready between the uprights of the gallows. Ropes dangled from the cross-tree above, two of them. The hangman stood in the cart, grinning. He had been called from his supper and promised a gold piece for his efforts. The task was not new to him, but the gold piece was. He had a reason to grin. A man sat on the driver's seat of the cart behind the two horses, his whip poised. Just at his back in the cart was a box, wide enough to receive two bodies.

"Hanging, then cremation outside the town walls," the Duke remarked to Lir. "The customary procedure."

Lir discovered his legs had given way. The sergeant was bellowing some order to his men. Lir straightened himself. They hadn't tied his hands. Surrounded by guards as he was, it had perhaps seemed unnecessary.

Two soldiers marched Lir up to the cart; one of them was the man nicknamed Lank. The single soldier had already carried up Lilune by means of a short ladder. They thrust Lir up the ladder alone.

Lir was stupidly gazing around. Through the sea of faces, shadows, torch-light, he sought desperately for Lilune's Black Soul. He was praying for rescue, even though it could not and would not happen. Even rescue by the Dark One himself seemed preferable to death. Even rescue by a fiend.

The cart was crowded now; the soldier and Lilune, Lir, the hangman.

The hangman leaned across. He let the noose drop casually over Lir's head.

"Say you forgive me," demanded the hangman.

"I hope you may be damned."

The Duke laughed stridently at Lir from the front of the pack of soldiers just beside the gallows. But even as he laughed, a black billow surged from nowhere, covered him, bore him under, and his laughter changed to howling.

The soldiers involuntarily jumped away.

The Duke howled, thrashing, falling. Though insubstantial, the phantom appeared solid. It smothered the Duke like a large writhing blanket.

A soldier lifted his sword. The sergeant caught his wrist. "Don't cut at it, fool! You'll chop our Duke in two."

The howling had dwindled into groans and whimpering. Everyone stared at the spectacle, petrified. The hangman, his mouth ajar, stood transfixed.

Lir pulled the noose off his neck. As the hangman half turned towards him, Lir grabbed the rope and swung himself forward. The harp on his back leant him extra impetus. His knees jammed into the hangman's belly, and as the man folded, the rope carried Lir over him, flying off the cart.

Lir dropped from the rope. He wrenched a torch from someone's grip, and sprang with it to land beside the heaving mass that was the Duke.

Instantly, the mound of darkness shrank and lifted. Its female shape became clear; It was the more terrible because of it.

"No, you don't love fire, do you, night-thing?" Lir said. He whirled the torch and the shape withdrew further. It stretched out ghastly hands.

Behind him, Lir heard a movement. He flung aside at the same moment the sergeant roared: "Leave him alone, Lank. Can't you see he's the only one can master it?"

Lank backed off, snarling.

The Duke lay on the dirty floor of the market. His face was as parchment-pale as Lilune's and he whined like an animal.

On the gallows-cart, the soldier held Lilune in one arm.

Lir darted once more up the ladder and snatched the girl from the soldier, and pushed him out. Below, the *thing* gazed up at them. Ignoring the Duke, It started to eddy towards the cart.

"Come, then," Lir said to it. He raised the torch away from himself and the girl, invitingly.

He was trembling with reaction, his hands so cold he

could barely feel the torch he held. Somehow, he knew the thing grasped what it must do, as It had grasped its part before. He sensed a revolting link with It, but this was not the time for revulsion.

It rippled over the edge of the cart. It came in like a tide. Lir cringed a little, but Its stretching hands fastened on Lilune. It sank into her like an indrawn black breath, and was gone.

"Take note!" Lir shouted. The trained voice went to every corner of the market place. "Let us go, you'll be safe. I give no guarantee if we are hanged."

He stepped along the cart, kicking away the ladder as he went, his heart in his mouth, praying again. He laid the girl beside the box which had been brought for their corpses. There was also a spade by the box. To bury ashes? The driver had prudently vacated his seat. Lir appropriated the reins and the whip. He looked up and swallowed hard. No one had moved.

He raised the whip and cracked the air above the horses' heads.

The ranks of the soldiers parted.

The spirit of the riotous flight swept Lir with it. For a while, nothing seemed impossible. Even getting through the town gates. Which, as it turned out, was simple. They were anticipating the cart, loaded with dead witch and warlock, making haste to cremate the dangerous bodies. Lir pulled his cloak over his head to hide his conspicuous fair hair, and drove straight at the gate, cracking the whip and bawling: "Open! Open in the Duke's name!" The gates slammed back and the cart plunged through and away up the road and into the woods.

Lir kept the horses going at breakneck speed until the well-ordered, grassy tracks, used for the Duke's hunting, began to deteriorate. Then he slowed the horses to a trot to let them breathe and to take his bearings. The Duke would be after them; that was a certainty. The only thing Lir was unsure of was precisely when. He might send men at once, or he might be too weakened and too afraid to decide on it just yet. Lir had a strong suspicion the sergeant wouldn't encourage pursuit. The sergeant had had personal doubts about the hanging. He also apparently agreed with Lir's statement that it was better to let the phantom be removed as far away as possible. But the Duke would never feel safe until witch and warlock were truly destroyed by rope and fire.

Lir had a few times driven a cart and horses in former years. But it was strange to be doing it again. Odd to recall that not so long ago he had been rejoicing in the carelessness of his wandering minstrel's life and his lack of burdens.

Finally, he let the horses rest. The trot had cooled them off, and they stood patiently, in a bored but uncomplaining way. They had got used to unpredictable rushes, extended trots and boring waits in the carter's trade.

Lir stepped over into the cart and looked at Lilune. Her head cradled on a pillow of plaits, she seemed peacefully asleep. Who would guess what hideous power lay coiled within her. It was dark under the trees, and Lir wondered for a second if the phantom would emerge again, perhaps attack him. But he remembered the unwelcome link he had felt with It. No, It accepted him as servant, saviour. Him It would never harm. All the same. . . .

He leaned over Lilune and shook her. When she opened her eyes and smiled at him, he wanted to hit her.

"It was all a dream," she said. "I kept wishing it were. And it was."

"What dream?" he said.

"I dreamed you threw the chest into a river, the chest the villagers gave me."

"Not I. But the villagers did it. They meant you to drown."

"And did you mean me to drown?"

"No. But that wasn't all your dream, was it?"

Her face clouded. She sat up and stared into space. "A stag," she said. "The Duke's court went hunting a stag. But the stag and I were the same, and they were hunting *me*. And next I dreamed—it must have been a dream—I was screaming, but instead of me it was a woman in an alley. She screamed because she had a black cloak wrapped around her." Lilune stopped. She did not seem to realize what she was saying, yet some part of her realized, for her hands were knotted and her teeth chattering.

"What else did you dream?" he asked, softer, laying no stress on the word "dream".

"I was in the forest—no, that was before. It was another dream I had once. I saw a man running through the forest, a pedlar—but that was when I was ill. I never remembered it, till now."

"Do you recollect waking in the Turret and speaking to me?" Lir said.

"No," said Lilune. Her teeth were chattering so violently he could hardly distinguish what she said. He tried to take her cold hands in his, which seemed even colder, but she pulled her hands away. "I saw you on a gallows," she announced. "And—*myself*." The shock of this shocked her into calm. Levelly, she went on, "The Duke was wrapped in a black cloak, like the woman in the alley, and he fell over. And then I dreamed you woke me up, and you had."

There were gaps in her "dream", and a lack of comprehension that reassured him. Though she had partially seen through the consciousness of the Black Soul, she had not been wholly one with It. He would have to explain it all to her. She had to know, or she had no chance to survive. He couldn't be sure she could grasp what he said. He couldn't be sure she could fight what was in her, if, indeed, it were possible to fight such a possession. While she was awake, the monster was trapped inside her, but the power It could exert, though trapped, he had experienced. But she must be told. And he must make the best job of telling this story that any harper with a story, and trained to give value to each word, had ever done.

She listened, silent.

This was not the Lilune he had met before. The alteration was abrupt, but not unnatural. Events had caught her up: the chains she had escaped in her Castle, the terror of freedom; the sun, the river, the chest. Not least the court which had pampered and then turned on her. And last, worst terror of all, the terror that she herself was. For obviously she believed what he related. It came to him that maybe he had alerted in her some ancestral memory, lingering in her blood, enabling her to glimpse those others who had suffered the affliction before her. Was everything settling, grotesquely, into place in her mind?

When he had finished, she was a lost child, looking at him dumbly.

"That's why the hags bound me, watched me, shut me in. No wonder. I'm horrible, disgusting. Oh, it's not fair." That was still the child. Then, with no warning, there was a woman where the child had been. And the woman said to him: "Please kill me, Lir. At once. I'm too afraid to do it myself."

It staggered him. Idiotically, he burst out laughing.

"That's the first time I ever heard you say 'please' for anything." Her eyes and mouth widened. "No," he forestalled her. "If you're valiant enough to ask for that, you're so much more worth saving."

"But you can't save me!" she wailed. The child was back.

"I'll try," he said. "And you'll attend to your side of it. Sleep by day, but stay awake at night. Resist. Come, you're tough enough, my lady, aren't you, if you beg for death rather than inflict evil?"

Lilune was numb with fear. But somehow his laughter, nervous though it was, had bridged her despair. It wasn't like the unreal laughter of the Duke.

She lifted one of her plaits from the bottom of the cart.

"Golden bees," she whispered, indicating the plait's decoration. After that, she stayed very quiet. She had to brood on the truth, digest the confusion of it. She felt ashamed as well as fearful.

To give her privacy, Lir went to see how the horses were. presently, he drove the cart on through the forest.

* * *

Around midnight, the Duke's woods broke up among valleys. The extended palisade of trees retreated eastwards and the up-and-down lands began that Lir had encountered on his way to the town. The woods had led them northeast, so that now the eastern villages where he had idled and played songs lay all over to the west, and the country was unfamiliar. Still, there was a fine road. On either side, pale ghostly fields of wheat were tinged by the moon; here and there a ditch gleamed with shallow water. There were wind-breaks of poplars like tall black feathers.

Lilune watched everything as avidly as before, too avidly, as if she would see none of it again.

They did not speak to each other. There seemed nothing to say.

When the sun rose, Lir turned the box, that had been intended for their corpses, on its side. Lilune crawled into the box, and Lir pushed it flush with the side of the cart. The box seemed sufficiently heavy to remain stable, but he drove the cart more slowly, as a precaution. In the afternoon, they went through a village. Lir bought feed for the horses. Nobody asked about the sideways box in the cart, or the ominous-looking spade. They asked Lir if he were a harper and if he would give them a song. He told them his sister was sick in the north and he was hurrying home. He lied too well, and became embarrassed when they showered him with sympathy, bread and pears, and even a small carved wooden saint to pray to for his sister's health.

In a stand of trees in a meadow he tethered the horses, fed them, and stretched out on the grass to catch some sleep. He willed himself to wake at the sun's decline.

He did not wake up till dusk, and jumped up frantically, but Lilune had managed to release herself from the box and was patrolling the meadow like a cat. She had been more determined than he to keep the evil trance at bay. Her slight silhouette passed to and fro against the green sky. Soon she saw he was awake and walked over.

"I've been thinking," she said. "About resistance. So I want to do everything differently. I have to face as much of the sun as I can. I have to try to eat the sort of food you eat. Will you teach me to drive the horses? Will you get a knife and cut my hair?"

"If that's what you want," he said.

The resolution he had glimpsed in her formerly was now gritty and earnest.

He handed her a pear. She held her breath as if in fear, and bit into it. After a few bites she ran away up the meadow and fell to her knees. He realized she was being sick. She crept back, wretchedly.

But when they went on, she insisted he show her how to drive the cart and horses, and sat proudly, flicking the reins.

They drove through the night, taking turns. They started to have a conversation. She recounted things about the old women, things nasty and often funny, always bizarre. In exchange, he offered his life-story. She listened hungrily.

When the sun had risen, she sat angrily in the cart until she blistered. Lir was awed, almost distressed, by her courage.

They had made good headway. Shortly before noon, Lir saw a distant dark bank looming on the horizon's edge: the forest, north and east. But instantly he saw it, he felt oppressed.

The road had petered out into a track, the track into a steep hillside. Having coaxed and bullied the cart and horses to the top of the hill, Lir looked back. The view was vast, sweeping. He even identified the far western glint of the river. But something else quickly claimed his attention. Away along the road they had used previously, a white ball of dust was fraying out into the fields. It was the mounted soldiery of the Duke, swift horses kicking summer's dry powder off the road. Half an hour's ride behind the cart, less, if they maintained their speed.

Lir cracked the whip. The horses pelted forward. Lilune's box rattled against the side of the cart.

Lilune thrust against the side of the cart, levering the box backwards. When the gap was reasonably large, she hauled herself out. Black boughs shut out the twilight. The cart was jolting to a halt, unevenly, in a tunnel of forest.

Lir turned to regard her. His face was grey and exhausted, alarming her. She had relied on him. She had relied on his being always the same.

"The Duke's men are after us," he said. "I've kept the horses going all day, with just a minute's rest here and there to save them dying on us." He lashed the reins and the horses moved off again, but plodding, their heads drooping. "We have to keep on."

She sat in the cart, not knowing what she should do, doing nothing.

The horses went gradually more and more sluggishly.

Her heart seemed to beat in time with them. When they stopped, so would her heart.

Then through the trees, echoing, she heard the yap of a hunting horn.

"Lir!" she screamed.

"Yes. It's their game. Ever since the light started to go. But it sounds closer than they really are. They won't catch up to us." At least, he thought, not for a mile or two.

Lilune stared at Lir's shoulders as he hunched over the reins. Lir's strength was all that stood between her and the nightmare. And Lir seemed crumbling with fatigue, like a tired fire. She wished she had learned another spell instead of the spell of Calling. But she remembered that in any case magic might be connected with the Black Horror which possessed her. She felt she ought to tell Lir to leave her for the Duke's men and go on alone. But she hadn't the nerve left to face death a second time.

She tried not to weep.

A quarter of an hour after, the soft thunder she had been ignoring exploded into the noise of hoofs. Amid the idiot yapping of the hunting horn, seventeen men crashed out of the trees, whooped, spurred their mounts, surrounded the cart.

At their head was the soldier called Lank. He snarled as he looked at them, the exact snarl he had snarled when

Lir evaded his blow in the Duke's courtyard. As if Lank had never stopped snarling since, and never would.

Lank sat and stared at Lilune.

Behind him, firelight flickered where the soldiers had made their camp.

"Tonight, or maybe tomorrow, we'll burn the two of you," Lank stated softly.

"It isn't his fault," Lilune said. "I bewitched him."

She meant Lir. Lank knew who she meant, for she had said it many times, and once, she had cried. She was unsure why it had become so desperately necessary to protect Lir, more necessary than to protect herself. Probably because he, in turn, could protect her.

Lir was tied around the chest and legs to a tree. The harp had been removed from his shoulders and from its box. They had discussed the ripping out of its strings, but nothing had been done. It was a magic thing. Best toss it on the fire tomorrow with its owner.

Lir hung his head, reminding Lilune of the weary horses in their last trudging. He had said little, only something about the forest, the north, the proximity of the Castle. He had said the soldiers were fools, and Lank had hit him in the jaw with a: "Not fool enough to burn for witchcraft."

Lank went on staring at Lilune.

She thought of the two old women. She wished she had learned a spell to petrify Lank.

He hadn't struck her. None of the men had touched her. They were all afraid of her . . . but not afraid enough to go away and leave her alone. They were afraid of Duke Dark-and-Pale, too, who had instructed them to hunt down and slay her.

"Here, you," Lank called over a couple of the other soldiers. "Come and tend this snivelling witch while I have my food."

He went off, and the other soldiers crouched about thirteen feet from Lilune and began to play a game with dice.

The moon was sinking and had appeared through a gap

in the trees westward. Like a generous shaving from a pale gold coin, the moon was. By the hour of its setting, she might be dead.

Suddenly, Lilune felt a passionate longing for her Castle. She wanted, how she wanted, to be there. Safe in her lidded bed in the tower. Safe, safe, with the two old women to guard her and care for her, and protect her from the world and from herself. There had been no witch hunt in her Castle, no exposure to the sun; no threats of burning. Even the chains by which the hags had bound her to the bed seemed a security. Yes, Lilune would be thankful to be locked into the tower, bound by iron and magics—yes. If only. . . .

And then the revelation came to Lilune, as if it had simply been waiting there in the darkness of the forest for her to acknowledge it. She could work the spell of Calling. All she had to do was to Call the two old women.

The Power in the Castle of Dark, which had previously thwarted the hags, would not thwart them now. Because the Power in the Castle would desire Lilune's escape from death, would it not? But suppose the hags were unable to reach her in time? She could not estimate how far away the Castle was. No matter. The old women's sorcery, if not they themselves, could span distances easily, as the spell of Calling itself did. Lilune set her doubts aside. She bowed her head, concentrating.

Lir had been watching the soldiers' fire as it shone through the harp. Lir was dazed. He anticipated all manner of misfortunes, nothing lucky, and he had no hope left. He was too tired and the odds seemed too great. He cared about the girl and about the harp. He wished he could be angry, rage, curse, anything rather than this stupid void in which he had sunk. To begin with he had tried to think of some trick or plan. No longer.

The fire seethed, reflected slowly over the strings of the harp, and abruptly there was Wild-Eye walking out of the fire and out of the harp. Wild-Eye with his cloak blazoned by yellow serpents and his own yellow bone harp-box on his shoulders. He looked precisely as he had when Lir had first beheld him, offering the bone harp in the night-market to the young men of the Minstrels' School.

"You, the fair-haired boy," Wild-Eye said to Lir, banteringly, as he had then. "You've got yourself in a hot kettle of a mess. Did I confirm you a harper for this?"

"You are just my dream," said Lir.

"And maybe I was just your dream that other night. Recall the yellow gem that shrivelled to an acorn. Recall how I lessoned you in the making of your harp, that lesson, which you have never forgotten, nor ever will."

"I bid you welcome, dream or not," said Lir. "For whatever else, the harp gives foretelling dreams. Why are you here?"

"To remind you of what you are. A true harper. Did my harp not prove so? And has your year's wandering not proved so? And a true harper has the uncanny gift of his music. Such music belongs to the elder glamours of the earth, and you should know it. He may harp in the Dark One's Hall and take no harm, who is a true harper. I swear it, who have done it."

"Then your harper's magic is at ease in Hell? I don't fancy such talent."

"What's Hell?" inquired Wild-Eye. "You should visit before you pass judgement on a place. And have you never heard it said, the Dark One is a gentleman?"

Lir considered it silly that he was having a philosophical argument with Wild-Eye in his sleep.

"I'm to die tomorrow," said Lir. "This is nonsense."

"Brother my brother," said Wild-Eye, "ask for your harp and see if you die. And later, under the ground, recollect what I taught you of the building of harps."

Lir lifted his lids, waking confusedly. The forest was swirling with something that appeared to be sheer sorcery made visible. Then he heard a soldier grumble in consternation: "This fog, it's getting thicker by the minute, Lank."

"Night mist, blowing from some marsh by the river," said Lank. "You can smell frogs in it."

Lir turned his head. Lilune was seated like a small

stone image. Her head was bowed, and instinctively he guessed the nearness of Dark had inspired her to create magic. The soldiers seemed not to guess. He wondered what they would do if he asked for the harp. Though he was tied, the cords knotted the other side of the tree trunk, his hands were free. But surely, to offer the warlock the prime instrument of his trade would not appeal to them. No, the dream had been ridiculous.

"Let's have the harper give us a tune," someone cried.

The others laughed nastily.

"Yes, lazy devil, while he lives he might as well be useful."

Lank got up and brought the harp to Lir. Lank gave a mocking bow.

"Drive the fog away, harper."

Lir realized the aura of sorcery had not been an illusion. The soldiers were acting out of character. He thought of the old women in Lilune's Castle, how they had pounced on him, bleating for a song. And when he played, the Castle played through him, drugging them, enabling him to rescue the girl from their clutches. And now, the Castle reached out to save the girl, and again he was to help the Castle.

"Come on," said Lank, thrusting the harp on Lir, even loosening the rope about Lir's chest to make it handier for him.

"Gladly," said Lir.

He accepted the harp, not bothering to tune it. He struck a chord, coldly curious as to what would happen, and if the demonic force would take over his will on this occasion.

The music came flowing off his fingers. It was savage and set him meditating on lions, conflagrations, storms, war. He experienced no psychic invasion. The thing which was the power of the Castle of Dark assisted, but did not rule him.

The effect on the soldiers was extraordinary.

Initially, they glanced about, and started to beat the fog from their faces with their hands, as if this might clear it.

Then one man said: "I swear I smell smoke." And another: " The wood's on fire—the summer heat—" Another yelled: "No, it's the town. The houses are burning and the boats on the estuary. I can see it!" Some jumped up. Two or three dashed to their horses. The horses, infected by the mood, snorted and kicked at the turf. With only this as a prologue, madness broke upon the soldiers. All sprang to their feet, running this way and that. A high-voiced man screamed that the enemy were upon them, and drawing his sword, cut about him insanely. The fog kept coming in in swathes around the trees, and the riot was blurred. A man hurtled through the fire. His tunic caught. He rolled almost across Lir's feet, beating out the flames. "The gates are down!" he bellowed. "The Duke is slain."

Lir, his fingers flying on the harp, said to the man, "Unbind me, friend, or the enemy will murder me."

"Surely," the soldier declared, and slashed Lir's ropes with his sword, before plunging on into the fog.

Lir left off playing.

It apparently made no difference to the soldiers. Now they were bounding to horse. From the uproar, it seemed they believed they were racing to the defence of their town.

In a whirlwind of hoofs, the soldiers tore blindly, and howling, away into the fog, southwards, leaving behind them an enormous silence.

Lir stepped cautiously over to Lilune. She was standing by a tree, frightened and exalted.

"I Called to the old women. They heard me, and sent their spells."

"The Castle," Lir said. "Not the old women. The Castle."

"That terrible, fierce tune you played," Lilune said. "Look. The fog's already lifting." To Lir, the fog was, if anything, more intense. He took Lilune's arm to guide her, but she shook him off. "I can see the cart and the horses," she said. She turned and ran off through the trees, unhindered. But Lir had to edge his way. For him, the fog had become denser than velvet.

"Wait for me," he called to the girl. As he called, the

truth came to him. He did not need her responding shout: "No, Lir. I release you from your service to me." Her voice had cracked as she said it. Next came the crack of the whip.

The cart snagged through the wall of the fog, in which now only Lir was lost.

PART FIVE

15

Lilune: Iron

The cart horses were rested and the soldiers had fed them. They went swiftly through the forest. When dawn came, Lilune drew them to a halt and worked her way into the box. Her own independence impressed her. But when she thought of Lir, tears rolled down her cheeks and stained the bodice of her green court dress. She did not need his service further, and she had had to leave him behind. He had come near death for her sake, and she couldn't bear the idea of his dying. Better to return alone. In any case, he could not be intended to travel further in her company. Her adventures in the world were over. The old women had decided on that. Or was it the Castle of Dark?

The Castle of Dark.

When she woke, and night canopied the forest, she drove the horses on. She knew her direction as if she had travelled this route a hundred times. The Castle drew her to itself. She also knew that Lir, if he tried to follow her, would find it hard. His journey would become confusing, tortuous. He would not catch up with her. But then, he had probably already gone south, glad to be rid of his burden.

In the cart, the spade beat a rhythm against the box. Lilune sang to the horses, a song she had heard at the Duke's court. As she sang, she wept. The skies wept too. The first rain of that long, dry summer month blotted out the half moon, and twanged the branches of the forest like one vast pliable wooden harp.

In the minutes before dawn, under a pearl sky, she emerged from the woodland, and saw the lake. It lay, itself like a pearl, faithfully copying the sky's colour. Along the curve of the shore, the empty ruined houses. Down there the tree stood over the well, the tree that had been struck by lightning seven times, the last on Lilune's birthnight.

Between lake-shore and woods, on its pinnacle of bare rock, her Castle.

Lilune released the horses from the cart. They picked off along the slope, grazing greedily. Lilune walked towards the Castle. She was still some way off when she saw the two old women in the southern gate.

Their raggedy ringlets and clothes were flapping in the dawn wind. Soon their arms rose and flapped too.

She came up the rock. When she was a few yards off, they stole out to meet her.

"There's a clever precious," said one of the old women. "All the way home on her own, the wicked darling."

"Make haste," said the other. "The sun will be here shortly."

"I'm quite ready to be bound," Lilune said. "I'm ready for the iron chains."

"There's a lamby."

"Thank you," said Lilune, thinking of Lir, weeping, "for the magic you sent to rescue me."

"*It* wanted you safe," said the first old woman. "*It* saw your danger."

"Hush," snapped the other, as they conducted Lilune through the dilapidated porter's door into the bailey.

"But she's learned her nature," said the first old woman. "Hasn't she, the foxy?"

The smell of ivy, black-green in the rainy morning, mingled with the scent of Lilune's own tears.

"We'll keep you snug," said the old women as they tottered along with Lilune between them. "There, there," they soothed her.

They were crying too, and Lilune suddenly perceived that they loved her, in their awful eldritch way. And she hugged their skinny knobby shoulders as they staggered on together towards the keep, the tower, the lidded bed, the spells of binding and the heavy iron chains.

16

Lir: The Ground

Softly, and warm, the rain slid over the archaic woods, the slope, the rock with the Castle. The moon gazed through the rain. It was a strong, waxing moon, about three days from full.

Lir sat in the south gateway of the Castle of Dark. The porter's door would no longer open. He had also attempted the larger northern entrance, but that was similarly closed, and besides, rusted irrevocably into its sockets and hinges. Lir had grown weary of banging on the doors and shouting. He was wet through, quite soaked by the rain so that he had ceased to mind it. He had fought his way north in the fog, let alone the rain. The rain, and a day's moist sun had dispersed the fog. He still wasn't certain if the fog were an illusion, or reality, or partly both. Frankly, he was uncertain about everything, least of all why he was here.

He had arrived at midnight, having mislaid a couple of nights, a couple of days, trudging about the woods. He had supposed sorcery was being used against him to prevent his tracking Lilune. This supposition was so positive that maybe it was merely that which kept him going round in circles. But, whatever, he determined to reach the Castle, and reach it he had.

At the edge of the woods he came on the deserted cart, though the horses had vanished. It was all the proof he needed that the girl was there before him. He strode to the Castle walls. And here he sat, locked out, semidrowned, brooding.

Finally, the rain stopped. The night was warm as the rain had been. The forests steamed eerily.

Lir took the harp from its box.

Like a beautiful sulky animal, the harp disliked the wet. The strings had slackened and its tone would be flat. Lir tuned it carefully, petting the harp. He began to play, for once, with absolute forethought. It was a galloping, bawdy melody. The song entreated some cold cruel lady to look out of her window on the languishing minstrel below. As each verse progressed without the lady's deigning to appear, the languishing minstrel became more and more uncomplimentary in his remarks on her person.

Lir had no notion if anyone would answer this challenge. When he noticed, through a crack in the doors, a ghostly light drifting across the bailey court, he stepped up the volume of his song.

The light swelled through the crack. Abruptly a tiny spy-hole whipped open in the ivy-clad porter's door. A mad old eye peered out.

"Pesty, go away."

Lir went on playing, left off singing, said, "I'm waiting for the lady Lilune to look out of her window."

"She won't. Granny won't let her. Granny won't even let her hear you. Run! Run for your life!"

"No," said Lir.

A muted squabbling and hissing occurred in the bailey. Both hags were present.

"We shall witch you if you don't go," said the voice—their voices were identical; it might be either one.

"Thorns shall claw you and beasts gore you. Fly or die!"

"Last time I played this harp, the Castle played through me and we had the better of you."

"No more. We are protected now by spells."

"And is Lilune protected by them?"

"Bound by magic and by iron," the hags creaked in chorus.

Lir's stomach turned over inside him.

"And that's your permanent solution, is it, you two foul crones? Chain her up in a living death?"

The old women spat at him. Had there been no door between them, he could imagine their scratching out his eyes. Then:

"There's no other way. Even the mother abandoned her baby in our care. Charm and chant is all that will keep the demon in. The dark Castle, the Castle of Dark. Evil's built into the stones of it. But it's the ground, the very ground where it stands. The ground is evil—soil, rock, tree. Before ever men were in the world, as we know men, there was evil at Dark."

Lir listened, conscious of the resemblance of these sentences to those the chief-man's wife had spoken in the woods-village. They all knew the tale, it seemed. But none of them knew how to end it.

Lir took up the story. With his trained harper's memory, he could about repeat it word for word.

"And those who dwell in the place are liable to be tainted with its evil. Not all. But always some, one by one. Tainted. A hundred years ago there was one who bound the village in the woods. He said all travellers must be sent to him at Dark. It was a pact and they kept it. Go north, they told the travellers, and north the travellers came. After that evil one was gone, there were none, not for forty years. Then another was born. There was the sign. The lightning struck the tree. The mother herself, when she saw her child scorched by the sun, fled the Castle. They say she left two guardians—"

"Silence!" screeched a hag.

The other rasped: "*It* wanted to get out into the world and It let you help it. But now, for a space, It fears the world, It lets us bind it. Be off before It begins to covet the world again."

"But It is a nonsense."

"What? What?"

"It appears like a phantom and absorbs the strength from those It attacks. It houses itself for protection in a human body. But what is Its aim or purpose?" The old women made incoherent noises. Lir said: "It robs men of their vitality presumably in order to sustain itself, in order that It may survive. Why then does It give warning by a sign? Is it true lightning strikes the same tree whenever this creature manifests itself in a man or woman—or a baby? This tree is a falsehood, isn't it? Simply a bit of extra drama added to the tale to make it prettier. And I don't recollect seeing a lightning-blasted tree hereabouts."

"The town!" a hag squealed through the door.

"A tree above a well," said the other. "Go and find the tree and leave us alone. Or lions shall eat you."

"And it shall snow stones."

A stone came whizzing at Lir out of nowhere, a small sharp stone which smashed against the south gate. Three more followed, and one drew blood from the palm of his hand.

Inside the bailey, the hags cackled.

It was beginning to rain again.

He could seek shelter in the ruinous town, tree or no tree. When the sun rose, he had a better chance of breaching the Castle, for the hags had seemed to sleep through the day, or most of it, as the girl did.

He slipped the harp into its box.

"I'm leaving you, gentle ladies," Lir called, retreating down the rock.

They didn't cackle again. Somehow, he had the distinct impression that they regretted his departure, the brief diversion he had provided.

And was there a lightning-blasted tree in the deserted town?

He found the tree. It stood against the well on a little patch of ground between the ruins. The well was dry. At the base of the shaft, rain pocked a floor of black mud. As with his return to the Castle itself, he was unsure what significance the tree and the well had for him. Some significance, however, there was. He stared at the tree, dim-shining in the rain. At the very top, its branches showed bone white; lower, the tree's limbs were charred and blackened. Blasted seven times. Yet upright. Burnt, but intact.

Then he became aware of something wrong with the tree.

The evidence of the seven lightning strikes was clear upon it, but only to a certain height. Further up, the tree was whole. Which meant, impossibly, that the lightning had not struck the tree from above. But from *below*.

He walked off a way and squatted in the shelter of a doorless house, with his mind buzzing, his heart throbbing. The lightning did not come from the sky but up from the well itself. Out of the ground. . . . . . . *it's the ground, the very ground where it stands* . . .

Through the doormouth and the rain he could see the Castle with its many towers, crouched on the bare pillar of rock, along the shore and the slope. . . . *the ground is evil* . . .

Not the Castle, the ground. The ground beneath.

Lir felt a sapping wave of dread go over him. Was it the force of what lay there in the earth pushing him back? Or only common human fear? But it wasn't really important which, for he would have to ignore it.

He got up, and the rain again stopped, as if in sympathy for his task. He must search the ruins now, and, if the search proved vain, the Castle, when and if he got into it after sunrise. Then he remembered the abandoned cart on the hill and the grave-digger's spade left lying in the cart. He would not have to search after all.

The distance from the well's head to its floor was perhaps twenty feet. The walls were slimy and eroded. The bottom of the well was a foot or so deep in mud and moss, a small swamp made extra vile by the rain. Lir sank in this swamp, having climbed perilously down to it. Some of the roots of the lightning-tree struck through into the interior of the well. These, too, were scorched, but had offered a sinewy handhold here and there; crumbling earth and lumps of stone were risky footholds. Of course, only a madman would have entered the well. The way up would be a thousand times more treacherous than the treacherous descent, probably impossible.

Lir dug himself free of the floor with the spade he had brought below with him, tied on his shoulder with the harp. He had also supplied himself with a bundle of the charred branches from the tree. One of these he now pushed into the mud, and with flint and tinder ignited the damp wood. Reluctantly, with a greenish flame, the makeshift torch gave him light.

The sense of dread came at him in steady pulses. If anything, it would be of assistance to him, for, as the dread increased, so he would know he approached his goal accurately—whatever the goal was.

In the deceptive flickering light, he stared at the well-sides. Before him, to the left of the tree-roots, lit up by the smoking stick of wood, was a slender mossy aperture, no larger than his fist.

Through this aperture had rushed a shock and charge of energy, of sheer power that, flaring upwards and out of the well, had struck the tree. It had appeared like lightning, had scored the tree as lightning would have done. It was not quite lightning. What was it? There was but one way to discover.

Lir began to dig at the packed earth about the hole.

Sometimes loose earth, dryer than the rest, showered outwards. Sometimes the spade clanked on stone. Then, with his fingers, and with the haft of the knife he had broken in the Duke's Turret, Lir would pry out the stone and sling it aside. Luckily the stones were never huge. It was very hot in the well, and dank. Periodically, the lit branches guttered out. Once or twice, accidentally, he put them out himself when casting shovels of earth backwards. He had a feeling of familiarity, and could not think why. He had never mined the earth, never dug graves, nor even a field or vegetable-patch since his earliest childhood.

Twenty feet overhead, the small upside-down pool of the sky started to silver.

He had considerably enlarged the hole, but it gave no clue yet as to its contents. He had paused a minute, leaning on the spade, when there was a sudden low rumbling in the soil. Next moment the entire wall that he had been digging at subsided.

When the black dust had settled, Lir beheld an opening, a tunnel-like fissure in the ground beyond the fallen wall. The dull light could not penetrate this opening, but it was high enough for a man to stand upright in it, and from some way along it came the sound of water.

Taking the spade and the remains of the kindling, Lir went forward into the passage. The last burning stick he plucked from the mud and held up to show him the way.

There was air in the gape before him, but still, hot air, perfumed with damp clay. As he advanced, there began to be a secondary light. Poisonous-looking grey mushrooms and fungus draped the tunnel, giving off a phosphorescent glow.

Presently he found himself stepping through a series of inky glimmering ponds.

Lir paused, staring at the water. It was moving, flowing slowly across the passage and away into darkness. He realized, suddenly, what must have happened. At some point, far back in time, a stream or river had pierced through into this ancient passage, filling it with water. Later, when the town was founded and the Castle built, men had sunk the well to tap this undergound stream, undreaming of the ancient walkway it had sealed off. But eventually the stream grew shallower, and in time had died away to this dark trickle. The well-sides dried to mud, concealing the passage that once had been. But through that shoring of mud, a burst of Power—the lightning—had forced a narrow, violent exit. . . .

Lir walked on. Beyond the trickling ponds, he trod on rock. The walls of the channel were rock. Hewn rock. This place was hand-fashioned, immeasurably old. There was no knowing its age or what manner of people had crafted its rough walls. On the rock, Lir could see streaks, burn marks. This was the path the lightning had come. He thought of the small hole in the well-side, puzzling why such an explosion of energy had not blasted a broader one.

Then he recalled how the whole wall collapsed at once when the spade had loosened it sufficiently. After all, between this dawn and the last lightning strike, the mud had had sixteen years to heal its wound.

The sound of water faded behind him. It was quiet now. He could not swear in what direction the channel was leading him, but logically it had to be south westward. The branch went out in his hand. He did not bother to light another, relying instead on the glow of the fungi.

The waves of dread had become a continuous rhythmic sea through which he waded. Strangely, he was not troubled. It was what he had expected. He could even ignore the dread, shut it out, for he had become accustomed to it. And at the same moment he searched for phantoms, almost methodically. He was not afraid of dark places and this dark place, which probably *was* haunted, had begun to fascinate him. He wanted to learn its secret.

It surprised him to realize he had temporarily forgotten about Lilune, his sole reason for entering the dark. The dark had become a reason in itself. And then he was aware that beyond the pulsing dread, no obstacle hindered him, nothing thrust him away. Was something again Calling him, drawing him on?

He judged he had journeyed about a mile when he came on the runes.

He knew them for runes—and yet did not know them. They had been cut very deep, in that immemorial beginning. Now they had weathered, crumbled, were indecipherable. Yet he knew, as if they whispered it to him, that they were Runes of power: a power once greater than the power of what lay beyond. But time had ground them away, blurred and disfigured them, and in doing so had robbed them of their power—though *only* time had been able to do that.

They had been meant to keep something leashed and bound. Now time had worn them out, and they could not longer leash that thing.

Lir forced his eyes from the runes, and went on between them. In a minute more, the passage flared wide into a vastly tall and exaggeratedly conical cave.

High up, beyond the fungus glow, there was a renewed murmur of water, concealed in some vein of the rock. Beneath, facing Lir across a space of smooth, fire-tarnished stone, was a chair.

At least, it seemed to be a chair. But a chair of a design so alien and unlikely, and of a material so unrecognisable, that Lir would never have known it a chair, if something had not been sitting in it.

Not a live thing. Bones, a skeleton. And the skeleton was brown with its centuries, brown and shattered, and scorched like everything else—the monstrous chair, the floor, the walls. At its feet, if they were feet, was an array of metal objects strewn about, that might have been utensils, ornaments, before the lightning-bolt, erupting from the heart of the seated thing, had smelted and fused them.

The sea of dread abruptly evaporated.

Lir, no longer feeling anything of particular depth, observed the skeleton blankly.

He understood, for it was simple.

As once before, he had dug his way into a burial place. This chamber was older than the mound in the rank wood to which Wild-Eye had sent him; it looked and seemed to be more ancient than time itself. This mound contained the buried remnants of what might have been a man and might have been some other entity.

An entity which, though fleshly dead, remained psychically alive.

A million years ago, perhaps, the burial and the walling up had been. Later, much later, the channel-entry to the passage of stone had sunk into the earth. About it, on every side, the soil had crept close to robe and amalgamate, and the forest had crept after. As the runes, which were the guardians of this place, gradually wore out, the ground itself became the guardian of this chamber; imprisoning and holding close, lapping it round with new soil and forest, to be forgotten, while cupped in its pinnacle of stone, the power still seethed. At length, unaware of it, men set a castle on its head.

The rocky upthrust on which the Castle of Dark had been constructed was a prehistoric burial mound, visible yet disguised, in which a jet black magic lay fermenting.

The ground is evil.

Yet Lir felt now no surge of malevolence, not even of power, and no surge of fear in himself. Only the devastating quiet, tinged faintly with water-sound. Only the sight of lightning-seared and broken bones.

And standing there, the dream Lir had had of Wild-Eye rushed back to him, pristine and decisive. He almost heard Wild-Eye's dream voice in his ear:

"And later, under the ground, recollect what I taught you of the building of harps."

Lir found he was contemplating, with a steady, calculating eye, the brown skull of the being in the chair.

17

Lilune: The Lion

Behind the cellar door, the two witch hags were wheezily conferring together.

For some reason, Lilune was able to make out every word they said. Which should have been impossible, since she was lying, chained to the lidded bed in the dusk, within the tower room.

"I saw him prowling about the ruins. He didn't come away. He went to the well. Pale and shiny as a fox's coat in the moonlight, that hair of his."

"How did you see?"

"By the Craft, in a dish of water. But when he reached the well, the picture wrinkled."

Both hags clucked irritably.

"That was two nights back. He'll have left by day, no doubt."

"Never. Can't you tell he's still near, the foxy? Can't you feel it?"

"When I drew water from our well at sunset," said one of the hags, after a pause, "I heard a noise far below in it, under the water."

"What noise?"

"A crack. The crack of a bone, snapping."

"A sign. It's a sign. The evil keeps him in its thrall. We must get rid of him. Root him out."

"Yes, poor sweetheart. How shall we do it?"

"It must be death. He must die."

"Ah, the pity, poor lamby. Granny must kill him. A Sending?"

"Or a Calling. A lion. They'll be restless, now the summer's fading. Call a lion."

"Yes, a lion. It will eat him, shameful thing."

"It must be done. Begin now."

"Yes. Begin now."

Lilune woke in panic and confusion. Chained helplessly by the iron fetters, to which she had willingly submitted herself, she writhed and struggled. They were going to destroy Lir. They were going to Spell Call a lion to slay and devour him. They would manage it, she knew. And he would have no warning. She could not warn him.

She had not thought he would follow her. And he had followed her into the very trap she had tried to spare him—death.

In the slot of window, the star which always shone there at this time of year went on shining complacently.

How had she heard that terrible conversation? It was no dream. Could it be that the Castle had enabled her to hear; the Castle's sombre, dangerous magic, pouring into her as before? But why? The evil genius that possessed the Castle, that possessed her if it was permitted to do so, could surely care nothing for the fate of Lir. Only she cared. Frantically.

She wanted to scream, But during her adventures in the world, she had learned that screaming was not necessarily of use. What could she do that was useful?

She forced herself to lie down again, and tried to sink into the dozing state a second time. That way, she might eavesdrop some more on the activities of the old women. But the doze wouldn't repeat itself, and the hearing-ability did not return.

The evening sky became a void beyond the window. She lay and glared at the star, hating its emancipation and indifference.

Below, the tower door gave at a push, as it always did. Lilune's sharp ears picked up the rustling decrepit steps creeping into the tower. The two old women had completed their Calling, for the moment at any rate. They were bringing Lilune her drink.

The ring-handle turned on the flimsy bed-chamber door. The hags entered.

They were smiling. They appeared pleased and satisfied. The Calling must have given evidence of success. Already the lion, greying over its tawny coat, changing colour like the leaves, might be padding towards the ruined town and towards Lir.

Lilune smiled dreamily at the hags. She had also learned to improve on her knack of pretending.

"Here's our own Lilune. Sit up and sup your drink."

Lilune stared at the black drink with the head of creamy foam. Shavings of chestnuts decorated it. Her eyes swam with tears.

"Have you been busy?" Lilune asked politely. "Tell me all you've done."

The hags, unsuspicious, beamed. They no longer kept her in complete ignorance, for she was fettered now. They recited their chores. "Tomorrow night," added one, "we must cast a precautionary spell over our precious girl. It's full moon tomorrow."

She could not trick them into any admission regarding Lir. They had not even told her that he had come after her.

Later, they fell to reminiscing. It was obviously a relief to them to speak without the restraint which had hampered them before. They even spoke of Lilune's mother. But Lilune, to her dismay, had discovered she wasn't very interested in this mother who had deserted her in alarm a few days after her birth. And tonight, she was less interested than ever.

In the end, Lilune feigned drowsiness. She slept a lot, and would need to sleep more than she did, as a caged animal trains itself to do. Somehow she had not, until this hour, faced the bleakness of her future, not actually *pictured* her life, which would all be spent chained to this bed.

When the old women shuffled out, Lilune lay like a stone, and she did picture it. Her existence would be good for nothing, neither for herself nor for any other. And there was no chance of rescue. She could never get away, *must* not. Dare not. She was ready to cry, but tears seemed as useless as everything else.

She considered Lir, who should live, and would die in the lion's jaws. She considered herself, who would be better dead.

She, too, could activate a spell of Calling. She had Called the pedlar, and Lir. Though the power of the Castle had assisted her, she still believed herself a witch. And now she would Call the lion, away from Lir, to herself. It would come by day, while the hags slumbered and while she slumbered. It would thrust through the porter's door, through the door of her tower and of this chamber. It would wait patiently, scenting flesh, for the lid of her bed to lift. If she were fortunate, it would slaughter her before she woke. Lir would survive.

She had never acquired in-between shades of character, had not had the opportunity. She had been utterly selfish, and was now selfless, because she had never become a whole person, did not like herself;, or know herself. Nor had she ever gained sufficient wisdom to be properly horrified at what she meant to do. She couldn't think that intensely.

Accordingly, she stretched on the bed, afraid but resolute. And Called the lion.

The lion was already making roughly towards the Castle. It was far off, still, on the northern shore of the lake, where the trees were yellowing and papery leaves falling down. Now it hesitated in its advance, vaguely conscious of a fresh motivation. It did not foresee the Castle. The promise of food had started it moving, the idea of appeased hunger, for the woods were empty of things it could kill, except for the littlest beasts and the tiniest birds. As for the doors of the Castle, it would merely throw its strong body against them when it met them. The motivation would see to that. And the doors would yield to the lion, even the door of the keep, even the porter's door, which the hags had generally given over barring. They reckoned Lir shortly to be dealt with, and disliked manoeuvering the bars with their stiff fingers as they went in and out to collect herbs and weeds for their potions.

But the lion did not guess its luck. It was only lured, though not by scent or instinct, towards a location where it might feed.

And the lion ran on eagerly through the starry night.

18

Lir: Black Soul

He had sat down on the floor of the burial chamber and gone through his itinerary carefully. He had listed for himself what the underground place could give him, what he himself had brought to that place that could also be used. And what he would have to improvise, do without. He was slightly taken aback by the amount the site could offer that would aid him. He was slightly, foolishly, nervous, almost shy, wondering if he had forgotten those essential bits of trades he had been tutored in over a year ago.

It appeared to him that no hint of the supernatural lingered, or maybe he had grown immune to it.

Lir raised the spade and struck off the head of the abhuman skeleton. Antique tales of rousing the undead recalled themselves to him. But nothing happened, beyond the brown skull's striking the floor, rolling a short distance, juddering to rest.

Lir took up the skull. It felt like part-fossilised wood, or stone. He carried it back through the channel to a spot equidistant between the bottom of the well and the subterranean ponds. He would require water. He had searched for the water that rustled above the roof of chamber, but it was securely enclosed, perhaps the water-source which supplied the Castle well. In any case, to return along the passage was a wiser plan. Through the well's high opening there would be evidence of the coming and going of day and night. There was also the generous store of tree-roots to be hacked off freely in the well, for a fire. Because fire was as vital as water.

Lir seated himself on a slab of rock in the tunnel. There was an inconclusive quarter-light created by the fungi on one hand, the diffused glow from the small well-opening on the other.

He lifted the harp from its box. As he set to work on it, the first rush of positive alarm went through him. But it was not agitation at what was to come, it was a loathing of tampering with the harp. The harp was his security. He had no other.

He partially unstrung the harp. With one of the fused metal objects he had selected in the chamber of the mound, he started to prize the rivets from the smooth honey-coloured plate over the sound-box.

When the bone was loose in his hands, he used it as a guide in marking the brown skull. It was far larger than the skull of a man. The apex was domed and ridged. The fall to the floor had not chipped it. Lir, having scored the necessary shape on the skull, began to peck at the shape with a second length of metal. The metal was lustreless, unidentifiable, but very sharp.

He had none of the specific acids or delicate implements of the ivory-worker. Not even the carpenter's humblest mallet.

The day which had lit the well-opening wore out.

Aching, yet indifferent to it, Lir found himself in a deeper dark. He drank from the trickling pools and ate a wizened pear that had survived from the last friendly village. He slept with his shoulders to the rock. The summer was losing its heat. In the night's centre it got cold in the guts of the passage. He woke, half frozen, and strode about to warm himself, not wanting to waste a fire. As he strode, he had another abrupt attack of insecurity and nerves. Again, not at the Powers looming in the mound, but at his own actions. He asked himself if he had gone mad. Yet somehow he could not keep a hold on this dismalness. It went off, like nausea.

Eventually, he did set and kindle a fire, and crouched

by it, scratching on at the stony skull. And soon he spoke the charm over it, the Charm for the Bone, that Wild-Eye had taught him, essential in the harp-making of the true harper.

The sun lifted and the passage lightened and stealthily changed into a furnace.

After a long while, Lir walked through into the muddy well to breathe the cooler air. Then he strolled the length of the passage to ease the cramp of his immobility, to the burial chamber and back, as if it were only some familiar street.

It was now afternoon, to judge from the glare of the well-opening. Lir built up the fire and coaxed it, sweating, to its maximum. He pushed the brown skull into the fire to bake.

He sat and watched the skull in the fire.

Once more, stories of prowling vengeful ghosts drifted to the surface of his mind. But then, he knew this ghost—if ghost it were—meant him to do as he did. It instructed him. Am I yet enslaved? Lir thought drily. And what will be the finish of it? Deep within him something—conscience? —jabbed like a sore muscle. *Resist, fight, deny the force that controls you. It will escape* through you. Its energy, mostly contained till now, will run riot. . . .

Lir dreamed of Wild-Eye. Wild-Eye was harping in Hell-Hall. Sulphurous pits puffed between the rocky pillars, and yellow bats dripped from the rafters. The Dark One was nowhere to be seen, but Lilune sat on the dais. Her dress was the colour of red burning, and it smoked.

Lir awoke. The sky above the well was red as Lilune's Hell-dress. From the skull in the fire came a sickening cooked stench. Lir dug the skull from the fire with the spade, and ran forward with it, balancing it, further into the channel. When he came to the pools, he lowered the smoking skull under the water.

A ferocious sizzling answered and steam and bubbles fleeced over the spot. Then there came a savage crack. The channel seemed to crack itself with the noise, magnifying it out of all proportion.

Lir drew out the skull on the spade.

Coughing, his eyes dazzled, he leant over it. The sculpted piece had broken away, jagged but entire. Even the holes he had scraped for the rivets were cleaned out.

He hammered the rivets home with the spade handle. As the points grated through the bone into the wood of the harp, Lir's spine crawled. But he went on with the charm, the marvellous potent gibberish in which Wild-Eye had lessoned him.

And now, all he had to do was climb out of the well and wait for the night.

In the channel, the fire died. The broken skull, its relevant portion removed, sat where he had discarded it, Stars looked in at the well-opening.

He had reckoned it would be impossible to climb out of the well. It was impossible. Of course it was.

Staggering with fatigue and cramp, and saddled with the harp, he grabbed the lower protruding roots of the lightning-tree, and hauled himself upwards. The tree, laid bare by the collapse of the well wall, provided a better ladder than the wall had done. The ascent was not difficult.

When he dragged himself out on to the stone lip of the well, the stars seemed to tilt crazily over his head as if they laughed at him.

He couched in an overgrown garden and slept peacefully, the harp in its box beside him.

Asleep, he did not see the lion, which, just before dawn, trotted along the lake-shore.

By the lake, the lion paused to drink and snuff the air. If it caught the scent of a man nearby, it paid no heed. Rather slowly, for it was hungry and weary, it moved on along the shore towards the slope and the Castle.

Lir idled the day away. Above ground it was golden but no longer hot. On the trees the colours seemed to have altered overnight. Yellow apples had plumped in the grass. Whole rose-heads had tumbled beside them.

Lir sang by the lake, through the edges of the woods

which here and there stole to the water's brink. The songs were melancholy but sweet, like the ending of the year.

He was carefree, the burden was to come. Tonight, and perhaps ever after, he would carry it. And perhaps he would not even live to carry it. But he knew the utter liberty of the slave, who has no motive now to search his heart. Right or wrong, the choice was not his.

Ultimately, the sun set. The full moon stood alone in the dusk, a moon red-gold almost as the sun had been.

The earth veiled itself in shadows and Lir went towards the Castle of Dark.

He had thought of climbing the outer walls by the south gate, where the ivy was thickest. But when he came to the south gate, the porter's door hung wide.

It was like an invitation, and startled him. Were the two hags in the toils of the Power again, obeying it, to let him in? There was a diluted animal reek about the door, but he paid it little heed. He didn't see the scratch of lion-claws on the black wood.

Silence, undisturbed, had gathered in the bailey court along with the darkness. Above, the sky glowed with its blueness, its jewels of stars and moon.

Lir sat down in the midst of the bailey, and took the harp from its box. A little while he held the harp. He ran his fingers over the piece of ridged, unpolished bone. Then, as he tuned the harp, each note rose into the silent dusk, and each note had a new voice that the brown bone leant it.

But when he had tuned the harp, he put it off. He didn't want to begin. Yet he felt the Castle, waiting, and all the things in the Castle waited, too. The rats in the cellars, the pigeons clustered on the towers. Perhaps the elderly women waited, and Lilune herself in her arbour of chains. Each caught in a spell of waiting, and only he could release them, for good or for ill.

He struck the initial chord. In that solitary gesture, as he had anticipated, the piece of bone mastered the strings and mastered him, hands and brain and soul. "What the harp will give," Wild-Eye had said. And it was the harp, had always been the harp, more than the harper. For the true harper did not make music, he invoked it, as any magician invoked the magics of the earth, to the limit of his skill. And now, through the new-ivoried harp, Lir invoked the Force of Dark, and it answered.

At first, there was only the music that poured from the harp.

It was a weird and ancient music. It seemed to have no form, yet it had a pattern. For harmonies it rendered discords. Yet the discords were apt. The music suggested the moaning chant of many throats, of pipes hollowed from stems or the horns of enormous beasts. And under it a tempo of staves beating on granite.

Lir had closed his eyes, but through the lids, he had sight. Not of the Castle. It was a murky landscape, foggy, a swamp with soaring trees that seemed to probe the sky, and in their nets an engorged red moon, floating. Against the moon, a stone edifice. Hard to pinpoint in the fog, against the swimming moon, but quantities of people appeared going back and forth, shapes, shades . . . and the music was theirs.

Rationally, Lir surmised: Is this the burying? But he was bemused. He opened his eyes and the scene winked out and he had the Castle in view once more. But in the Castle too, a murky fog was rising.

The fog, smelling of the marsh, breathed from the walls of Dark. And in the fog, the moon grew red and swollen. The towers of the Castle had the semblance of soaring trees.

Lir was not afraid. He had known he would be protected from fear. His fear had no role in what this Thing wanted of him.

And thus he experienced no fear when the music boiled up over the harp like scalding pitch from a cauldron and he was carried up with it into the swirling mist.

He glimpsed himself, beneath. A white faced harper, his hands racing on the harp-strings.

Then the brown bone which had become the speech of

Dark, spoke in Lir's mind, or in his spirit. There were no words. There had been no words in that time, when the bone dwelt in the head of a living being, nor any necessity for words. It was a time before time began. Lir understood everything. For one instant. And then understanding deserted him, and the wordless speech of the bone deserted him, and he fell back into himself.

The thing at Dark, the thing buried in the rock, aeons dead, yet psychically alive, had wished, in the end, simply for freedom. Any magician, if he had been wise enough—or foolish enough—could have freed It. Once the runes had worn away, It had tried to free itself. These attempts had come at irregular intervals, as desperation galvanised It into activity. A convulsion had followed, of which lightning had been the by-product, not the warning, of Its upsurge. The thrust of energy did not, however, unshackle It. The freedom It attained was a false one, the possession of man or woman, which freed a fraction of itself, no more. It could no longer think or reason. Its cravings were blind. And It craved only to exist, and to be free. So, roaming by proxy through the medium of those It possessed, It slew other men, draining their energy to fuel its own—mindlessly and stupidly, but without evil intent. It killed as one starved must eat bread if it were placed before him. Nor did It plot to kill or desire to kill. It did not harm those who were its hosts or protectors. Instinctively, it accepted their value to its survival. But It had no logic.

There had never been a magician, till Lir. Not a true magician.

Not immediately, but eventually, It had sensed his worth, the hope It might uncover in him, in the same blind way It sensed sustenance. A slender layer at a time, It pervaded the will of Lir, now holding him off as It strengthened itself to rule him, now attracting him to itself to bind him. Lir was the pivot of Its salvation. probably the last opportunity It would have, in a world where true magic was dying by the hour.

It wanted only to be free. Not free to wreak death on the earth. Free to *escape* the earth. . . .

Lir lay on his elbow, his head ringing. But he played on, and though positioned awkwardly, yet he played deftly. He could do nothing else. Nor could he stop till the music was done.

He did not cease playing either when he raised his head, and *saw*.

Darkness was gushing upwards from the Castle, up into the evening sky. The stars were blotted out. A distance off, in the ruined town, a tongue of lightning exploded from the well, striking the tree; the eighth lightning strike. And in the bailey court, the Castle well spat up the water from the vein below, and after that a shower of debris, rock, mud, and lastly a white fork of fire that dashed into the air and split the fog a moment, and vanished in it. The ninth lightning.

And then there was no sound.

And no fog, for the fog was not a fog. It was *Itself*.

Black as a black pit in the sky, It rested over the Castle like a gigantic plume. It moved a little, as a snake might move. Just a little. It had no absolute form. It was like the music that had called It. High in the mile-high height of It, two stars came visible, but they were not stars.

Lir had understood, for an instant.

Now he did not understand as the blackness drifted from the Castle into the night. It was as if the moon called It, like the music; summoned It. The moon with which It had affinity, as It had shunned the sun. It ascended. It seemed to pull the raw roots of the Castle after It, and the roots of Lir's bones, and the very fabric of the ground. The ground shook. Small stones crashed. The towers swayed for a second, and grew quiet. The music stopped.

Blood ran from under Lir's nails. The strings of the harp snapped and the bronze pegs rolled on the bailey court.

The moon shone from a clear sky. Then the sky clouded over again. A thin smoke of bats streamed up out of the well and across the moon. The pigeons surfaced from the ramparts next, and flew away.

The night was hollow as an empty jar.

Like a sleep-walker, Lir went through the open door

of the keep. He looked across the inner courtyard, dazed at being alive. Dazed because his heart was not heavy, his conscience at peace, though blood still oozed from his fingers' ends. As he leaned there on the ivy-massed wall, a light bloomed in the Hall doorway.

The two old women, one shielding a feeble lamp, stared at him. Then they commenced squeaking. Like two tattered tiny grey rats they launched themselves in his direction. Scampering, they swarmed over the courtyard. They arrived at his side. They grabbed him with demented claws.

"Lovely precious!" one screeched.

"Cunning foxy!" put in the other.

They embraced him. Their skinny arms were like sticks, their sharp elbows were digging in him, their withered faces were insane with joy.

"He has slain the dark, the blessed lamb."

Now they were gambolling with him towards the solitary tower in which Lilune had been chained. With confused shame, Lir realized the hags were supporting him. He tried to steady himself, but couldn't quite do it.

Now one hag sprang ahead to push open the tower door. The door had already been ajar, and banged inward. The hag wailed like a high-pitched whistle and cowered aside.

Within the tower, crouched on the stair, a shadow within shadows and two eyes gleaming like flat silver coins.

To Lir it seemed it was the Black Soul, that extension of the Force which had possessed Lilune. Utter despair threatened him. He had set free the Force yet the nightmare remained. And then he perceived, through a blur of wretched shock, that it was no uncanny thing inside Lilune's tower. It was a lion.

The lion glared at them, its feral eyes sliding from one to another. Presently it slunk down the stair, out into the moonlight.

It had been hungry, the lion. Now it seemed not to be hungry. The impulse to vacate the Castle, which had set the bats and the pigeons flying, had affected the lion, too. It went by them. Its jaws looked matted, wet. . . . With a whip-thong smiting of tail on side, it bounded forward, through the door of the keep, away into the night.

The two old women clung to Lir in horror, mumbling and mouthing. He eased from their clutches.

He dragged himself up the stair of the tower on legs that had no sensation in them. The old women didn't come after. He didn't blame them. The upper, flimsy door had been knocked off its hinges by the muscular leaping body of the lion when it plunged into the room. Something must have driven it to that leap, more than hunger.

Lir stood in the doorway, as he had before, striving to evolve features from the almost lightless chamber. Now, as then, gradually, the bizarre draped and lidded bed emerged on the gloom.

He did not want to go to the bed. She had been chained, she would have had no chance. He asked himself how long the lion had been here, feeding, and a whiteness went over his eyes. Then the whiteness ebbed, and his sight returned.

There was a shallow pool of liquid by the bed, but it was not blood. The dregs of Lilune's witchy drink, for a goblet lay beside it. The lion had been sampling the drink; had the drink been what made the lion's mask wet and sticky?

Lir advanced, halting step by step, not trusting to hope. But abruptly the chains rattled in the bed and a pale face broke from the smother of hair, and a pale hand, and a voice.

"Lir?"

He managed to reply to her: "Yes, I'm here."

With a muted, stifled fright she cried:

"Be careful! There's a lion. It will mean to kill me when I wake—"

He comprehended. She had slept till this minute, slept in the trance-state in which the Force of her possession could maintain her. Even when the lid of her bed moved upwards, the lion had held off. It was the most basic woodscraft Lir had learned. Lions did not attack the sleeping thing. On this night of its release, the Force at Dark had kept her safe, in trust for itself, as a precaution. But when the Force had been released from Dark, it left her yet sleeping, yet safe. A coincidence, or a gift? He could not divine. Nor would he ever risk saying, unequivocally, if the Force were evil or merely elemental, if he had driven it out upon men, or only unlocked the fetters that had trapped it in the rock, and thus freed the world of it forever. Or if Hell were a wicked place, for that matter, or just the misunderstanding of men as Wild-Eye had suggested in the dream.

He was sufficiently near that he could take her hand.

Lir was past amazement, and so was not amazed when the chains crumbled from her wrist.

He had never supposed he liked her much. But liking had nothing to do with what he felt for her. She was a part of him, and he had not guessed it.

She seemed totally awake. Though he couldn't perfectly see her, the pressure of her hand was constant. She too, perhaps, was past amazement. She asked no explanation. As if, suddenly, she knew it all.

"Tomorrow," she said decidedly, "when the sun rises, I needn't hide. It won't hurt me any more. I can walk by day under the sun. Can't I, Lir?"

He nodded, wanting, as he had never wanted anything in his life, that it would be true.

It was true.

Prince on a White Horse

Contents

1

The Waste

The prince had been riding a featureless track over the dry and empty waste for ten hours. A cold wind was blowing through the rocks, and snapping nastily at the occasional leafless tree, of which there weren't many. The Prince didn't know who he was or how he had got here. He had been puzzling over it for several minutes now, and once he had thought of an acorn, but that hadn't made sense, and he had forgotten it again. Apart from this, he could make out only that he was a prince—though who? —that he was riding a white horse—though whose?—and that they had been going through this waste for ten hours—though why? Perhaps he was here on a holiday.

"And I don't even know my name," grumbled the Prince. "Could it be Richard? Or *Cecil*?"

It was getting dusky and cold, and the Prince—Alexander? Cuthbert?—stared up at some dark unfriendly-looking mountains in front of him on the horizon.

"Now is that East or West? Or North?" worried the Prince. "If only I had a compass. Perhaps I have." After rummaging for a moment, he decided he hadn't. He leaned over and looked at the horse. "Excuse me, horse, but can you tell me why I'm here, and who I am, and where this is?"

But the horse couldn't, or wouldn't. It stared up at the mountains and flared its nostrils.

"Or South?" added the Prince.

Just then there was a kind of whirling in the air in front

of them, and after a moment a girl stood on the track. She wore a scarlet dress with a golden girdle, and every strand of her long black hair sparkled with bits of gold shaped like little beetles.

"Who are you, and whom do you seek?" cried the girl.

"I don't know," said the Prince, admiring her grammar.

The girl blinked, but she went on determinedly, "Ahead lies the Castle of Bone, guarded by the Dragon of Brass. All the secrets of the world are hidden there, but all who seek them perish in the Dragon's jaws."

"Well, in that case," said the Prince, "I think I'll leave it."

The girl blinked again, and frowned, and said sternly, "Then, if I cannot dissuade you, take this magic sword."

There was another whirling in the air, and out of it the girl snatched a sword of white metal, set with rubies at the hilt, and thrust it on the Prince.

"Thank you," said the Prince. "Who are you?" he added.

The girl smiled. He had obviously said the right thing at last.

"I am Gemael the Red, brave prince, the Lady of the Waste."

"Do you happen to know who I am?" asked the Prince.

The girl stamped her foot, pointed at the mountains, hissed "Godspeed" in a cross voice, and disappeared again.

"Well, it certainly isn't a holiday," said the Prince.

The sky was by now a dark and murky blue, and the mountains stood out black against it in sharp, dangerous shapes. Half way up one of the nearest the Prince could now make out a weird shifting light, which he didn't like the look of one bit.

"That must be something to do with the Castle of Bone," said the Prince. "Or the Dragon. Well, I don't have to go there," he told himself, and yet he had the most unpleasant feeling that he did have to. "Well, I'll make camp here for the night, and worry about it in the morning."

But just then he noticed that the air around him felt very prickly and strange, and the wind seemed full of squawks and squeals and howls, and the darker it got the louder they got, and some of the rocks seemed oddly luminous, and he didn't think, really, he wanted to stay here after all.

He urged the horse on. It was very richly decked out in white and gold, and so was he, which surprised him.

"But then," he reasoned, "I am a Prince. Am I? It's a pity," he said to the horse, "you can't tell me what all this is about—if only I could remember." He was really talking to keep his courage up, because he was certain he could now see shadowy figures and red eyes glinting in the darkness. "It must be a spell, or perhaps a blow on the head—that thing when you forget everything—amsneezia, is it?"

"Amnesia," said the horse.

"Then you *can* talk!" cried the Prince delightedly.

"Of course I can't," said the horse. "Whoever heard of a horse talking?"

"Oh," said the Prince.

They hurried on, and the track was much steeper now, and the mountains loomed close.

Presently the Prince thought of something.

"But you just did."

"No," said the horse.

"But you did talk—there, you did it again."

"You imagined it," said the horse.

Just then a ghastly white lightning opened the sky. The horse reared, and apologised. In the lightning, which seemed to last a long time, the Prince saw the outline of a huge white castle on the mountain slope above, with a black causeway curling round the rocks right up to its gaping doormouth. A cold glow slid from every chink of it, and it seemed to be built entirely of the bones of colossal ancient monsters. When the lightning went out, the glow went on, and staring at the bone towers and ribcage walls and vertebrae palisades, the Prince was sure he didn't want to go anywhere near it.

"Now what do I do?" cried the Prince in despair. Horrible shapes quivered all round him, and the only refuge seemed to be the awful castle.

"Draw a Bezzlegram," said the horse.

"You spoke!"

"I didn't," said the horse.

"What's a Bezzlegram?"

"It's a circle with a seven-pointed star in it and drawings of safe signs in between the points. It keeps Bezzles out."

"What are Bezzles? And I can't! And does it matter?"

"Yes," said the horse. "The things you can see all around you are Bezzles. They're demons of the Waste, and they'll attack any minute unless you're inside a Bezzlegram."

"Well, I'm not and I won't be," cried the Prince in a panic.

The horse proceeded to draw a Bezzlegram in the dry ground with its hoof. It looked just the way it had said it would, a circle with a seven-pointed star inside. The 'safe signs' were a dot, a cross, a square, an oblong, a thing like the letter T, a thing like an H, and a thing that didn't look like anything at all.

"What's that?" asked the Prince, pointing at this thing.

"I don't know. I couldn't remember the last safe sign," said the horse unworriedly, going and standing in the centre of the star. "This Bezzlegram's a bit messy really altogether, but it'll keep those Bezzles out anyway. They're very ignorant. Beezles, now, or Buzzles, they're much harder to fool."

The Prince soon realised the horse must be right, because the awful cries and howls had died down to a whispering and wailing, which still made his hair stand on end, but didn't seem so close. After a time, when it got completely dark, the Prince could make out a ring of eyes all round the Bezzlegram, but they were a safe three or four yards away. He didn't like them much, even so.

"Will they go away again at daybreak?" he asked the horse, finally getting off its back.

"Oh yes, or the moonlight might drive them off."

"Ah. When does the moon rise?"

"Which one?"

"How do you mean?" asked the Prince. "You know, the moon, that round white thing."

"*Which* moon, I meant. There are three, and none of them is round."

"They must be," said the Prince.

But he was wrong. Just at that moment one of the moons appeared over the mountains, and it was an almost perfect square.

"That's silly," said the Prince. "It can't be that shape."

He said this again, later on, when the other two rose. One of them was an oval, and the other was a heart.

"It's obvious to me," said the horse, sitting beside him in the Bezzlegram (the moonlight hadn't driven the Bezzles off), "that you come from quite a different country."

The Prince put out his hands to the small fire he hadn't been able to light, recollected, shivered, put them back and said, "If only I could *remember* where I came from."

"Well, you do," said the horse. "At least you remember things like a round moon. How daft that must look."

"That's different," said the Prince. "Well, at least tell me," he added, "how I got to be sitting on your back."

"I can't *tell* you anything," said the horse with dignity.

"Oh, very well. How did I get on to your back?"

"You were just there," said the horse.

"What, out of nowhere?"

"Precisely," said the horse.

"That's silly," said the Prince, but he caught sight of the three moons again, and he thought perhaps it wasn't so silly hereabouts.

"Didn't you mind?" he tried.

"No," said the horse. "When you arrived I suddenly

had all these white and gold trappings. I don't mind people dropping in when they bring presents."

"Before I came," said the Prince, "what were you doing?"

"Being a lion," said the horse.

The Prince was interested despite himself.

"Can you change at will?"

"Always. Everyone can."

"*I* can't," said the Prince.

"You haven't tried," said the horse.

But when the Prince tried, he still couldn't. He went on being a Prince, instead of a tiger or a wolf or an ostrich and all the other things he had tried to be.

"It's because you come from another country, I expect," said the horse consolingly.

The prince thought a moment. A cunning look crossed his face.

"If I come from another country," he said, "which country is this?"

"It's simply here," said the horse.

"Hasn't it a name?"

"Oh no," said the horse disdainfully.

"Well, it's like being in the back of beyond, if you ask me," grumbled the Prince.

"Whose back?" enquired the horse gently. "And if it were, wouldn't you be *on* it, not *in* it?"

Despondently the Prince rolled himself in his cloak and lay down to sleep. The ten hours' riding he knew he had put in had tired him out, not to mention Gemael the Red, the castle, the Bezzles and the horse. Despite the cold he grew drowsier and drowsier. The very last thing he saw as his eyes closed was a silver chariot, shaped like an open flower, being pulled over the sky by three silver horses with fiery wings.

"That's pretty," he murmured, and fell asleep.

2

The Castle of Bone

"A silver chariot shaped like an open flower, being pulled over the sky by three silver horses with fiery wings!" cried the Prince, sitting up with a terrific start. "That's silly! Oh, no it isn't. I forgot."

It was dawn and the sky was gold, with clouds like huge red roses floating about in it. The Prince nervously stared to make sure they weren't actually roses, but they were clouds all right. A big lion was sitting a few yards away, outside the Bezzlegram, washing its paws.

The prince was rather scared, wondering if it might be hungry.

"Good morning," he said very politely. "Do you speak too?"

"No," said the lion.

"Ah—ha," said the Prince. "It's you. You're being a lion again."

"I'll be a horse when you want to ride me," said the lion.

The Prince stretched, wondering why he felt so well and cheerful when he was in such a ridiculous place, and didn't know the first thing about himself.

"I see the Bezzles have gone."

"Mostly," said the horse-lion. "I had one for breakfast."

The Prince didn't like to think about this.

"Did you see the silver flower chariot?" he asked quickly.

"Yes. It's one of the chariots of the Sky People."

At that moment the sun rose over the Waste, and the

Prince was certain, before it became too bright to look at, that the sun had a hole in the middle just like a doughnut. He decided not to mention it.

"What do we do now?" he asked the horse-lion.

"I thought you wanted to go to the Castle of Bone."

"Not really, I just felt I had to. I still do, in fact," added the Prince gloomily.

"Well, it's quite safe by day," said the horse-lion, giving itself a shake and turning back into a horse. "Look."

The Prince did look, and the castle still seemed ancient and peculiar, but the bones were lacquered golden by the sun, and the cold light was gone from the windows.

"Right," said the prince bravely, and swung himself into the saddle.

The horse started forward at a brisk trot. They crossed the rocks and were soon on the smooth causeway, riding upwards. In spite of his cheerful mood, the Prince couldn't help noticing the bones lying about by the side of the road, and the broken-off swords and crushed helmets rusting in little piles.

"Would that be the Dragon of Brass, do you suppose?"

"Who else?" said the horse.

After travelling for about half an hour, they reached the huge doorway, filled by a massive black door with brazen studs. The Prince felt he ought to knock on the door with the hilt of the sword Gemael the Red had given him. When he did so, a great clanging boomed and echoed through the castle.

For a long while nothing happened, except that the echoes died away. And then there came the sound of heavy footsteps on bone floors, and a chink of metal.

The Prince got nervous.

"I've changed my mind," he said urgently. "Can we ride away rather fast—or could you draw another Bezzlegram or something?"

"I don't think it would be any good," said the horse. "That sounds more like a Beezle to me."

Just then there came the scream of a key in the lock, and the door was flung open.

Framed in the doorway stood a gigantic muscular creature, covered from neck to knees in a sort of furry tunic, with a brass studded belt at its waist. Arms, legs and a head just as furry as the tunic protruded through holes; but the tunic fur was white and the rest black. Long yellow eyes and teeth glittered in the fur. A single horn stuck out where its nose should have been, and a club was thrust through its belt. In one taloned paw it carried an enormous key-ring, in the other a mop and bucket.

"*Is* it a Beezle?" whispered the Prince anxiously.

"No, a Buzzle," said the horse.

"That's worse isn't it—" began the Prince, but was interrupted by the Buzzle, which roared out, "WHAT DO YOU WANT?" At which the causeway trembled, as if in an earthquake, from the noise, and the Prince almost fell down.

"Is this—is this—the Castle of Bone—wh-where all the secrets of the w-w-world are hidden?" he got out at last.

"YES," thundered the Buzzle, though more quietly. "WHAT ABOUT IT?"

"Well, can I come in?"

"I DON'T SEE WHY NOT," shouted the Buzzle, "AS LONG AS YOU WATCH OUT AND DON'T DIRTY MY FLOORS."

It waved them in and shut the door with a terrible bang.

"I—er—won't have to fight the Dragon of Brass, will I?" asked the Prince.

"NO. THAT'S ONLY AT NIGHT."

Having got them inside, and decided they were "VISITORS", the Buzzle became quite jolly, and took them into its "ROOM". It said it was the caretaker of the castle, and offered the Prince breakfast. The Prince gladly accepted, but it turned out that the Buzzle thought raw eggs and watercress were what he wanted (which they weren't). The Prince managed to tip them out of a window when the Buzzle wasn't looking.

* * *

"YOU SEE," screamed the Buzzle, as it took them on a guided tour of the castle some twenty minutes later, "IT'S QUITE NICE FOR ME TO MEET SOMEBODY FROM OUTSIDE, AND YOU A PRINCE AND ALL."

"And the horse," put in the Prince politely.

"OH, HORSES AREN'T ANY GOOD. YOU CAN'T TALK TO A HORSE."

"Quite right," said the horse approvingly.

"But if the castle's safe by day, don't you ever get anyone calling here then?" asked the Prince.

"NOBODY EVER GETS HERE BY DAY," yelled the Buzzle, "ONLY BY NIGHT."

"Always?"

"ALWAYS."

"But that's sill—" began the Prince and stopped.

"But supposing they stay in the Waste until morning?"

"THEY GET EATEN BY BEZZLES, THEY DO."

"I didn't, said the Prince.

"YOU DREW A BEZZLEGRAM."

"Oh yes. No, I didn't, the horse did."

"HORSES DON'T DRAW. YOU MUST HAVE DONE."

The Buzzle led them up many flights of bone stairs into a long bone gallery. Here were several statues in a row, all painted and dressed in beautiful clothes. The Prince thought they must be past lords and ladies of the castle, but the Buzzle said it didn't know who they were, and hurried them on. There were several other places where the Prince would have liked to stop—rooms of magnificent furniture, and caskets of jewels—but the Buzzle said they didn't want to bother with those; what it was going to show them was much more interesting. The Prince became very excited thinking it was about to reveal one or all of the hidden secrets of the world.

Eventually they came to the top of a high tower.

"THERE!" boomed the Buzzle rapturously.

The Prince looked round the room, and it was perfectly empty.

"Where, exactly?"

"THERE! THERE!" And the Buzzle ran forward and

clasped something in its paws. "BEYOND PRICE. YOU MAY HOLD IT."

"Thank you," said the Prince, and took the thing. He thought it might just be invisible, but it wasn't even that. It wasn't there at all. He caught the Buzzle glaring at him, so he said, "It's really lovely. You must be very proud."

"I AM," howled the Buzzle.

"The point is," ventured the Prince, "I was hoping to see some of the hidden secrets of the world."

"OH, YOU WON'T SEE THOSE IN THE DAYTIME, THEY'RE ONLY HERE AT NIGHT, ALONG WITH ALL THE FRIGHTFUL THINGS."

The Prince felt very dismayed, because he had begun to realise that what he probably had to do at the castle was to see these secrets of the world, and now he would have to spend a night here, after all.

"Is that when the Dragon's about?" he asked.

"YES. NOT TO MENTION THE SKOLKS AND OGGRINGS. I ALWAYS HIDE, BUT THEY DON'T HALF MAKE A MESS OF THE PLACE—AND ALL THOSE BONES AND BITS OF ARMOUR LEFT LYING AROUND JUST ANYWHERE—"

"This is awful!" lamented the Prince. "I do so want to run away, and I don't seem able to."

Remembering the mess the Skolks and Oggrings made, however, the Buzzle suddenly became very efficient, and hurried off to mop and dust everything. The Prince sat on the floor with his head in his hands.

"Whatever shall I do?"

A kind of whirling began to happen in the air. After a moment or so, a girl in a red dress appeared in the centre of the room.

"Who are you?" she cried. "And whom do you seek?" And then, "Oh, it's still you. Have you killed the Dragon yet, oh brave Prince?."

"No," said the Prince.

Gemael the Red looked surprised and annoyed.

"I gave you the magic sword," she shouted, and the sword rattled on its own in the Prince's scabbard. "Use it on the Dragon tonight, or you will rue the day we met. Godspeed," she finished, and whirled herself away.

The day went by very quickly as the Prince wandered worriedly about the splendid rooms of the castle. By the time sunset showed in the windows he was very hungry and very, very frightened. The horse had turned into a lion again in the afternoon, and gone off somewhere. The Prince thought it would probably go back into the Waste, and draw a Bezzlegram, and stay there all night if it had any sense.

The majestic shadows lengthened in the rooms, and some stars sneaked out over the Waste. The Prince ran up and down the stairs, looking for the Buzzle. Finally he found it hastily locking doors with its key-ring.

"Almost time, then?" said the Prince unhappily.

"CAN'T STOP NOW," yodelled the Buzzle, and ran past him down the corridor. The Prince ran after it. "HAVE TO LOCK UP THE VALUABLES, AND THEN I GO AND HIDE IN MY ROOM."

Just then they reached the "ROOM". The buzzle dived inside, and suddenly there was only a blank wall with no door in it at all.

"A friend in need is a friend indeed," said the Prince sourly.

At that instant, the last purple glimmer faded from the sky. It grew very quiet and dark, and then an icy wind came rushing from nowhere, sweeping like a great cold broom through every crevice of the Castle of Bone. The Prince shuddered, and pressed himself back against the wall to let it past, because he felt the wind knew he was there, and would be angry if he didn't show it proper respect. After the wind, he began to hear a lot of strange noises, a sort of creaking and groaning like a forest of old trees, and he didn't like it at all.

"I must try to find a candle or something, now it's got so dark," he muttered and, squaring his shoulders, and putting one hand on the hilt of Gemael's sword, he went back up the corridor in the direction of a big hall he thought he remembered seeing earlier.

It was now as black as the bottom of a tar barrel. The Prince had to feel his way with his hands and stumbled over stairs and furniture all the time. He began to count his steps aloud to cheer himself up. When he reached one hundred and seventy there was a distinct echo to his words, and he thought he had got to the hall. He remembered there had been brass candlebranches in the walls, each with about fourteen bone white candles apiece, and after a lot of accidents, he managed to find one and get it down. Then he recalled he had nothing to light it with. He was standing there, feeling stupid, when he realised there *was* a light in the hall, and it was gliding towards him.

"Get back!" cried the Prince hoarsely, drawing his sword. But the light took no notice, and floated nearer. What was more, it made a peculiar noise at him. "Go away!" yelled the Prince. "Beware of my sword!" The light didn't.

The Prince broke into terrified flight. He fell over hundreds of things, and candles rained from the candlebranch, and all the while the light clattered after him, making the most horrible sounds. Finally, the Prince hit his head on something, and sat down abruptly on the floor. The awful creature rushed up, stamped on his sword arm, just as he was trying to use it, and lit the three candles left in the candlebranch.

The Prince found he was staring up at the horse, which held a lighted taper in its mouth, and had therefore been unable to speak properly. The Prince removed the taper, and the horse said, "Fire is an important protection against the dark powers of the castle. The Buzzle lent me a flint, but it took ages to make it strike."

The Prince looked round the hall, and it was vast and shadowy. He had hit his head on a huge carved chair with a canopy, and spilled candles lay everywhere.

"What do I have to do?" asked the Prince. He had come to rely upon the horse, and was very glad it was here.

"I think you should draw a Draxagram on the floor, and

get inside it," said the horse. "Then, with the help of the four elements, you'll be as safe as you can hope to be. Do you have any chalk?"

"No, I don't. What four elements? And what's a Draxagram?" enquired the Prince, feeling happier already.

"A stick of charcoal would do," said the horse. It turned abruptly and gave the chair a dreadful kick. One leg collapsed at once. The horse picked it up, held it awhile in the candle flame, and then proceeded to draw on the floor with the charred end. The Draxagram seemed to be a collection of eight circles, each one with bits overlapping into the other seven, which should have been impossible. When it was done, the horse shook some earth out of its hoof into a small pile inside the Draxagram, spat on it (the Prince hadn't realised horses could spit), breathed on it, and then rested the burning taper on the top.

Just as it finished, a dull ominous booming sounded from somewhere above, the doors of the hall flew open with a thud, and a great crowd of black flying things whizzed into the room. The Prince ran inside the Draxagram, still clutching the candlebranch and the sword, aware, with a cold sinking feeling, that the terrors of the night had truly begun.

3

Ysome

The Prince and the horse sat inside the Draxagram in the flickering circle of candlelight. Round and round the Draxagram on the outside beat the black flying things, glaring with unpleasant fierce eyes, and squealing with rage because they couldn't get at them.

"Are they bats?" asked the Prince.

"No," said the horse, "Oggrings."

After a time the Oggrings settled in flocks on various pieces of furniture, rustling and shrieking in the dark.

The awful booming came again from the heart of the castle.

"What now?" wondered the Prince.

Through the open door ran twenty skeletons, dressed in brazen armour and carrying great axes. They rattled and clanked across the floor and surrounded the Draxagram.

"Surrender!" cried the captain skeleton in a high whistling voice. "Come out and you will be shown mercy."

"It—er—seems like a fair offer," said the Prince.

But the skeletons shifted their axes to get a better grip, and the Oggrings rustled excitedly.

"As long as you stay in the Draxagram," said the horse, "you'll probably be safe. If you leave it, the skeletons will chop off your head and the Oggrings will eat you."

The skeletons gnashed their teeth unmusically. They lifted their axes in both hands and began to leap all round the Draxagram in a whirling circle that made the Prince feel dizzy and confused.

"Take no notice," said the horse.

But the Prince couldn't seem to take his eyes off the skeletons. Soon he began to turn round and round in circles himself, and each circle brought him a little closer to the edge.

"Join the dance," invited the captain generously.

"Why, thank you," said the Prince.

The horse got hold of his sleeve and pulled him back just in time. The Prince fell over, and the horse sat on him. The Prince struggled and complained until quite out of breath. Seeing he wouldn't get away, the skeletons stopped leaping about, and went and leaned on their axes in the shadows.

The Prince came to his senses at once, and the horse let him get up.

"The thing that bothers me," said the Prince, trying to pretend nothing had happened, "is that I shan't get to see any of the hidden secrets of the world if I'm stuck in this Draxagram all night."

"And you won't if your head's chopped off either."

Just then the darkness began to lighten.

"Is it morning already?" asked the Prince hopefully.

But it wasn't. Through the door came a troup of maidens, clad in filmy white, some carrying lanterns shining with a soft pale light, others playing little harps and pipes so that a peculiar sweet music filled the hall. At once all the skeletons froze in attitudes of fright, and, as for the Oggrings, they lifted in a frenzied cloud and fled out of a high window.

Among the maidens walked the most beautiful girl the Prince had ever seen. At least, the most beautiful he could ever remember seeing. She had long fair hair plaited with pearls, and a primrose yellow dress with a girdle of silver lilies, and she held out one hand to him, and came towards him, smiling.

"Brave Prince," cried she, "you have overcome the terrors of the Castle of Bone. I am Ysome the Saffron, the Lady of the Castle, under a spell all day, but freed by night if a brave man dares to visit me. Now, be my guest, and we will eat and drink and make merry until the stars fade, at which time I will show you all the secrets of the world which lie hidden here."

It was a very long speech to make while you were walking rather fast, and she didn't get at all out of breath, so the Prince admired her even more. He was just about to take her hand and step out of the circle, when the horse caught hold of his tunic and almost succeeded in sitting on him again.

"It's only a trick to get you to leave the Draxagram," said the horse, "because the Oggrings and skeletons have failed."

"Nonsense," said the Prince, gazing at the lovely girl, and thinking about the eating and drinking she had mentioned. "Besides, you said fire was a protection against the dark powers of the castle, and so this lady wouldn't be likely to have lamps, if she *were* a dark power."

"Those aren't flames in the lamps," said the horse, "only elflight or phosphorus."

"Oh, what's *that?*" snapped the Prince.

"To whom are you talking?" interrupted Ysome the Saffron.

"This horse—Let go!" cried the Prince.

Ysome gave a tinkling laugh.

"But, dear Prince, horses don't *talk*."

The Prince shook the horse off.

"No, they don't," he decided. And he stepped out of the Draxagram, and clasped her hand.

"Now there'll be a thunder clap, and she'll change into a monster," said the horse, but there wasn't, and she didn't. She led the Prince gently from the hall, her maidens gliding behind, swinging their lamps and playing their harps.

The horse might have thought it was mistaken, but, just as the lamp-glow was fading from the doorway, several of the skeletons sneaked out after them, grinning skull grins, and it noticed that some of the Oggrings had flown back in and were following the procession too.

The horse shook itself into a lion, picked up the taper in its mouth, and went after everybody else, with a stealthy lion tread.

Ysome the Saffron conducted the Prince through many twisting passages and up countless steps into a gigantic banqueting hall. The walls were hung with silver cobweb draperies, and bone chandeliers rattled in the ceiling lit by hundreds of luminous green beetles.

The Prince was seated at one end of the long table and helped to wonderful food on silver dishes by Ysome's maidens. She sat at the opposite end and gazed at him fondly, as he stuffed himself with roasts and pies, and drank rare wines by the jugful.

Finally he leaned back in his chair and thanked Ysome warmly.

"That's quite all right, dear Prince," said Ysome. "It was all magic food, and now you are completely in my power. I can make you do whatever I like."

And so she could. No sooner had the Prince tried to draw his sword than he found she had made him put his hand in the gravy instead, and when he tried to run at her he ran into a hanging and became completely tangled up.

"Now," said Ysome, clapping her hands (at which all her maidens turned back into the large lizards they had presumably been all the time), "I am indeed the Lady of the Castle, and I could have you killed at once, and in lots of revolting ways, but I don't think that would be so much fun as letting you get away—no, don't thank me, I haven't finished yet—and then letting the Skolks and Oggrings hunt you down."

The Prince became aware that the Oggrings had flown in at the doors and windows and were perched on the chandeliers, occasionally eating the beetles. Two skeletons dragged him roughly from the cobweb.

"Be careful not to damage him!" screamed Ysome angrily, and they cowered, and dusted him down. "Now, when I give the signal, oh Prince, you may start to run away. You can go anywhere you like, and hide anywhere you think you might enjoy, but the Skolks will find you, you can be sure. Come, my Skolks."

And through the door slunk ten hideous animals, rather like enormous jackals, with big blazing eyes and evil teeth. They stared at the Prince, and snuffled towards him to get the scent, then licked their jaws and smiled.

"When I say 'go'," cried Ysome, "the Prince will run out. All the rest of us will cover our eyes and count to a hundred, after which the Skolks and Oggrings may give chase. Any cheating," she added, "will be severely punished. I like to see fair play."

The Prince tried to throw a plate at her, but found he had dropped it on his foot instead.

"Cover your eyes!" shouted Ysome, and they all did. "Go!"

The Prince spun round in a panic-sticken circle, then, with a cry of angry despair, fled out of the banqueting hall, certain that all the Skolks were peeping.

He tried to count too, as he ran, and he had only reached eighty-three when he heard the first cries behind him.

"They *did* cheat," he wailed. "Oh! If only I'd listened to the horse."

He stumbled up and down stairs, leapt over thresholds into empty rooms, where things mumbled and shrieked at him, and leapt out again. He found some of the beetles had fallen on his head and so he could see where he was going by their light. Unfortunately the Skolks and Oggrings would also be able to. Every so often he was positive he felt hot breath on his heels, and could hear the flap of wings in his ears. Then he would put on an extra burst of speed.

"But it's no use," he panted, "no use at all."

Dashing round a corner, he plunged into a whirling thing which became Gemael the Red even as he collided with her.

"Who are you?" she gasped, "and whom—haven't you killed the Dragon *yet?*"

"Oh, for goodness sake," cried the Prince and rushed past her. Gemael ran after him.

"You must destroy the Dragon, and then the castle will fall, and my sworn enemy, Ysome the Saffron, will perish. Do you hear?"

But he didn't, and fairly soon Gemael caught sight of the Skolks, and disappeared at top speed.

The Prince now realised he was going downwards, all the flights of stairs had led this way for a long time, probably because he had found it easier to run down these than up the upwards ones.

"I shall be trapped in a cellar," he shuddered, but he couldn't turn back.

And then suddenly he ran slap into a closed door. He rubbed his nose and stared at the door. It seemed to be made of ebony, and was bolted seven times and barred seven times on his side. With frenzied fingers he strained open the top bars and bolts, and pulled the middle ones, and scrabbled at the ones at the bottom, which were very stiff. Just as he got to the last one, he heard a joyful snuffling behind him, and turned round to see three of the Skolks grinning in the passage, each with an Oggring perched on its back.

"Look," said the trembling Prince, "do Skolks talk?"

"No," said the nearest one, dribbling.

"Oh good, well in that case, I hear there's a lot of treasure here, and wouldn't you like some of it—half of it—all of it, then? Just think of the meals you could buy with a whole castle full of treasure. Eat me, and I'll be gone in a flash, all over, only a memory—"

The Skolks only smiled, and began to pad forward, the Oggrings flapping over their heads.

"Shall we eat him all now?" asked a Skolk. "Or save some for later."

"All now!" squealed an Oggring. "Before the others come and want their share."

The Prince drew his sword in desperation and lunged at them, and, as he did so, another shape burst into the passageway. He thought it was a Skolk too, but it was the horse-lion.

"Jewelstar!" shouted the horse-lion, which was apparently some kind of battle-cry, and jumped on two of the Skolks.

"Jewelstar!" echoed the Prince and, finding it made him feel braver, he chopped off the head of the nearest Skolk with one blow, and clipped the wings of an Oggring which flew into his face. After that, everything seemed to blur together, and, when he next looked round him, he and the horse-lion were standing by the door with five dead Skolks and a great pile of Oggrings in the passage.

"Quickly, open the door," said the horse-lion. "There'll be worse than Skolks in a minute."

The Prince obeyed, and they dashed through it and slammed it shut behind them. Amazed, the Prince heard it locking itself on the other side.

When he looked around him, he saw that they were in a great courtyard with a tall bone tower standing remotely at the far end. It was walled on the other three sides by bone palisades, and was open to the sky. Stars and the heart moon gazed back at him, and washed the court with cool light.

"Where are we now?" asked the Prince, but the useful horse-lion was scratching a weird sign on the door with its claws.

"That will stop them unbolting it," said the horse-lion, "and we're in a courtyard."

The Prince shrugged, and went round the courtyard to see if he could find a different way out. On the ground, near the right-hand wall, was the remains of an old Draxagram someone had drawn but, judging by the bits of broken sword lying round it, they hadn't stayed in theirs either.

There didn't seem to be a way out, except possibly by the tower, but he didn't like the look of it for some reason. Turning back, the Prince found a large brass bell hanging from the wall. On it was inscribed: 'I AM HERE. SOUND THIS' AND I WILL COME.'

If the Prince had stopped to think about it, he would have realised that possibly he might not want to meet whoever was there, and would come, but somehow he didn't. He just reached up and rang the bell before he could stop himself. It gave off a most terrifying clanging that bounced from wall to wall, and the horse-lion ran up to him and cried, "You shouldn't have *done* that!"

"What will happen?" trembled the Prince.

The first thing that happened was that a great black crack appeared down the whole length of the tower, and out of it billowed rusty-red smoke. It filled the court, and turned the sky and the moon the colour of blood, and it smelled of hot metal and burning oil.

The second thing that happened was that the crack split wide open so that the tower separated into two halves, and out of the middle a glittering, huge, terrible thing uncoiled itself, its metal cogs grinding together, black steam puffing from its brazen nostrils, and fire flickering behind its empty hungry eyes.

It was unmistakably the Dragon of Brass.

4

The Dragon of Brass

"It's the dra—the dra—Oh! Can't we draw a Draxagrarn?" cried the Prince.

"No," said the horse-lion, "there wouldn't be any point. As you can see, the Dragon of Brass is made of brass. It's all machinery, and so a Draxagram wouldn't have any power over it."

"I don't see why not!" shouted the Prince. "I think you're being unreasonable."

The Dragon was now clear of the tower, and was coming across the court with a slow, metal-squealing tread. It lashed its tail, and brass plates rattled, and a brass forked tongue flickered noisily in and out of its hinged jaws. The red fire behind its eyes made them glow terribly.

"Look," said the Prince as they backed away, "it's got fire in it, so it can't be one of the dark powers–perhaps it's friendly."

"That kind of magic doesn't make any difference to a machine," said the horse-lion. "Besides, the fire is its combustion—"

"Oh, these long words!" cried the Prince.

At this moment they both banged into the courtyard wall, having backed as far as they could go.

Gemael's sword suddenly rattled by itself in the Prince's scabbard.

"Shall I–try this?" the Prince wondered, drawing it. "She said it was magic, after all."

"You've got nothing to lose," said the horse-lion.

So, clutching the ruby hilt and feeling cold all over, the Prince took a few steps forward to meet the Dragon. The Dragon seemed delighted, and speeded up. The Prince backed away again.

"It's not fair," he said to the horse, trying to press himself through the bone wall and into another part of the castle–any other part–"I thought it stayed *outside* to guard, like a—like a dog."

The Dragon now reached the wall, and so they began to back along it, which made a change, but still didn't really improve things.

"It hasn't attacked yet," whispered the Prince. "Perhaps it won't."

Just then it did. It reared up its frightful head and lunged at him. The Prince managed to jump aside, and, stung to action, brought the magic sword crashing down against the Dragon's bodywork. The sword promptly snapped in half.

"Oh, that's a lot of use!" yelled the Prince in horrified rage.

A gale of laughter floated down from the other side of the court. As he ran away from the Dragon, the Prince was able to look up and see Ysome the Saffron and her lizards, and several Skolks, skeletons and Oggrings having gleeful hysterics on top of one of the bone palisades.

"Fool, to trust the weapons of Gemael the Red!" howled Ysome.

Blindly the Prince rained another blow or two on the Dragon, and some more of the sword snapped off. He was just about to throw it away, as it slowed him down while he ran, when the smoky air began to whirl. Out of the whirling came a dim, trembling shape with long black hair. Gemael the Red looked very pale, and she cowered inside the whirling, never quite daring to form herself properly.

"A fine time to show up!" snarled the Prince. "And look at your useless sword!"

With huge fearful eyes fixed on the Dragon, Gemael gasped in a hoarse and angry voice, "Don't you know *anything,* you stupid creature. Don't hit the Dragon with the sword, *throw* it."

"Throw it where?"

"Oh! Down its throat, where else, you idiot!"

"She's quite right," put in the horse-lion across the court.

The Prince stopped running. He planted himself firmly, with what was left of the sword in both hands, and watched the Dragon lumbering towards him.

"I'll tell you when," hissed Gemael. The Dragon opened its jaws, and snaked its head down to them. "Now!" screamed Gemael.

The Prince threw the sword. It arched up and in, over the six inch long brass teeth, and went down the throat with a rasping, clattering sound. The Prince fell flat, and hid his face, and waited to be crunched up. As a result of this, he didn't see what happened to the Dragon. First it hesitated and looked surprised. Then it shook itself, jumped in the air, and kicked out its six legs, one after the other, and looked even more surprised. Then there was a thud inside it, as if something had exploded, a lot of white smoke came out of its joints, and bright flashes went on and off behind its eyes. It ran on the spot, ran backwards, tried to run backwards up the wall, fell down again, and finally stopped quite still. After this, it didn't move again, simply steamed gently to itself, and made soft sizzling sounds in a corner.

The Prince looked up at last.

"I think you shorted something," said the horse-lion.

"What?" asked the Prince. He was interrupted by a shrill scream from the palisade.

Ysome the Saffron, with a very white face, had lifted her arms to call down a ghastly curse on the Prince, but it was too late. The stars had begun to fade.

"Your power is gone with the night!" cried Gemael. "And now the Dragon is dead, you must leave the castle and wander homeless, as I have done all these years."

Ysome shivered again, and ran off the palisade, closely

followed by lizards, skeletons, Skolks and Oggrings, all squealing and grunting.

"Brave Prince," began Gemael warmly.

"I don't see," said the Prince with dignity, "if I was supposed to *throw* the wretched sword, why you didn't tell me when you gave it to me."

"I thought you knew," said Gemael humbly.

"Well, I didn't. And, anyway, why give it to me and not to all the other poor Princes who came to the castle and got eaten?"

"You were special."

"Oh, was I?" asked the Prince, thawing slightly.

"Yes," said Gemael, "though I don't know why."

And so saying, she disappeared.

"Well," said the Prince, "it's almost dawn. I shan't see any of the hidden secrets of the world *now*."

"Whatever makes you think that?" asked a voice.

A door that the Prince hadn't seen before had opened in the far wall, and there stood a tall straight old man. At least he looked as though he ought to be old, because his hair was white and there were lines around his eyes, but really you couldn't tell for sure. Out of the white hair at his temples grew two fine curling horns, and, instead of a garment, he was covered from neck to ankles with long, well-groomed white fur.

"Come with me," he said. "I can't show you everything because not everything concerns you. But what does, I *will* show you, I promise."

"But—" said the Prince.

The horse—it was a horse again–nudged him forward.

"It's quite all right. He's a Theel. They're incapable of harming another."

"Another what?" said the Prince vaguely.

The Theel took them into a round room. How they got there the Prince couldn't quite recall. In the middle of the room was a large cup carved of bone, but when the Prince peered down into it, what he saw was a smoky shifting mist. He had a sudden feeling he wasn't going to see anything special at all.

"Of course you will," said the Theel kindly, though the Prince hadn't spoken aloud. "However, you may not understand what you see, as yet. There are a lot of secrets, and all jumbled together like that they don't seem to be anything, but if you just stand here a minute, the ones that belong to you will arive."

At that instant, one did. Out of the mist appeared a distinct picture of the Castle of Bone itself, caught in the rays of dawn, and it was collapsing.

"Don't be afraid," said the Theel. "It won't be dawn for a little while, and you'll be well away by then."

"But what happened?" asked the Prince. "Is there going to be an earthquake?"

"Gemael told you that once the Dragon of Brass was destroyed the castle would fall. You ended the power of the Dragon–for the time being at any rate–so the castle *will* fall."

The Prince didn't really understand this, but he was getting used to not understanding things out here.

"What about Ysome?."

But just then he saw Ysome in the bone cup. She was sitting in the Waste, wringing her hands, surrounded by a lot of grumbling Skolks and other dreadful things the Prince didn't look at too closely. He didn't feel a bit sorry for her. But he wondered about the Theel, which seemed to live in the castle too.

"Where will *you* go?" he asked.

"Where I'm needed, just as you will."

"Will I?"

Surprised, the Prince caught a sudden glimpse of a marching army, waving banners, glinting swords, and there, at the front of it, was a young man in white and gold armour with a golden helmet on his head, and the young man looked just like himself.

"Jewelstar forever! jewelstar undaunted!" shouted the armies.

"Jewelstar?" muttered the Prince. "Where have I heard

that word before? Wait a minute, the horse used it as a battle-cry when we fought the Skolks. Why did you, horse?"

"It came into my head and seemed right at the time," said the horse.

"But where is this Jewelstar, and what is it?"

"Don't ask me," said the horse. "Not that you'd be so foolish."

But the armies seemed to know all about it, and they were yelling even harder as they faded back into the mist.

"And there's an acorn!" exclaimed the Prince. "Whatever's an acorn doing there? Or is it? Nulgrave! It's gone!" The Prince paused. "What do I mean by *Nulgrave*? It must be a sort of curse—Ah!"

What was presumably Nulgrave had appeared in the mist. The Prince drew away from the bowl, and turned pale. There was a black coiling *something* there, and the very sight of it made him feel that wherever it was he had come from, he ought to get back there very quickly, before he and the Something got any closer to each other.

At that moment the first pink jugful of dawn brimmed over the window sill and spilled on to the floor.

"You must go," said the Theel. "But no; wait one moment," and going past the Prince to the cup, he put in one hand and drew out an egg. This seemed so ridiculous that the prince laughed, though rather shakily. "Here you are," said the Theel.

The Prince took the egg, turned it over, and asked, "What do I do with it, actually?"

"In the Egg is your personal secret," said the Theel. "You can't break the shell until it's ready, but when it's time for you to know what your secret is, it will hatch out on its own. Until then, simply keep it with you. If you lose it, you may never find out, and others might discover some way to destroy the Egg—which could do endless harm, particulary to yourself."

"But do you mean," said the Prince, "that when this Egg breaks open on its own, I shall remember who I am, where I came from and what I'm supposed to be doing here?"

"Yes," said the Theel.

There came an abrupt, uneasy rumbling from under their feet.

"We must go now," said the Theel.

"But what am I to do?" cried the Prince.

"What you feel you must," said the Theel. "That's the only thing to do at any time."

Having said this, he went to the window and, to the Prince's horror, stepped out.

The Prince ran to the sill and looked down to see how badly the Theel had been hurt when he hit the ground twenty feet below, but the Theel wasn't there. He was floating gently away into the Waste on a morning breeze. He smiled and raised his hand in farewell.

"Oh, this is awful!" shouted the Prince to the horse. "I'm even more confused than before. All I've got is this stupid Egg—and—and—" –the Prince went pale again– "this feeling that I've got to get on your back, and ride over those mountains towards—something I'm not sure I'm going to enjoy. When I think I thought all this might be a *holiday*!"

There was another thud in the foundations of the castle. The Prince stopped worrying about riding and eggs, and dashed down the stairs as fast as he could, the horse behind him. They burst out of a small door, and across a bone drawbridge they hadn't seen before, which led over a frightening gap between the castle mountain and the mountain behind it. Oggrings and Skolks and skeletons and others rushed by, carrying pieces of furniture and jewels from the castle and taking no notice of anything else.

Once on the other mountain, the horse and the Prince scrambled up a winding path to put as much distance between themselves and the castle as they could.

"There's the sun now," said the Prince, looking back.

A golden slice of it had slit the horizon.

Immediately the bone castle tottered, cracked, heaved and crumbled. Bone towers and halls fell inwards, bone stairways buckled, roofs crashed, and a white cloud of bone dust hid the sun.

A sound of wailing and cursing and crying came from below.

As the dust settled, various creatures came crawling out, hiding their eyes from the light. Last of all came a big furry thing in a white furry tunic. It clutched a key-ring, but, after a moment, flung it down on the ruins. Obviously there were no more rooms to lock and unlock.

"It's the poor Buzzle," said the Prince. He had forgotten about it and now wondered what it would do, as the castle had been its home as well. Then he heard its voice booming over the crowds of Ysome's minions.

"OUT OF MY WAY. NO MORE MESSY FLOORS TO CLEAR UP FROM ALL YOU MESSY MONSTERS. GET OUT OF IT! NONE OF YOUR LIP!"–shouldering a Skolk out of its path–"FREE AT LAST!" And it strode off into the Waste whistling. It seemed to understand the Skolks had no power by day.

"Well, someone's happy," said the Prince.

He felt nervous. He put the Egg in his pocket and cleared his throat.

"Over the mountains then," he said. "It's bound to be an awful journey. But at least," he comforted himself, "I've got someone to talk to."

The horse, naturally, made no reply.

5

Vultikan's Forge

The climb over the mountains took several days, and the Prince didn't actually ride on the horse because the horse said it found it easier to climb mountains as a lion.

It wasn't so much that it was a difficult climb, just thoroughly unpleasant. The mountains were black, sharp and spiky, and there were sharp spiky winds as well. At least there weren't any Bezzles at night, though there were wolves.

Occasionally they came to a small pool with some thin bushes growing round it. On these bushes might be a blackberry or two, and this is what the Prince lived on; the horse, when it was one, tore up the scrubby grass. Once they came to a hut, and the Prince knocked on the door, but no one would let him in. Several times they passed caves with the black wolves in them who prowled round them in the dark. The wolves snarled, but said nothing. They didn't like talking to people they might be eating later.

On the third day the Prince noticed a strange muddy-red glow on the tip of the highest peak ahead.

"What's that?" he asked the horse-lion.

"I don't know," said the horse-lion.

"At one time you seemed to know everything," remarked the Prince tartly.

"At one time I did, but we're all entitled to forget, I suppose. Besides," it added, not unkindly, "I only seemed to know everything because you knew nothing at all."

As they got nearer, the glow became brighter. At night it was like an orange star at the bottom edge of the sky. By the time they reached the mountain where it seemed to be, and stared up it, the glow was very fierce, and strange hot smells blew down to them on the wind, along with a lot of cinders.

On the sixth day they came to a steep rocky path, and began to climb it. Twilight fell, and the Prince grew uneasy.

"I think we're climbing directly towards that red glow, and we should turn back, or go sideways or something. Listen!" he added.

A dull thudding, like blows, sounded from above, and echoed away among the peaks.

"I think it's a volcano," cried the Prince, "and it's about to erupt."

"Volcanoes," said the horse-lion, "don't sing."

And the Prince realised that a loud thunderous voice had started up overhead, in time to the blows.

"Toil! Toil!
Furnace boil!
Shape and hammer,
Hew and hoil!"

"He hasn't got much of a voice," said the Prince, who was feeling angry because he didn't want to go anywhere near the singer and he was already hurrying up the rock terraces towards him. "And what does 'hoil' mean?"

"It means he's a blacksmith—a hoiler, it's called up here. So it must be Vultikan."

"Who's Vultikan?"

"I don't know. I just thought it must be."

The singing had meanwhile got louder and louder, and, rounding a spur of rock, they came suddenly out on to a plateau. All around it lay massive furnace pits, ablaze with orange and scarlet flame, and pouring out purple smoke. In the middle stood a colossal anvil, and, hammering on it with a colossal hammer, was a gigantic figure. It wore a black tunic, leaving bare its muscle-packed arms, and ragged red hair flapped down its back.

"Ho!!" it howled, and the Prince dived behind the rocks, but it was only another part of the song.

"—hoil and hew,
And hammer and shape,
To forge a sword
None shall escape!"

And it brought the hammer down with a final ringing blow.

"Here you are," cried the smith, turning round and holding out a sword towards the place where the Prince was hiding. "Come on now. A sword forged by Vultikan the Smith, and you won't take it!"

The Prince, feeling silly as well as scared, got up and went between the fire pits.

"Are you sure it's for me?" he asked.

"Oh, it's for you all right," said Vultikan, who had a red beard and yellow eyes, and was just as awesome from the front as from behind.

"But how did you know I was coming this way?"

"Nice night," said Vultikan, obviously thinking this question totally stupid and best ignored.

The Prince took the sword. It had a gleaming blade and a hilt shaped like a dragon which was made of silver inlaid with gold.

"It—isn't magic, is it?" asked the Prince.

"No," said Vultikan. "It'll cut through anything, and nothing'll cut through it. Very useful you'll find it."

"When?"

"When you get down there," said Vultikan, pointing over his shoulder at the other side of the mountain.

The Prince went across the plateau and looked down. In the light of the square moon he could see sweeps of wooded country, and what looked like the thread of a river, gleaming like black glass in the distance.

"I don't expect you can wait to get down and get to grips with all those monsters, and all that bad magic," said Vultikan, throwing some metal pieces into the nearest furnace.

"Is that what's down there, then?" asked the Prince. "Because if it is, I'm going the other way."

Vultikan clearly thought this was a great joke. He roared with laughter.

"Sit down," he invited. "I've not finished your armour yet."

"I don't want any armour. I'm not going to *need* any armour. I'm going to find a nice quiet spot, and—"

The Prince was interrupted by a furious scream from across the fires. He would have recognised it anywhere as the scream of Ysome the Saffron. And sure enough, there she stood, quivering with fury in the firelight. There was a lot of dirt on her face, and all the pearls had fallen out of her hair, and her dress had been badly torn as she scrambled up the mountains. And she was quite alone.

"Were you following me all the time?" asked the Prince curiously. "I didn't even see you."

Ysome took no notice.

"Vultikan the Hoiler," cried she, pointing at him, "I am Ysome the Saffron, Lady of the Castle of Bone, and I have work for you."

"You'll have to wait your turn," said Vultikan, stirring the metal in the furnace.

"I am Ysome the Saffron, and I *command*—" Ysome broke off, seeing Vultikan didn't care. She rubbed her hands over her face, straightened her hair, and came daintily over to the Prince.

"Sir Prince, I appeal to you! We have been enemies in the past, but can I believe you ignoble enough not to aid a lady in distress?"

"You can believe it," said the Prince. "I suppose you've come to get that Dragon mended. Well, you'll have to wait until my armour's done," he finished smugly.

Ysome began to cry. She sobbed that all her Skolks had deserted her, she had no home, and no one to love her or take care of her. The Prince started to feel uncomfortable. But just as he was getting ready to ask Vultikan to see to the Dragon first, the hoiler broke into song once again and drowned Ysome's crying. Ysome stopped crying and went up to Vultikan and yelled at him, and nobody could hear what she yelled over the noise. Eventually she went and sat on the other side of the plateau with her face turned away, scowling.

The Prince fell asleep, leaning against the horse-lion. When he woke up Ysome was on his side of the plateau again, and there were three or four wolves sitting opposite her. They had told Vultikan they'd come about a fitting for iron claws, but they were gazing at the Prince hungrily.

The reason the Prince had woken was because Vultikan had stopped singing and hammering.

"Here's the armour then," he said. And there it was.

It lay in a heap before the Prince, and it was white and gold, and on top was a golden helm.

"I saw myself in this in the cup at the Castle of Bone," said the Prince. "If I put it on, I'll end up at the head of an army going to fight something."

"That's right," said Vultikan.

"Well, then, I won't put it on. That's that."

"Doesn't he know," said Vultikan, addressing the horse-lion, "who he is?"

"No," said the horse-lion.

"He's only pretending he doesn't, so he can trick people," said Ysome.

"I'd better tell him then," said Vultikan, taking no notice of Ysome as usual.

The Prince felt anxious and rather sick. He had a feeling he didn't want to find out.

"You," said Vultikan, "are the Looked-for Deliverer."

"What?" asked the Prince. It sounded like the name of a town, or a very old book nobody ever bothered to read.

"It means," said the horse-lion, "that you're going to help everyone, and that they're expecting you."

"But—but what am I supposed to deliver everybody from?"

Vultikan folded his great arms and glared down at the Prince.

"Nulgrave," he said.

The effect was amazing. The wolves uttered yelps of fear and ran off among the rocks, Ysome clapped her hands to her ears and began to scream again, and even the fires cowered down in their pits. The Prince felt very worried, and he couldn't help remembering the black coiling *thing* . . . .

"But I don't even understand what it is."

"You'll find out," said Vultikan. "And now, take your armour and go on your way."

The Prince, however, sat on in bewilderment.

"Now," he heard Vultikan say, "about your Dragon. Where is it?"

Ysome stopped screaming.

"In the Waste."

"Well you can't expect me to mend it if you haven't brought it with you."

"But it's huge," Ysome cried. "I thought you'd come and fetch it."

"Well I won't."

Vultikan looked around, saw that the wolves were gone, and, without a second glance at Ysome, he blew out each of the fire pits in turn with a colossal breath. Then, shouldering his tools, he strode off down the mountain. His gigantic strides had soon taken him out of sight, and well out of range of Ysome's curses.

"I suppose we'd better stay here the night," said the Prince, wishing Vultikan hadn't blown out all the fires, and that Ysome would go away, and that there weren't so many wolves about–even though he couldn't see any, he could hear them howling to each other in the distance.

He looked at the horse-lion and it already appeared to be asleep. The Prince couldn't help feeling that if the horse felt that it was safe to go to sleep, it must be, so he lay down next to it and did the same.

6

The Honnerdrin

In the morning the sky was green, and Ysome was gone.

"I think," said the horse-lion, "I heard her screaming in the night. I suppose she was being carried off."

The Prince felt quite pleased until he recalled the wolves. He didn't like to think of people being eaten, even Ysome.

"It wasn't wolves, was it?" he asked.

"I don't think so," said the horse-lion. "She didn't scream hard enough for wolves."

"Perhaps it was someone she knew," said the Prince, telling himself she was probably screaming 'Hello!' at them. After all he had enough to worry him without worrying about her as well.

They had breakfast off some squashed berries they had saved from yesterday, and, carrying Vultikan's armour between them, set off down the other side of the mountain, towards the woods.

It was a steep and dangerous mountain, but after a time they found a winding track which curled all the way down to the valley below.

The doughnut sun was high in the sky when they reached the mountain's foot. Before them lay a slope of parched grass, which gradually tumbled off into pale brown, silent oak woods and shadows.

"I don't like the look of those woods," said the Prince. Something about them made him want to shiver and, although none of the trees were dead, they didn't look as though they were alive either.

"This is where you put on your armour," said the horse-lion, becoming a horse.

"It'll be too hot to wear," said the Prince, for it felt very hot in the valley, and close, as if just before a storm.

But the horse went forward and cropped a little of the dried grass and there was a rattling noise, and suddenly all the bits of armour flew up at the Prince and clasped themselves on to him. The breast-plate clattered on to his chest, and the greaves crashed on to his legs, and the gauntlets whizzed over his hands, the sword sheathed itself with an angry rasping noise, and the helm came down on his head with a thud that almost knocked him unconscious. The Prince was terrified. It felt like suddenly being done up in a tin can.

"What? What? Help! Why did it—!" he cried, staggering after the horse.

"That's better," said the horse. "Now get up on my back."

"I can't. I'm too heavy."

"Try," said the horse.

The Prince put one foot in the stirrup, and tried. He found he wasn't too heavy. The horse began trotting towards the woods.

"I don't think—" said the Prince, but it was too late. The dark shadow of the wood fell over him, and shut out the sun.

It was hot, but shivery hot, as if the wood were feverish. The trees all looked the same as each other, with their smooth, acorn-coloured trunks. There was no sound at all, except for the hoofbeats of the horse, and the dull rustling of countless withered yellow flags of leaves. No birds sang.

"Why aren't there any birds singing?" asked the Prince in a nervous whisper.

"There aren't any birds," said the horse.

"Well, what is there then? It feels as if there's someone about."

And it did.

"Honnerdrin, probably," said the horse.

"Wh-what are h-honner—what you said?"

"Tree people."

"Are they—friendly?"

"No," said the horse.

"Couldn't we," said the Prince, "go some other way to get to the place we're going to–wherever it is?"

Just then the visor of the Prince's golden helmet came down over his face with a bang. The Prince panicked and shouted, until he realised he could still see out of the eye-holes in it. What he saw was that he and the horse had emerged into a clearing. At the far end stood a tall pavilion of scarlet velvet with some frightful-looking monsters embroidered on it in black. Next to the pavilion a gold bell hung from a solitary tree.

"I bet that bell says, 'I'm here, sound this and I'll come out and kill you', or something," said the Prince irritably. "Well, I'm not going to be caught a second time."

But he was, though in a most unexpected way. A thin brown hand came sneaking around the trunk of the tree, snatched the bell-rope and tugged it. The bell clanged noisily.

"Did you *see* that?" gasped the Prince. "That's not fair—" but there was no time for more.

Out of the pavilion came striding a terrifying figure in coal-black armour, scarlet plumes, and wielding an enormous axe.

"Who dares challenge me, the Champion of the Wood?" it roared. "Dismount and fight!"

"I didn't challenge you— It was—" began the Prince.

The figure roared at the horse. The horse reared. The Prince fell off.

The Prince picked himself up. He was certain the horse hadn't needed to rear at all; it couldn't have been that scared.

"Look," said the Prince reasonably, "I really didn't touch that bell. This hand came out of nowhere—" he broke off to avoid a ferocious axe blow.

The Prince drew the sword Vultikan had given him.

"Well, he said it would cut through anything," said the Prince doubtfully, and aimed. Both he and the Champion were very surprised as the sword sheared off the axe-head. Of the two, however, the Prince went on being surprised the longer, which allowed the Champion to hit him rather hard with the haft, and then jump on him as he fell over. The Champion's armour was very heavy and the Prince could hardly breathe, let alone move, but he cut about weakly with the sword, and presently the Champion said quite pleasantly, "I say, you can leave off now. You've wounded me badly and I surrender, only I can't get off you because of my armour."

The Prince wriggled and struggled and finally crawled out from under the Champion, and rolled him over on his back. The Champion pushed up his visor with one feeble hand, and smiled at the Prince in a 'don't worry about me, only a scratch, I'll be all right in a minute' kind of way.

"You needn't think I'm sorry for you," said the Prince angrily, "you started it."

"I didn't realise who you were," said the Champion.

"Who am I?" yelled the Prince, in a mixture of hope and foreboding.

"The Looked-for Deliverer, Slayer of the Dragon of Brass, Bearer of the Sword of Vultikan."

"Oh," said the Prince. He wiped his sword on the grass, and began to feel rather concerned after all.

"Do you want a doctor?" he enquired after a moment, and then wondered where on earth he would find one if the Champion said he did.

"No, no. I heal up very quickly–it's a spell my sister put on me when I decided I wanted to be a Champion and fight people. She likes magic and that kind of thing. Just give me a second, and I'll be as fit as a fiddle. Oh dear," he added apprehensively.

The Prince couldn't believe his eyes. Out of the trees came a violin, hopping along, coughing and sneezing and moaning that it felt sick. It crossed the clearing, and vanished among the trees on the other side.

"You have to be careful around here," said the Champion in a low voice, "not to say things like fit as a—well, like what I just said. They always try to show you up."

"Who do?"

"The Honnerdrin. They can take any shape they want, you see, and they listen to everything. When I decided to be a Champion, I thought this wood looked ideal, but if I'd known *they* were about, wild horses wouldn't have dragged me here— Oh!" he cried in despair.

Six neighing black stallions burst into the clearing, picked up the Champion, dragged him round his pavilion twice, dumped him back at the Prince's feet with a crash, and made off among the oaks.

"You see how it is," groaned the Champion.

The Prince helped him up and into the pavilion. The Champion sat on a scarlet chair and took off his helm. He had rather a nice, kind sort of face and black hair.

"If it's as bad as it seems to be here," said the Prince, "why don't you go somewhere else? And what do you want to fight people for, anyway?"

"Well, you have to choose very early on," said the Champion sadly, "and I thought it was a good idea then. But really, you know, I'd rather talk to people than fight them. They won't talk *after* a fight–they get huffy, or else they run away."

"Why don't you stop being a Champion?"

The Champion brightened.

"Do you know, I'd never thought of that? Why not, indeed? I won't be a Champion another minute."

All his armour immediately fell off on to the ground. Under it was a scarlet tunic with golden beetles embroidered on it.

The Prince looked at the tunic and said, "You didn't tell me your name, by the way."

"Oh, didn't I? It's Gemant the Red."

"Your sister," said the Prince, "is she, by any chance, *Gemael* the Red, the Lady of the Waste? She whirls about a lot."

"That's it. Have you met her, then?"

"Several times," said the Prince.

"Yes. Nice girl," said Gemant. "Of course, I haven't seen her for ages, with her living in the Waste and me here in the woods, and all those mountains in between. She doesn't like whirling across mountains. How is she?"

"She seemed all right when I saw her last."

There was a clang from the bell outside. Gemant jumped to his feet in horror.

"There's a challenge, and I'm not a Champion any more! What shall I do?"

The Prince looked round the entrance flap and saw a Knight in purple armour in the clearing. He was riding what looked as if it might have started out to be a horse and then had changed its mind. It was bright mauve in colour with frightening yellow eyes, which it rolled around, and awful pointed teeth, which it snarled. Instead of a mane and tail, a hard spiky crest stood up on its head, and hard spiky things rattled behind it. Draped across it, in front of the Knight, was the form of a fair-haired maiden, presumably in a maidenly swoon.

"Are you the Champion of the Wood? If you are, come out and fight," cried the Knight in a menacing voice, having caught sight of the tip of the Prince's nose.

"Er, no," said the Prince, making the best of things, "I'm afraid he's not here at the moment–gone to visit a sick aunt."

"When will he be back? I'll fight him then."

"Let me see," said the Prince. "I should try again in five days' time. He's bound to be here by then."

The Knight gave a sound that might have been a growl of thanks, or a growl of anger, or simply just a growl. He wheeled the horse-thing, and they galloped off, sparks flying up all around them.

"You should be able to get away in five days," said the Prince to Gemant.

The horse put its head into the pavilion.

"Did you happen to notice," it asked, "that it was Ysome the Saffron he had in front of him?"

"Look," said the Prince, "really, I shouldn't bother if I were you. She's an enchantress–a bad one. She had me hunted all through the Castle of Bone–it's her Dragon of

Brass I had to fight! *And* she was your sister's sworn enemy, Gemael told me so—"

"No, no," said Gemant firmly (he already had his armour on again and was running about packing things into a bundle), "I can't refuse to aid a lady in distress. I just couldn't face myself."

A Honnerdrin promptly walked into the pavilion, looking exactly like Gemant the Red, went up to him, stared him in the face, and walked out again. Gemant was too busy to notice.

"I'll have to get a horse somewhere," he worried, "and a sword now my axe has gone."

"You can have my sword," said the Prince. "*I'm* not going after her. You didn't *see* that purple knight."

"No, I couldn't take your sword. If Vultikan the Hoiler made it for you, I wouldn't be able to use it. Now, let me see, Gemael told me a spell for getting a horse . . ."

He wandered outside and began to say odd-sounding things with no result.

The Prince sat down and ate some fruit that was on the table in a golden bowl. But he had a feeling he was being watched, even though he couldn't see anyone, which must have been Honnerdrin.

After a time he got rather angry, and had an angry idea. He was tired of things happening to him, and he never seeming to make a decision of his own. So he got up, went out, looked at the oak trees, and said in a loud voice, "I know you're there, you Honnerdrin, and I suppose you know who I am–the Looked-for Deliverer, Slayer of the Dragon of Brass, Bearer of the Sword of Vultikan. Everyone else seems to think that's important, so I don't see why you shouldn't as well." The trees rustled noisily. "As you can change into any shape at all, I suggest," the Prince went on, "that one of you change into a horse and another of you into a sword so Gemant can rescue Ysome. You can't mind that. She's just as much a troublemaker as you all are."

There was a long silence. The Prince noticed the horse staring at him in surprise, while Gemant looked positively terrified. The Prince had begun to wonder if he had done the right thing, when out of the trees came a black charger with red trappings, and a bright sword hopping along behind it.

"It, er, may be a trick," Gemant whispered to the Prince.

"No," said the Prince, feeling sure of himself all at once. "My name seems to be a powerful one, for some reason. perhaps because of this Nulgrave thing they think I'm going to deliver them from."

"Ssh!" hissed Gemant, paling. All the trees seemed to shudder.

The Prince felt rather pale, too, suddenly.

"If you're all so scared of it, what is it?" he asked.

"No one knows," said Gemant, "but it's absolutely *awful*."

7

The Oak Wood

Gemant the Red and the Prince rode through the shadowy oak wood until it grew dark with evening.

"Are you sure we're going the right way?" asked the Prince, who wasn't sure of anything himself, especially as to why he had gone to look for Ysome after all.

"Oh, yes. You can see the hoof pocks and the scorch marks the Drumbil made quite clearly."

The Drumbil was, apparently, the awful mauve horse-thing the Knight had been riding.

The Prince wanted to stop and rest for the night, but Gemant said they ought to press on a bit farther, so they did. Blue starlight trickled down the trunks of the trees, and later the three moons appeared, one by one, and hung like peculiar white lanterns in the upper branches.

Soon after this, or so it seemed, the Prince woke up with a start, and realised he had fallen asleep on the back of the horse, and that it was now dawn. He looked round at Gemant, but *he* was very wide awake, and was urging the Honnerdrin horse to gallop, which it wouldn't.

"Look ahead!" he cried excitedly.

The Prince rubbed his eyes and did so. The oak trees came to an abrupt end at the edge of a broad river. On the far bank, a hilly heath toiled in grey-green folds towards the distant sunrise, and on the horizon stood up a curious, crooked black shape. The Prince realised several things at once. First, that Gemant seemed to think the shape was where the purple knight was; secondly, that Gemant was trying to ride straight into the river, which looked dark and dangerous; and thirdly, that the sun seemed as if it might be rising on the wrong side of the sky.

He grabbed Gemant's bridle, seeing this as the most important thing at the moment, and said, "You can't, it's too wide to jump. You'll be drowned."

Gemant stopped bouncing about, and looked crestfallen. "However shall we cross?" he asked.

"Easy," said the Prince. To the wood he called out, "Remember me? One large boat, please, and an oar."

After a moment a boat appeared, and flopped into the water with a splash that wetted the Prince and Gemant from head to foot. The oar was next and managed to fall on the Prince's toe as he was dismounting.

"They don't like obeying anyone," said Gemant anxiously.

But he and the horses got into the boat, and the Prince rowed them all across, which took a long time. When they had struggled out of the water-reeds on the other side, and climbed a little rise up on to the heath, the Prince suggested they have breakfast. Gemant was unwilling to waste time, but the Prince insisted.

When they had finished, it was quite warm and sunny. Gemant lay down, and said, "Just rest for a moment," and fell asleep.

The Prince, delighted at any delay, followed his example. The Prince had been dreaming about splashes and thuds, and it was a particularly loud thud that woke him. He sat up with a start, but everything was silent and very dark. It seemed odd, because he had been sure it was quite light when he fell asleep, but then it was probably only the wood, shutting out the sunlight.

Then he remembered that they had left the wood at the river bank.

"Gemant!" cried the Prince, in a loud, trying-to-be-quiet voice. Gemant took no notice. The Prince unkindly shook him, and Gemant woke up with a yell.

"Ssh!" warned the Prince. "Look!"

Gemant stared around them, and saw that they were surrounded by trees again, and by hot, shivery shadows.

"Well, there's the river behind us," he said, "and this is the heath. And you can just make out the knight's hold, still."

"I am holding still," grumbled the Prince.

Gemant looked confused, and decided to pretend the Prince hadn't said anything.

"The wood doesn't stretch very far up the heath, you see," he explained. "The trees end just in front of the next rise."

There was a colossal splash behind them. They both turned back and gawped at the river. Two or three oak trees seemed to be growing in it that hadn't been there before. Gemant and the Prince shrugged.

The Prince found his horse, but the Honnerdrin horse had vanished. So had the Honnerdrin sword. The Prince didn't ask for replacements.

As they were walking over the heath towards full daylight, several thuds happened behind them. Whenever they looked round, everything was still. After a time they stopped looking round.

"Do you know any songs?" the Prince asked Gemant very cheerfully.

"Oh, lots," said Gemant, very cheerfully.

There was a silence and three or four thuds.

"Sing something," said the Prince, very cheerfully.

Very cheerfully, Gemant began to sing.

> "I met a maiden, fair and good,
> With long yellow hair, in the acorn wood,
> But when I asked with her to walk
> She changed me into an apple stalk."

"That isn't the sort of song I meant," said the Prince.

There was another thud.

"Anyway," said the Prince loudly, "she couldn't have been fair and good if she turned him into an apple stalk."

"Perhaps she thought he might enjoy it," said Gemant lamely.

"You know," said the Prince, "I think it would be fun to have a race–to the end of the wood. Ready, steady, go!"

He and Gemant broke into a lurching run in their armour, and the horse shot ahead. It wasn't far, and soon everyone was out of the tree shadow into the noon sunlight.

"I won," said the horse.

"It doesn't matter who won," said the Prince, "we got out of that wood. Do trees always hop about like that?"

"Honnerdrin trees do," said the horse.

"Well, we're safe now," said the Prince, turning his back on the last tree.

They strode over the rise, and down the other side.

There were three loud thuds, one after the other.

"What?" said the Prince.

He and Gemant hurried on after the horse.

Thud! Thud! Thud! Thud!

"Don't look back, you'll only encourage them!" said the Prince. But Gemant did look back, and there were now five large oaks standing at the top of the rise, which had previously been treeless.

"It's no use, Horse," said the Prince. He scrambled into the saddle and helped Gemant scramble up behind him. "I know we're heavy, but do your best."

The horse broke into a slow walk.

"Faster! Faster!"

The horse trotted, sighed, and began to gallop.

Thud! Thud-thud! came behind them.

Gemant looked back and howled. The wood was no longer pretending not to move, for it too had burst into a gallop, and with its trees bounding over the ground in huge hops and leaps, leaves flying in the wind, branches snapping furiously, it was in close pursuit.

"What are we going to do?" despaired the Prince.

"When we get over the next rise," said the horse, "there'll be a ditch. Roll off into it and hide."

"How do you know there'll be a ditch?"

"How do you know there won't be?" asked the horse. "I shall ride on, and the wood will chase me, not having noticed the two of you are gone."

"Of course it'll notice. And besides, I need your help, and you may not come back."

Just then they rattled over the rise, the horse gave a peculiar wriggling rear, and Gemant and the Prince fell off into a ditch. As they lay there among the dead leaves and the mud, the oak wood went thundering by, each tree jumping over the ditch without pause. It was quite terrifying, however. Any minute it seemed one might misjudge the distance and land on top of them in the ditch instead. Finally it was over, and the cracking and thudding died away. They looked over the edge of the ditch, and saw the last trees thumping across the heath away to the right, which still left them a clear road to the hold of the Purple Knight (unfortunately, thought the Prince).

They crawled out and pulled the leaves from their hair. While they were doing this, the Prince suddenly noticed one solitary sapling standing quite still, behind them, on the other side of the ditch. He drew his sword.

"Stay where you are!" he yelled.

The sapling obeyed. But someone didn't. Around the side of the sapling, seeming to appear out of its trunk, came a thin, brown child with long, acorn-coloured hair and greenish-yellow eyes. It regarded the Prince with an amused sneer.

"This is my tree," it said, "and it didn't follow you. It's always been here by the ditch."

"Oh," said the Prince.

"B–be careful," whispered Gemant nervously. "It's a Honnerdrin child. They never appear in their true form unless they mean really bad mischief."

The Honnerdrin child looked at Gemant thoughtfully, and Gemant paled. Then it looked at the Prince and said, "Nulgrave is coming. You'd better be quick and stop it."

"What do you know about Nulgrave?"

But the child had disappeared, and there was only the oak sapling standing by the ditch.

8

The Tower of the Purple Knight

The Prince hadn't at any time liked the look of the Knight's hold, and now that he was close enough to see it properly, he still didn't like the look of it.

It was a tall tower made of some black metallic stuff, and out of its sides grew lots of other small towers, all craning and leaning and twisting in every direction. At the back of it the heath fell down into a dismal-looking chalk quarry. Round the foot of the tower was a circular black moat, and on the near side of this was a black stone with a black bell hanging from it.

"I suppose you have to sound that when you want to be let in," said Gemant.

"Well, I don't trust bells," said the Prince.

They stood about by the bell for ten minutes or so, and then Gemant said, "I say, I really think we ought to try. I mean we are supposed to be rescuing Ysome."

"Go ahead," said the Prince, edging back several places.

Gemant strode up to the bell and struck it. There was no sound at all, but an opening appeared suddenly in the tower, and out slid a drawbridge over the moat. Gemant marched straight on to it.

"Come back, you idiot!" yelled the Prince. But Gemant didn't, and so the Prince reluctantly followed him. They walked off the drawbridge into a totally black space, and in another second the drawbridge was drawn up behind them, and there was no light at all.

"Where are we?" cried Gemant, and his voice echoed back nastily four or five times.

"Where are *you*?" cried the Prince.

Next minute they collided with an armoury clatter, and nearly went deaf from armoury clattery echoes.

"I knew this was a mistake," muttered the Prince.

Just then an awful booming voice called out, "Who dares the hold of the Purple Knight?"

"If we keep quiet," whispered the Prince, "they might think there's no one here after all."

But Gemant wouldn't.

"I am the Champion of the Wood!" cried he, "and I have come to rescue the Lady Ysome."

The voice laughed horribly, and this time an opening appeared in one part of the darkness, filled with a bright purple glare.

"Enter, fool!" invited the voice.

"I wouldn't," said the Prince, "really–especially when he's being so rude."

But Gemant charged forward. The Prince ran after him, trying to pull him back, and the next minute they were through into a huge purple hall full of purple pillars, and purple light and purpleness.

The opening shut behind them with a bang.

"Trapped," remarked the Prince, without surprise. He sat down on a purple chair, feeling on the whole too fed up to be frightened. "I don't see why you had to rush in here, Gemant."

Gemant looked worried.

"I couldn't seem to help it," he said. "I didn't want to. And I didn't want to call out who I was either."

The Prince remembered how he had pulled the Brass Dragon bell in the Castle of Bone, and felt more sympathetic.

Just then two purple doors rolled open at the far end of the hall. Gemant and the Prince clutched each other, waiting for Something–probably a monster–to come slithering or crashing or leaping through, slavering at the jaws and with its blazing eyes glazed with hatred and blood-lust. It didn't. Nothing came through, in fact, except a stream of normal-looking light.

"Now don't—" began the Prince–but it was already too late.

And, as he ran after Gemant, it occurred to him that he didn't seem to have any choice either.

Beyond the door was—

"Aaaah!!!" cried the Prince.

"Whaaah!!!!!" cried Gemant.

A great white wind rushed up from their feet, their hair blew up from their heads, and the walls raced past at a terrific rate. They would have liked to say to each other, "Help! What is it? Help!" but the speed made them speechless. And then suddenly it was very dark, there was an awful splash and a lot of water in their eyes and ears, followed by a nasty, wet, dripping silence.

"What happened?" the Prince asked the darkness eventually.

"I think we fell down something," said Gemant. "Into something."

"Water. Only I can't understand why we're floating on top of it and not sinking because of our armour. And it's as black as when we first got into the tower."

"Not quite," said Gemant.

And after a time the Prince found he could just make out a dark rippling pool in which they were, with dim walls all round, and a very big circular black hole about five yards away.

"I wonder if that's a way out," said Gemant.

"Or a way in," said the Prince, and wished he hadn't.

"A way in–for what?"

And they both thought about the slavering monster with blood-lust glazed eyes they had been expecting upstairs, and wondered if it would come through the hole instead.

"You know," said the Prince, "I'm sure there's some way we could get out of this if we really thought about it." He was trying to ignore the fact that a faint light seemed to be coming out of the hole which hadn't been coming out of it a moment ago. "If only I could reach that brickwork higher up–it looks as if it might give a handhold. I wonder what would happen if I crawled up on top of you–?"

"I'd be pushed underwater and drown," said Gemant sadly.

The light was quite unmistakable now. It poured out from the hole and made silvery lacework on the water.

The Prince splashed hurriedly over to the far side of the pool.

"Look out!" he warned.

The next second something came out of the hole.

The Prince tried to get up the wall and failed. After a while he stopped trying and began to wonder why he hadn't been eaten. This was when he saw *what* had come out of the hole. It was three beautiful girls covered entirely, except for their faces, by long lustrous dark fur. Out of the fur at their temples grew two fine curling horns which reminded the Prince of someone or other, but in addition there were delicate gills fluttering just under their chins, and they seemed to have furry fish tails below the water. The silvery light came from a small globe the nearest one had on a thin chain around her neck.

"Who are you?" asked the Prince.

"We're a monster," said this girl, and they all tittered.

"Are you?" asked the Prince doubtfully, prepared by now for almost anything.

"Well, *he* thinks we are," said the girl scornfully.

"Do you mean the Purple Knight?"

"Yes. When we saw something moving about in the pool he thought it must be a monster, and so he built this tower all around the water, and he lures people, and has them thrown in here all the time. They don't drown because we put a magic on the water to keep them up, and then we come and show them out the back way. But *he* thinks the monster's eaten them." And they all giggled again. "Actually," added the girl, "we're Water Theels."

The Prince then remembered the white-haired Theel in the Castle of Bone, who had also been kind, if a little odd, and he wondered why such nice creatures always seemed to live in bad places with wicked things going on all around them.

"That's easy," said the girl, seeming to read his thoughts as the other Theel had done. "The bad places are where we can do the most good. Now come with us, in case *he* turns up to see if there are any bones floating about or anything. You'll have to hold your breath for the first part because that's under water, but it isn't very far."

It was rather farther than the Water Theels thought, being used to underwater, and it was very cold. But eventually the Prince and Gemant arrived in a dry warm cave, hung with pretty water-weed curtains, and with flowers growing out between the stones. A few globes like the one the girl carried, only larger, floated about in the roof, giving a soft clear light. The Water Theels sat with their furry fish tails still in the pool, and said a spell all together to make the Prince and Gemant dry again.

"All you have to do now is go through that opening there and down the passage, and you'll come out to the quarry behind the tower. There's a magic over the door so you won't be able to see the entrance once you're outside."

"This is very kind of you," said Gemant. "But can you tell us if a maiden was thrown into the pool yesterday or today–we came to rescue her, you see."

The Water Theels looked at each other.

"Do you mean a girl with fair hair and a yellow dress?"

"*That's* her," said the Prince with distaste.

"We don't really think she needs rescuing," said the Water Theels, "she seems to be enjoying herself here."

"In that case," said the Prince, "I feel like rescuing her just to annoy her." He explained about the Castle of Bone.

"We can show you a way into the Knight's tower he doesn't know about," said the first Theel, "if that would help."

The Prince didn't really know why he wanted to get mixed up in more trouble, he thought he'd had enough, but suddenly he realised he had to go back into the tower. 'It's all this Looked-for Deliverer business again I suppose,' he thought mournfully, as the Water Theels said a spell at the wall and showed him a flight of stairs once the stone had disappeared.

As they climbed the stairway the cave wall appeared again behind them so they could no longer see the Theels. They climbed and climbed and grew very tired.

"I wish that horse hadn't run off," said the Prince, "it nearly always seemed to know what to do."

Finally they came to a blank wall.

"Now what?"

"Look," said Gemant, and the Prince saw that there were several small round holes cut in the wall. Peering through one he found he was staring down at the purple hall he and Gemant had seen earlier, although now they seemed to be very high up near the ceiling. The hall was rather different too, because it was lit by hundreds of gold and rose-coloured lamps which made the purpleness rather attractive, and there was a huge table draped with cloth-of-gold and laid with gold dishes and whole-amethyst cups. Just then a fanfare sounded, and the awful booming voice they had been terrified by before called out rather soppily, "Honour and joy to His Glorious Worship the Purple Knight!"

Through some doors–not the ones through which Gemant and the Prince had fallen into the monster pool– came pipers blowing pipes, drummers beating drums, girls strewing ribbons, and, last of all ("Well, look at *that*!" cried Gemant) the Purple Knight, this time in purple velvet and a lot of gold embroidery, with Ysome the Saffron walking beside him, holding his arm. She had pearls and amethysts in her hair, and a new dress of primrose yellow velvet, and she was smirking.

"When I think," cried Gemant, "how much we endured to save her!" And he smote the wall a blow with his gauntleted fist. Which must, unfortunately, have set working some hidden spring, for, an instant after, he and the Prince, instead of leaning on the wall, found themselves falling from a height down into the hall, and landing with a frightful crash on the table among all the golden dishes.

Ysome and the ribbon-strewing girls screamed.

"Guard!" bawled the Purple Knight, and several large shadowy figures strode forward through the doors. "Explain yourselves," said the Purple Knight furiously.

The Prince and Gemant rolled around on the table trying to get up, and sending cups and plates spinning in all directions.

"No need for them to explain," said Ysome in a cold, spiteful voice. "Do you remember I told you, my lord, of the man who razed my castle to the ground, and then abandoned me in the Waste–homeless, and without any of my dear friends left to help me? This–is he!"

"Which one?" asked the Knight.

The Prince managed to get off the table.

"She means me. However, I only followed her to rescue her from you–I thought you abducted her."

The Knight looked uneasy.

"Well, er—" he began.

"It was a mistake," said Ysome, "and anyway he's my friend now and my protector. I'm going to teach him all my magic."

The Knight looked pleased.

"So," he remarked, "there's nothing left for you to do. Shall we throw them to the monster, my dear?"

Ysome beamed. But Gemant, skittering off the table with a clatter, cried, "That already happened to us, and there isn't a monster there at all so your evil plans aren't worth a fig!"

"Oh Gemant," groaned the Prince. Gemant was surprised.

"Did I say something wrong?"

"No monster?" croaked the Knight. He looked shattered and near to tears.

"There are worse things," Ysome hissed in his ear. "Boiling oil-baths, vats of venom, drumbil dinners . . ."

The Knight cheered up.

"Of course there are, my dove. How silly of me. Guard!"

The guards advanced into the lamplight and the Prince

saw them properly for the first time. They were seven feet tall, covered in iron armour, and under their helmets poked long-snouted faces with cold, glittering eyes, and ghastly tusks growing where their teeth ought to have been.

"Oh," whispered Gemant sickly. "*Beezles*."

The Prince desperately tried to recollect what the horse had told him about Beezles–if anything. He seemed to think they were worse than Bezzles and not so bad as Buzzles–or was it that they were better than Bezzles and *worse* than Buzzles, or was it that—? He stopped wondering as the two nearest seized him by the arms and dragged him out of the hall and up some dark stairs and finally, with a horrible gurgling growl, flung him face down on top of Gemant, and shut a metal door on them with a clang.

After a time the Prince sat up and looked around him. It was obvious Gemant and he were in some sort of dungeon. There was one small narrow window set in the wall. The Prince went over to it and looked out and saw a muddy twilight setting over the chalk quarry. Black things were flapping in circles over the quarry–they looked like Oggrings, but might only have been bats. From the distance came a faint roar of thunder.

Several wild schemes went through the Prince's mind. Could he squeeze through the window? Hardly. Could he jump the Beezles at the door? No. Did Gemant know any of Gemael's spells either for turning one small enough to squeeze out of narrow windows or big enough to burst open dungeon doors and frighten off Beezles? Gemant didn't. The Prince remembered the Egg which the Theel had given him at the Castle of Bone. He took it out and shook it and hoped it would break and his own personal secret–whatever it was–would hatch out and save him. Nothing happened to the Egg, so he put it back.

"I wish that horse was here," he said.

Footsteps sounded on the stairs. A Beezle threw open the door, and there stood the Purple Knight in full armour again.

"I have decided on your punishment," he cried.

"What's that noise?" interrupted the Prince, changing the subject. The Knight broke off and listened, and the Prince was rather surprised to note that there really was an odd noise. In fact, it sounded like the thunder he had heard before, except that it went on and on, and seemed to be getting louder and louder.

"A storm," said the Purple Knight. "Have no fear. You won't be bothered by storms much longer. I intend—" he broke off again, this time because the floor was very gently trembling. He strode to the window and looked out and gave a cry of alarm. Then, ignoring the Prince and the punishment he had in store for him, he turned and hurried out. The door was shut again.

The Prince and Gemant crowded to the window and stared down.

"Is it—?" asked the Prince.

"I think it *is*," said Gemant.

In the twilight it was hard to see for sure, but as the rumbling got nearer and nearer, they could make out what appeared to be a great dark cloud bouncing over the ground towards the tower, and at the head of the cloud, galloping very fast, mane and tail flying behind it, was a determined-looking white horse with white and gold trappings.

9

Grey Magic

"It's that horse!" yelled the Prince in panic, "and the Honnerdrin wood's still after it! Whatever has it come back here for? Haven't we got enough troubles?"

The horse was by now running round and round the tower, skirting the quarry, the wood in full chase behind. The dungeon floor shook under the Prince's feet in a most frightening way, and hundreds of cobwebs and spiders which had been up in the beams for five years or more were falling on to his head in a grey, grumbling rain.

And then, all at once, the awful thudding stopped. The oak trees seemed to be all round the tower, standing quite still, and somehow looking at a loss. The horse had disappeared.

"I expect it's changed into a lion again to fool them," said the Prince in disgusted admiration.

"Can it change at will, then?" asked Gemant with interest.

"Oh yes," and remembering an earlier conversation with the horse, the Prince added, "It said you all could here."

"*I* can't," said Gemant.

"You haven't tried," said the Prince.

"Oh, I have. Lots of times."

The Prince thought this seemed a silly sort of thing to be discussing at a moment like this. He peered through the evening darkness, trying to see a lion somewhere, but was interrupted by the door being opened once again. This time the four Beezles bowed very low and muttered, "Please—growl, follow us—growl."

Astonished, Gemant and the Prince obeyed, and were soon back in the purple hall. The instant they arrived they were greeted by an incredible din, which turned out to be the Purple Knight and Ysome the Saffron shouting furiously at each other.

"Why didn't you tell me he was a powerful magician!" the Knight was bawling.

"He's not and I did!" Ysome shrieked. "And you said you could fight anyone!"

Then they saw the Prince. The Knight promptly threw himself on his knees.

"Mercy, Invincible Sir!" he cried.

Ysome ran straight up to the Prince, clasped and kissed his hand, and, staring into his eyes, squeaked, "My deliverer!"

"Well really," said Gemant. "If anyone's that, it's me.

"Be quiet!" snapped Ysome, giving him a poisonous glare. Then, sweetly to the Prince, "He made me pretend I was on his side–but I knew you'd rescue me. Oh, do you think I could ever really have *meant* those dreadful things I said?" She uttered a tinkling laugh at the very idea.

There came a terrifying thudding from outside, louder than ever. The floor trembled, and gold plates the Prince and Gemant hadn't knocked off the table before now jumped off by themselves. The Knight fell on his face. Ysome paled, but grabbed the Prince all the harder.

"S–so clever of you," she gasped, "to make the Honnerdrin help you."

Then, of course, the Prince understood. The Purple Knight and Ysome didn't realise the oak trees were just as intent on having his blood as they were; they thought he'd brought them here on purpose to attack the tower.

"But they don't—" began Gemant, bewildered. Quickly the Prince kicked him. Gemant yelled, but luckily stopped telling the truth, though his eyes were full of reproach.

"I'm the Looked-for Deliverer, remember," said the Prince loftily to Ysome. "Naturally the Honnerdrin do whatever I desire. Now Gemant and I must go out and speak to them–persuade them not to get too violent. You'd better stay here with the knight–and don't look out of any windows or they might fly at you.

"We won't," promised the Knight.

"We'll go the quickest way," added the Prince. He hurried Gemant across the hall, through the doors–and in another moment they were falling once more into the 'monster' pool.

The two Water Theels who appeared this time didn't seem at all surprised to see them. They seemed to understand the Prince's idea perfectly, though he had to explain to Gemant.

"If we go out this way we can hide until the wood goes away–if we'd gone through the door the trees would have jumped on us in a moment."

In the Theel-cave they found the third Water Theel. She was hanging her fifth garland of flowers round the neck of a big lion.

"It's the horse!" cried the Prince. "How did you get in?"

"Through the cave entrance," said the horse-lion.

"But there's magic on the entrance so it can't be seen from the outside."

"That's right," said the horse-lion.

The Prince decided not to pursue this line of questioning.

"When will the wood go away?" he asked instead. He could still hear the thudding as all the trees angrily stamped on the spot, though it sounded much fainter here, and the floor didn't shake.

"Once the tower falls, probably," said the horse-lion. "They think it's ours, and we're all inside it."

"But how—" began the Prince.

A rattle of metal pieces falling off the sides of the tower and into the quarry interrupted them.

"You mean," said the Prince, "they'll shake the tower to pieces by thudding?"

"Yes. It's vibration."

"Who?"

"What about these ladies?" asked Gemant anxiously.

"Oh, we'll be quite all right," said the Water Theels. "The walls of our cave are very strong and we can soon clear our pool with magic."

From outside there came a tumbling crash, and a splash as something fell into the moat.

"There goes one of the towers," said Gemant with conviction. "Or perhaps it was part of the roof."

Things fell thick and fast after that and it became quite frightening–at any rate, the Prince thought so. He was sure that at any moment the cave would collapse all round them, but it stood firm. There were tremendous bangs and groans and concussions overhead, however, and eventually one really terrible explosive thud followed by clattering and rolling sounds, screams, yells, and, finally, total silence.

"Isn't it quiet?" whispered the Prince nervously.

He realised then that the oak wood had stopped stamping.

They went to the cave entrance and looked up at the top of the quarry, and the wood had gone away.

"Once the tower fell, they felt they'd done enough," said the horse-lion.

"I should think so," said the Prince. He went out into the moonlit quarry–now full of broken towers, metal plates, window frames and an armchair–and stared up at the heap of black rubble above. "You know, this reminds me of the Castle of Bone . . ."

It then reminded him even more, for out of the heap came crawling the Purple Knight in badly dented armour, and Ysome, her dress in rags and the remains of an ancient crow's nest caught up in her hair. She saw the Prince at once, and pointed her finger down at him.

"You!" she screamed. "Again you destroy my home! I will be revenged–I swear it–by–by–by Nulgrave I swear it!" Having sworn, she looked rather scared, but she only had to glare at the Prince to become angry again. "By the four elements–Earth, Air, Fire, Water–I will work Grey Magic against you because of this."

The Purple Knight seized her arm.

"No, no–too dangerous—"

But she shook him off.

"Boiling-oil, vats of venom–you'll be pleased to be put into them by the time I've finished with you, sir Prince!"

The Prince, who was quite worried by now, tried to get back into the Theel-cave and, sure enough, couldn't find it because of the magic on the entrance. Suddenly a lion's paw appeared out of nowhere, hooked its claws into his arm, and hauled him through a blank wall which turned out to be the cave opening.

"Ow!" cried the Prince ungratefully. "Now look what you've done! She's going to put some awful curse on me, and she's going to work *Grey Magic*– whatever that is."

A silence fell in the cave, a silence both deep and full of mysterious meaning. Feeling left out, the Prince demanded, "What is it?"

The horse-lion said, "Ysome is the key to the coming of Nulgrave. Once she works Grey Magic, Nulgrave will be free to sweep into the world."

"What? I don't understand. How do you know?"

"It came," said the horse-lion, "into my head, and seemed the right thing to say at the time."

"Are you sure this will work?" worried the Prince, draping the wet water-weed around his neck and trying not to scowl as it dripped inside his armour. The Water Theels had put a magic on it so that for a time he–and Gemant and the horse-lion, who were also wearing water-weed–would be invisible to the vengeful inhabitants of the fallen tower.

"Oh, yes. But only for a little while, so do hurry," said the Theels.

The horse-lion licked their pretty faces and patted them gently with a paw. The Prince had never seen it show affection before.

Once outside the cave, they struggled up the sides of the quarry. At the top the heath had been dreadfully churned up by the Honnerdrin trees. There seemed to be no one about among the rubble of the tower except two of the mauve horse-things with spikes that were called drumbils. They snarled and rolled their eyes at the sky, but didn't seem to see the Prince and his companions, which was no doubt just as well.

Soon the three were hurrying over the hilly heath.

"Will it be dawn soon?" asked the Prince.

"No. Why?"

"I thought I could see some light back there."

"The sun never rises on that side of the sky," said the horse-lion.

"Well it rises just about on every other side, then. And there *is* a light. Turn round and you'll see."

They turned and looked back. A kind of grey glow was curling up the sky behind them.

"That's where the Knight's hold was, isn't it?" asked Gemant.

"Lie down on the ground," said the horse-lion.

"On the ground?" said the Prince. "It's damp–and also it's very hard to get up again in this armour—"

He got no further. The horse-lion nudged him over and he fell with a rattle on the grass. Gemant went over next, and the lion jumped on top of them. The Prince had a sudden horrible thought that it might have decided to eat him, but then he stopped worrying about that. A huge howling wind came gushing over the heath, a wind that would have blown them all flat in any case if they had been standing up. The grass bent right over, and racing, black, tattered clouds swallowed the stars and moons. Things came blowing past–a few uprooted trees among them—and fell around them as the wind spluttered and died down as quickly as it had risen.

"What was it?" gasped the Prince. "Not–Nulgrave?"

"No," said the horse-lion.

"Then it was that Ysome and her Grey Magic I'll bet."

He sat up and looked behind him, but the glow had faded from the sky. There was an uneasy quiet.

"Let's get on then," said the Prince.

So, pretending to forget the grey glow and the wind and Nulgrave and all the rest of it, they got up and got on.

10

The Marsh

The Prince woke in time to see the real dawn. He was lying near the ashes of the fire Gemant had made the night before in a small valley, surrounded by gorse-jacketed hills. It was too chilly to sleep, but not for Gemant. The horse-lion wasn't there, but it tended to go off by itself in the morning, the Prince had noticed. The Prince lay on his back and watched the sugarpink sky and the lavender clouds wallowing in it like furry, disgruntled whales in a pink sea. There was a mist over the heath that made it difficult to tell where the sky ended and earth began, and suddenly a bright thing came glittering across the mist.

The Prince jumped to his feet. It was a silver chariot shaped like an open flower, being pulled over the sky by three silver horses with fiery wings. He remembered how he had seen one on his first night in this strange world, but he couldn't work out why he was so excited at seeing one again–unless it was because it looked so romantic and beautiful. And then the chariot dipped gracefully.

"They're going to land on the heath!" cried the Prince aloud.

Next second the horses had leapt forwards across the gold spokes of the rising sun and they and the chariot vanished in the mist.

The Prince scrambled up the side of the hill, stumbled over the gorse, aiming for the place where he thought they had come down. The mist was golden now and he couldn't see where he was going. He banged into a dead tree, and apologised, put his foot into a hole full of water, and finally got tangled in a bush. While he was getting out of this he saw a cool gleaming ahead of him, and heard a soft strange tinkling that would have scared him if it hadn't sounded so gentle.

The Prince swallowed and went towards the gleam.

The chariot had settled on the grass, the three horses rustling their flame-feathered wings slowly, and nodding their silver heads so that little drops of crystal on their bridles sparkled and tinkled. In the chariot stood a handsome man and a beautiful girl in curious rainbow clothes. They were very pale–almost transparent; his hair was a deep rich gold like the sun's rays, and hers a delicate lavender, the colour of the clouds.

The Prince's knees trembled and his mouth felt dry though he wasn't certain why because he wasn't afraid. He wanted to say something to the people in the chariot–the Sky People, the horse had called them–but he couldn't think of what to say.

And then the man shook the crystal-beaded reins, the horses lifted their flame-flower wings, and the chariot rose upwards, over the Prince's head, and was gone.

The Prince stared around him.

"But I didn't have time to ask—" he said. "I mean I wanted to say that—"

"What?" asked a big lion shouldering through the mist.

"It was them–the Sky people—" said the Prince.

"Oh," said the horse-lion, "they never talk."

"Where are you?" an anxious voice howled behind them. Gemant had woken up.

As they trudged on over the heath the Prince became irritable. The mist had lifted, but the air was damp and cold, and there seemed to be a funny sort of disturbance in it from time to time.

"Are you supposed to be going somewhere, Gemant?" he demanded abruptly.

"No," said Gemant. "I just thought I'd follow you."

The Prince stopped.

"We might just as well stay here then," said the Prince. "Or go back the way we came."

But as soon as he stopped he had that feeling again that he had to go on. So after a minute or so of grumbling he did.

"When Gemael and I were very small," Gemant said suddenly, "we were very close."

"What's that got to do with anything?"

"Well," said Gemant eagerly, "we always seemed to know when the other one was in trouble. I remember once I was playing with my pet Skook—"

"Your pet what?"

"Skook. And I—"

"What's a Skook?"

"Oh," Gemant seemed rather surprised the Prince didn't know. "It's a sort of round fluffy thing. All children have them; they play with you and teach you the alphabet and the eleventy times table–things like that. Well, as we were playing, I suddenly got a cold feeling just here—" he tapped the end of his nose, "and I thought: Gemael needs me!"

"Did she?" asked the Prince.

"Yes. She'd fallen into a pond. I rescued her," he added proudly.

The Prince thought Gemant seemed to have a thing about rescuing people. The annoying muzzy effect in the air started again just in front of him. The Prince rubbed his eyes. It seemed to be getting worse.

"And then there was the time," said Gemant, "that Gemael suddenly cried—I say, what's that?"

"What had she seen?" asked the Prince.

"No, I meant, I said 'what's that?' "

"What?"

"There," said Gemant.

They all stopped and looked at the muzziness.

"You know, it reminds me of the whirling that always happened just before Gemael appeared," said the Prince.

They stared at it expectantly, but after a moment or so it faded away.

"My nose feels cold," said Gemant worriedly. "It has all morning. I think Gemael's in danger and she's trying to appear here instead of wherever the danger is, and something's stopping her. What shall I do?"

"Think about something else?" suggested the Prince.

"But I'm worried—"

"Ssh!" interrupted the horse-lion.

They had just come over a little rise, and in front of them the land levelled out and became a dull wet green marsh with large areas of water glinting in the distance. Two perfectly ordinary-looking men in green jerkins were walking in the mud and reeds.

"Will they attack us?" asked the Prince promptly in a low voice.

"Probably not, unless you say something to upset them," said the horse-lion.

"Then why did you say 'Sssh!'?"

"You can never tell," said the horse-lion.

The two men had by now looked up and seen them. Instead of attacking they started to run away as fast as they could.

The Prince and Gemant walked over the rise, but the horse-lion became a horse first because it said it didn't like getting its paws wet. When they reached the nearest reed-bed ten green ducks flew up quacking, and fled away.

"Well, really," said the Prince. "We're not *that* frightening."

He could feel his feet sinking in the marsh and became nervous. He walked along staring at the ground and testing the mud before he stood on it, and so he wasn't aware of the *thing* until he banged right into it.

"I'm so sorry—Ah!" he yelled.

He had collided with a black wood pole, very slimy, and on top of it was a shiny green skull with long green hair.

After a minute or so he realised it wasn't real but a skull carved from a green stone, and the 'hair' was actually some lichen which was growing on it.

"Oh–ha!" he laughed hoarsely. He looked round and

saw Gemant and the horse had taken another path and were some distance away. "Hey! Come and look at this!" he cried.

Just then the green skull jaws parted and the skull said conversationally, "Whither goest thou?"

"What!" screamed the Prince.

"Whither goest thou?" obligingly repeated the skull.

The Prince backed away, slid on some mud and fell over.

"Dost seek the Mad Witch?" asked the skull kindly.

"Help!" shrieked the Prince.

"Her lair lies yonder," said the skull, and swung round to point to the right.

Gemant came charging through the reeds, trying to wield his axe, having forgotten he no longer had one. The horse came more slowly.

"It's only a witch-mast," said the horse.

"A w-witch what?"

"A witch generally puts one up near her lair so it can tell travellers how to find her."

The skull suddenly burst into maniacal laughter. "Oh, but she is a mad witch, by my troth!" it cackled.

The Prince got up angrily.

"Well, I don't want to know how to find her, thank you.

Gemant seized his arm.

"Perhaps she can help me rescue Gemael!"

"Perhaps she can't!"

"The Mad Witch doth know all. She will mayhap aid thee. Yonder lies her lair!"

Gemant hurried off the way the skull pointed at once. The horse leisurely followed Gemant.

Having no choice, the Prince stamped after them, feeling confused.

Soon there was a stretch of reed-fringed water, and in it lay a sort of island, very flat, with some odd-looking trees growing over it. There was another pole at the water's edge, but instead of a skull on it there was a round stone with strange signs carved into the surface.

"Well, that must be where her lair is, on that island," said the Prince. "And it's probably dangerous to swim out there–you never know what might be in the water!"

"I don't care," said Gemant stubbornly, "I've got to help Gemael."

And so saying he plunged in and promptly sank up to his waist.

"You can't swim in armour, anyway," said the Prince.

A weird noise came from the carved stone on the pole. Suddenly a narrow path appeared over the water, stretching from the shore to the island.

"It's a trick," said the Prince.

Gemant struggled up on to the path and began to hurry across.

"It must be like the tower again. He can't help himself."

The Prince got on to the path and followed, and the horse came daintily after him, shaking mud off its hooves. It took only a short while to reach the island.

The trees were twisted around each other and bowed together like a group of thin people with their arms linked, plotting something unpleasant. It was gloomy and green, and there were weeds which lashed out and stung them as they passed.

And then they had reached a kind of clearing, and at the other end of it was something that made even Gemant stop and wonder if he ought not to go away again rather fast.

11

The Mad Witch

A gigantic spider's web hung among the trees, the top of it lost in the top branches, the bottom brushing the ground, the sides of it stretching for several feet. There was a cold glitter all over it for it seemed to be spun of thin steel, and it shifted and whispered abrasively in the breeze. At the very centre of the net hung—

"What is it?" gasped Gemant. "It can't *be* a spider . . . can it?"

"Yes," said the Prince spitefully, "it could be and it probably is."

"It's a large oval thing, big enough to be a small house," said the horse. "Perhaps the Witch lives in it."

There came a scream of insane laughter from the oval thing, and then a sort of door was flung open in it. And there stood the Mad Witch in the middle of her steel web.

"Well, she's certainly mad," muttered the Prince. "She lives in a spider's web and she's dressed like a wasp."

The Witch heard him. She gave a shriek of joy or fury and jumped straight down from the web into the clearing, landing upright and with perfect balance. Her thin body was clad in a tight furry wasp dress of black with yellow stripes around it, and out of the dress poked incredibly long skinny arms and feet and neck, and a face that was all one long nose and one mad grin and two malicious black eyes. A cascade of fierce grey hair poured from the Witch's head to her feet, covered by a green lace veil made from weeds and secured in various places by the pincers of small green crabs. The Prince didn't think they were real at first but he soon noticed how they wriggled about and realised they were.

The Witch darted straight up to the Prince, poked him in the chest with a long forefinger and squawked, "I am the Mad Witch! I know all the hidden secrets of the world! What knowledge do you wish to beg from me? Eh? Eh?"

The Prince backed away.

"I don't want a thing," he said. "Ask *him*."

The Witch Promptly flew at Gemant.

"My sister is in deadly peril!" cried Gemant. "Please help me to save her."

"Nonsense!" screamed the Witch.

"But she is–truly–I've always known when she needed me—"

"Half a measure of eel's spit would do!" shrieked the Witch.

"She *is* mad," said the Prince.

"Silence, slave!" the Witch howled. "Or I shall sting you! Now. Sisters, sisters. How many do you have?"

"Only one–Gemael–and she—"

"Rubbish! Save her? Why?"

"She's very dear to me."

"I don't give my services for nothing," snapped the Witch. "What will you give me if I agree to help you? Bah!!"

Gemant seemed to have become used to the Witch's way of talking.

"Anything," he said.

The Witch pondered, a crafty gleam in her eyes.

"Then give me," she cried triumphantly, "the rose growing out of your forehead."

Gemant looked around him wildly, clutching at his brow.

"What shall I say?"

"Say 'yes,' " said the horse.

"Yes," said Gemant.

The Witch leaned forward, clasped the air in front of Gemant's eyes and tugged.

"Ow!" yelled Gemant in obvious pain.

"Got it!" screamed the Witch.

"I don't understand," said Gemant. "There wasn't any rose growing out of me, but it hurt when she pulled it off me–only she didn't."

"Now–nonsense!" cried the Witch, turning to the Prince. "What'll *you* give me? Eh?"

"*I*," said the Prince, "am not asking for anything, so I don't have to give *you* anything."

"You do, or I won't help your friend."

"What do you want?" asked the Prince incautiously.

"Your eyes!"

The Prince turned pale.

"Say," said the horse, "they don't work properly."

"They don't," said the Prince.

"Don't what?" demanded the Witch.

The Prince was trembling so much he could only say, "The horse told you—"

"Horses can't talk," shouted the witch.

"My eyes—don't work properly—" gasped the Prince.

"Ah!" The Witch seemed to accept this. "*Bah*! Wait!" She pointed at the Prince and made a circling motion with her finger.

> "Wrinkle skinkle twitcheth snout,
> Sniff and snuff and find it out!"

The Prince had a sudden horrible sensation as if a million small ants were running all over him, and then the Witch grinned very hard and said, "In your pocket is an Egg. *That's* what I want. Nonsense!"

The Prince looked at the horse.

"Now what shall I do? The Theel told me I mustn't let anyone else have it in case it hatched out and then they knew—" The Witch interrupted by leaping forward, grabbing the Egg out of his pocket and skipping back clutching it in her skinny hand.

The Prince ran after her and the witch spun round on one foot, pointed at him, and cried, "Zellezor-in-Parrapax!"

And the Prince found himself rooted to the spot, not able to move any part of himself except his eyes.

The Witch looked him over.

"Your eyes seem all right to me, young man. Two ounces of Rend-fangs at the double!! You!" She pointed at Gemant. "You will now toil for me for three days, after which I will work the spell to save your brother."

"Sister," nervously corrected Gemant.

"Blister," agreed the Witch.

"Couldn't you—do it first—only I think she may be in awful danger—"

"Very well," said the Witch surprisingly. "Where is she?"

Gemant explained as best he could between the witch's interruptions of "Brimstone!" and "Bah!"

The Witch gave a sudden great leap into the air, came down on her back on the ground, rolled her eyes and waved her arms, jumped up again, ran round in a circle three times and screamed several seemingly meaningless phrases.

" 'Tis done," she concluded, sounding rather like the green skull. "Thy sister shall be restored to thee in four days–when you've finished toiling. Until then she's in a safe in-between place and won't be hurt. And just in time," she added. Leaping into the air again, she wailed, "Nulgrave is come. Woe unto the Land of Sinners whom God hath forsook!"

The Prince, unable to move, blinked his eyes rapidly in fear. Nulgrave had *come!*

But the Witch didn't seem to care any more.

In a series of impossible bounds up to and down from her oval house in her steel spider's web she collected several peculiar objects and laid them at Gemant's feet.

"I expect hard work," she said, "or I'll reverse the spell on your blister."

The first thing the Witch wanted Gemant to do was nothing whatever to do with the objects she had brought. It was to chop down all the trees around the clearing, presumably to make it bigger. Gemant set to work with a will swinging the Witch's large axe (which he found hidden in a puddle) as he had done with his own when he was Champion of the Wood. However, his armour was rather a nuisance. Eventually the horse suggested that he say, "I don't want to *be* a champion, or fight, or rescue anyone," whereupon the armour fell off on to the ground.

The Prince felt rather angry because no one took any notice of him. He had a nagging worry they might forget him and leave him here for ever.

The shadows lengthened, and by sunset Gemant had felled all the nearest trees. The Witch came leaping down and said he could rest for the night. Gemant, who hadn't even paused for lunch, curled up by the horse and fell asleep at once. The Witch came up to the Prince, spun round on her foot the other way and said, "Pellepor-in-Zarrazax!"

The Prince found he could move again. He stretched and groaned and the Witch thrust a large jar at him.

"Don't think–Nonsense!–you're getting out of *your* toil. Take the jar and sprinkle the seeds in it round the clearing ten times."

The Prince didn't argue. He went round the clearing as she had told him, throwing out handfuls of seeds as he went. It seemed to take a long time and the jar never emptied. After the tenth circle he was only too glad to roll limply in his cloak on the other side of the horse and go to sleep as Gemant had done.

They were both woken early by the Witch who was dancing round the clearing and singing a mad song. Scattered about were the fallen trunks of the trees Gemant had cut down the day before, but the clearing was now ringed with an even thicker fuller growth of trees.

"It must have been those seeds," said the Prince.

"Awake! Ah!" cried the Witch. "Up, and cut down all the trees."

The Prince, who was thirsty, asked her for a glass of water. The Mad Witch snapped her fingers and produced one from the air. She then threw the water in the Prince's face.

"Better? Now. Here's a second axe. Off with you."

At noon the Prince insisted that he and Gemant rest, so they shared the last of Gemant's provisions and sat for ten minutes under a tree before the Witch leaped down and ordered them back to work.

As dusk fell the Prince and Gemant leaned wearily on their axes, having cut down all the new trees.

They slept soundly but dawn brought the Witch with two jars under her arm.

"Third day," she screeched in their ears. "Sprinkle this round the clearing forty times, then deal with what comes up."

The Prince and Gemant, sighing, got up and did so. It took until noon. They were expecting a new crop of trees to cut down, but at first nothing happened. Then suddenly all the fallen trunks bounced upright, twisted round each other and somehow joined together, and changed, slowly but horribly, into an enormous, long, greenish prickly snake-creature with a very large mouth full of thorns instead of teeth and a pair of leaf-green eyes.

There was nowhere to run because the snake-creature was all round the clearing where trees had been—and this meant all round them. It wriggled its 'neck' about and stared at them, blinking solemnly, and then pushed itself nearer until its huge face was resting on the ground a few inches from the Prince's feet.

"Heaven help us!" whispered Gemant. "It could swallow us whole."

"Try being friendly," said the horse.

"What? *How?*" demanded the Prince in a shaky voice.

"Pat it," said the horse.

Very, very nervously, the Prince sidled up to the gigantic prickly face, and patted its head. A fearsome growling immediately issued from the thorny jaws. The Prince yelled.

"It's only purring," said the horse.

The Prince patted again, and the noise got louder. He scratched about among the bristles, and the green, rather lovely eyes gazed up at him adoringly. The Prince's heart warmed to it, and he suddenly felt quite silly with relieved affection.

"You're a nice old thing, aren't you," he laughed. "Who's a nice old thing, then? Who is, then, is it you? Yes, of course it is, purr, purr. Who's a dear old prickly snakey?"

Encouraged, Gemant joined in, and the purring grew so loud they could hardly hear what they were saying to it.

After a while the tree-snake put out a delicate green tongue and panted gently.

"Perhaps it's thirsty," said Gemant.

"Well, it's no good asking that witch for any water. I wonder if the marsh water would be all right?"

Apparently it would, because the tree-snake became excited and licked him and wriggled about. So they guided it through the remaining trees to the edge of the island, where, with a delighted roar, it buried its head and golluped up a few gallons of liquid.

They passed the rest of the afternoon very pleasantly, sitting on the island's edge talking to the tree-snake and putting their tired feet in the cool water.

About sunset they heard the Witch shrieking for them and went back.

"Ah! Nonsense! You've done it!" she screamed, obviously pleased. "I've always wanted one of those. Bah!" She embraced the tree-snake, which wagged its tail and knocked Gemant over. "Right. Third day of toil finished. You can go. Rubbish!"

Gemant staggered as all his armour reloaded itself on to him.

"But my sister–where is she?"

"A quart of Stoat's bane, and stir it well!"

Gemant looked upset.

"You did say—"

"Brimstone! She'll turn up. Be off now! Or I'll reverse the spell! Nonsense!"

Gemant turned sadly away, but the Prince ventured, "About my Egg—"

"Eggs–pegs!"

"It's rather important—"

The Witch folded her skinny arms over her furry wasp dress.

"Zellezor—" she intoned slowly, "—In—"

The Prince fled.

Looking back a safe number of trees away, he saw the Mad Witch and the tree-snake chasing each other happily round the clearing to the accompaniment of thunderous purrs.

"Well, I'm glad someone's satisfied," he moaned.

14

The Kreeler

A copper-red dusk lay over the green of the marshes as they floundered through the reeds. Befor long they saw a village of strange round mud and stone houses built on a platform on stilts. A few men in green jerkins–just like those they had seen earlier—promptly ran out of sight, yelping in fear.

"Perhaps they think we're the Witch," said Gemant.

"We don't look a bit like the Witch," said the Prince thankfully.

He still hoped they might be able to stay the night at the village in the warm and dry, but a woman in a green kirtle appeared suddenly out of a house with a handful of sharp stones which she flung at the Prince.

"Be off!" she cried.

The stones clattered against his armour.

"We only wanted—"

"I know who you are–the Looked-for Deliverer–and I know there's a curse on you, and danger follows you like a hungry Skolk. We'll have none of that here. Take yourself away!"

And she threw a particularly nasty stone. The Prince ducked, and the stone hit Gemant's helm and knocked him over. The Prince, feeling guilty, went to help him up. When this was accomplished, the woman had vanished, obviously feeling she'd done all she could. And she had. They turned away into the red darkness and splashed through huge puddles the colour of bronze.

* * *

They spent a damp uncomfortable night by a smoking fire. The horse slept very well, but the Prince was too uneasy, and Gemant was too worried.

"If Nulgrave *has* come," said the Prince, "where is it?" He was hoping the Mad Witch had made a mistake. "And, if Ysome's out to be revenged on me–where is *she*?" He glanced round hastily, just in case. "Don't worry," he comforted Gemant, "Gemael will probably whirl in tomorrow. That witch may have been mad but her spells worked perfectly," he added with a shudder.

Towards morning they dozed.

The Prince woke about an hour after dawn to drizzle and a cold, salt-smelling wind. The horse was drinking from a pool nearby.

"I can smell salt," said the Prince.

"The marsh leads into the sea," said the horse.

"Which sea?"

"*The* sea. There's only one."

"Oh," said the Prince.

As they had no food, they didn't waste time on breakfast, and were soon moving on. Gemant looked very downcast.

"Do you know any more cheerful songs?" asked the Prince, hoping to make him feel better.

"Lots," said Gemant sadly.

After half an hour or so, the Prince suggested he sing one.

"I couldn't," said Gemant.

"That's that then," said the Prince, and himself broke into a song he said was called "Heave-Ho!", or "The Drunken Sailor", or something–he wasn't sure. He wasn't sure of the words, either, but it made a good deal of noise, which was what he felt they all needed.

The ground began to go up and down again, though it was still very wet. And then suddenly there was nothing ahead but some chalky boulders, a few reed-beds, and a long, cold, grey stretch of something the Prince had thought was part of the sky.

"The sea?" he asked.

Large grey clouds herded overhead and a wind was blowing up, pushing the waves against each other. To the left was a range of low cliffs over which the sun showed in a small bright circle.

Gemant took out a scarlet handkerchief and blew his nose.

"She had grey eyes," he faltered.

The Prince, scared Gemant would break down altogether, looked hastily round for something to distract him.

"Look at that rock on top of the nearest cliff," he cried. "It's shaped just like a gigantic man with a gigantic fishing net."

"It is," said the horse.

"Well, I just said it was."

"It *is* a gigantic man. And as he would look altogether silly holding a fishing net of ordinary dimensions, he holds instead a net of the correct proportions, which is therefore similarly gigantic."

The Prince, who hadn't understood a word of this, turned round and found it wasn't the horse who had spoken. *His* horse was being a lion, and frisking in among the wavelets despite what it had said about not liking wet paws. The newcomer was also a horse, and also white, but it had gills and little fins as well, and instead of back legs a pearly fish tail. It had swum up in the pool behind him, and was now lying elegantly on a reed-bed.

"I might add," added the new horse, "that he is altogether a repulsive creature, and what he is doing is quite repulsive. He catches sea-maidens in his net, *and* sea-horses if he can, but, being less stupid than the sea-maidens, we generally extricate ourselves in time. He is known as the Kreeler."

Again the Prince felt he hadn't really understood properly. The horse–sea-horse?–seemed to have an odd way of talking. But it also looked rather impressive, so the Prince said, "Thank you."

"Do not mention it," said the sea-horse. "One is pleased to be helpful."

But Gemant was roused to action.

"Do you mean to say that monster up there *catches* mermaids in his net? What does he do with them?"

"One does not like to think," said the sea-horse. "Certainly, they are never seen again."

The change in Gemant was quite astounding.

"Oh for my axe!" he cried. "Or a sword! Nay! I'll tackle him with my bare hands."

"Don't be daft," said the Prince.

Gemant was already plunging up the marshy shore, shaking his fist.

"What a courageous young man," remarked the seahorse. "He must be the Looked-for Deliverer."

"Thank you," said the Prince again, though rather angrily this time. He ran after Gemant shouting, "Come back!" and "Help, horse!"

The lion looked up from the waves, and trotted in a leisurely way after him.

As they got nearer to the cliff, the Prince was able to see the giant more clearly, not that he wanted to. He had thought Vultikan the Hoiler was enormous, but he had only been about nine feet high. *This* creature was much bigger than that. It seemed to be dressed in black clothes, and black hair flittered round its head in the wind like a flight of Oggrings. The long net was stretched from cliff to sea, and dipped into it, for here the water seemed very deep.

Gemant ran to the rocks that formed the base of the cliff and began to climb them, intending to arrive at the top behind the Kreeler. He made a frightful din, but the Kreeler was probably too large to hear it.

Eventually Gemant reached his goal and lay panting on the cliff among some boulders. The Prince dragged himself up beside him.

"Now what do you think you can do?" he demanded. "Look at the size of him."

The lion joined them, and sat washing its paws.

"I'll think of something," said Gemant deperately.

The Kreeler gave a yell. The cliff shook from the noise.

"He's caught something," said the Prince in horrified interest. "Look, he's started to haul the net up."

Sickly, they watched the great arms hauling, and then the net, dripping water and seaweed, appeared over the cliff-top. A huge wicker basket lay a few feet away from their hiding place among the boulders. The Kreeler now turned with the net in one brawny hand, and leaned towards the basket. The Prince nearly screamed in terror as the gigantic dark evil face came looming over him, its little red eyes winking with pleasure. The giant flipped up the wicker basket lid, emptied the net into it, and pulled the lid down again. Then, with a chuckle, the Kreeler took up his former position on the cliff edge, lowered the net again, and sat waiting for a new catch.

Gemant was up in a moment, straining to lift the wicker basket lid. The Prince and the lion pushed at the other two sides. Unwillingly, the lid lifted a fraction. They gave a thrust, and the lid flew up, poised for a moment deciding which way to fall, then flopped on to its back with a crash. The Prince waited in fear for the Kreeler to turn round but he didn't. The Prince thought he must be deaf as well as evil.

They scrambled up the wicker sides and peered into the depths of the basket, and there in the darkness was a green and blue struggling mass, weeping and shrieking to itself.

"Be quiet!" yelled the Prince into it, no longer bothering about the deaf giant. "We've come to help you."

The noise died away a little, and pale arms and fins waved at them and voices cried piteously, "Save us!"

They arranged that the lion should dig its claws into the wicker to anchor itself, and hold Gemant by his scarlet sash as he leaned down into the basket. He would then grab the mermaids one by one and the Prince and the lion would haul them all up. This they did. On the whole the mermaids were very good, and only started to cry again when they were out. There were ten of them in all, their skins various pretty shades of green, blue and violet, with tails and hair to match.

"We didn't realise it was a net," they sobbed. "It only looked like seaweed, boo—hoo!"

The Prince and Gemant comforted them and helped them into the boulders where they could hide.

"We'll have to carry them down the cliff and back to the sea," said the Prince, wishing their tails weren't so heavy. "And what about *him?* He'll catch a whole lot more in a minute."

At that moment there was an angry cry from the depths of the basket.

"What about *me?*"

"We've missed one!" cried Gemant.

They ran back and stared down.

"I can't see anything–she ought to be green or blue, and glittery like the others. Wait–there's something red—"

"Of course there is," snapped the cross voice. "It's me, you stupid creature."

The Prince scowled.

"I think I know who *that* is," he said slowly. "It's your sister Gemael."

Gemant gave a cry of joy, reached into the basket, and pulled Gemael up in his arms without any help, he was so pleased.

Gemael didn't seem surprised to see Gemant. She gave him a brisk hug, took out a pocket comb and began to tidy her long black hair. Then from the same pocket she took the gold beetles the Prince remembered and began to clip them on to the strands with efficient crisp little snaps.

"I've had an awful time getting here," she said. "All that trouble and then getting stuck somewhere for simply ages and then whirling through and landing in the sea, *and* in a net with a lot of screaming mermaids."

Gemant tried to persuade her to come into the boulders and hide in case the Kreeler turned round, but instead Gemael jumped down from the basket, and ran straight up to him.

Appalled, Gemant and the Prince watched the tiny red figure standing behind the giant.

"You should be ashamed of yourself," she was yelling at

him. A whirling appeared in the air beside her, and out of it she snatched a sword of white metal with rubies in the hilt.

"That's just like that silly sword she gave me to fight the Dragon of Brass with," said the Prince, dazed.

Gemael seized it with both hands, and threw it at the Kreeler.

With a terrific yell he leaped up–it probably felt like a wasp sting–and, losing his balance, fell over the cliff and down into the deep grey sea. Not that it would have seemed so deep to him, and the Prince waited anxiously for him to reappear. But he didn't. After a time the huge waves he had caused died down.

"Well," said Gemael, marching back along the cliff, "that's the end of *him*."

"How brave you were," said Gemant fondly.

"Ever since," said Gemael, "I had to help that stupid Prince deal with that Dragon I haven't been scared of a thing."

The Prince bristled. Gemael hadn't noticed him, and he was just going to stride up to her and say, "Oh, yes?" when she added more gently, "Though he *was* special, even if he was stupid. I don't know why."

"He's the Looked-for Deliverer," said Gemant.

"Oh, that must be the reason then," said Gemael. "Somehow I haven't stopped thinking about him since I whirled away and left him in the courtyard at the Castle of Bone. I wonder where he is?"

"Here," said the Prince.

Gemael gave a little jump, and then blushed. When this happened the Prince suddenly thought how lovely she was even though she was so cross and unreasonable, and how glad he was she had arrived at last, even though she would probably be very bossy and an awful nuisance. Then she stopped blushing, stamped her foot and growled at him, "It's rude to listen to what people are saying when they don't know you are."

And the Prince decided she wasn't lovely at all, and he wasn't glad she was there.

But Gemant was in high spirits.

"First we must take the mermaids back to the sea, and then we must have a party. Gemael, you'll say a spell for some food, won't you?"

At which the Prince decided he *was* glad she was there after all.

13

By the Sea

By the time they had carried all the mermaids down and found a dry piece of shore, the stars were coming out in the pale indigo sky. At least it had stopped raining.

Gemael muttered magic words and out of the air whirled a scarlet pavilion with an open front facing the sea, a beautiful warm fire, chairs, and a table with a damask cloth covered with steaming dishes of delicious food and gold jugs of wine. The Prince was rather impressed.

The mermaids and several sea-horses sat at the waves' edge and arranged some brightly coloured luminous fish just under the water to give extra light. They joined in the feast, and neighed and giggled and splashed because of the wine, and sang strange sea-songs about sunken ships and coral castles. Altogether it was a very happy party.

When the oval moon rose, Gemant turned to Gemael.

"You never did tell us, though, why you wanted to follow us. Were you bored with being the Lady of the Waste?"

Gamael frowned.

"It is a gruesome tale," said she.

Gemant and the mermaids looked very interested. The Prince pretended he wasn't.

Gemael began in her best gruesome-tale-teller's voice.

"When the Castle of Bone had fallen, and the Looked-for Deliverer had gone on his way to the mountains, Ysome's Skolks wandered in the Waste howling, and I was very glad. The days passed, as they had always done. But there was a sense of waiting and of disaster to come. And then—" Gemael paused dramatically, "—four nights before this night–there came a terrible humming from the sky and from the mountains. A grey glow shone beyond the peaks, and then there was the sound of a great rending–and–*It* came!!!"

"What?" cried the terrified mermaids and the disturbed Gemant.

Gemael, who had gone rather white, whispered, "*Nulgrave*."

The mermaids sank back in terror, and the luminous fish dimmed.

The Prince thought Gemael was overacting, and had probably imagined it anyway, and he was annoyed because it had been such a good party until she had frightened everyone.

"However," went on Gemael, recovering herself, "I scorned to stay in the Waste and perish. I willed myself to the side of Gemant my brother in the oak wood–and it was very difficult because of the power of—of—what had come. But I did it. I, to whom magic is an open book–and then you weren't there," she added accusingly. Gemant began to apologise, but Gemael, ignoring him, went on, "Then I simply tried to will myself to wherever you might be, but it was hard, and the–*power*– was creeping over the mountains, and I thought I should be no more. And in the midst of my trials I found myself in a No-Place–that is a place that is neither in this world, nor out of it. It was dark and silent, and strange winds blew. There I sat for longer than I knew, in despair. And then I found I could whirl again, and broke through into the daylight–and into the net of the Kreeler!"

The mermaids and the sea-horses applauded at this point because Gemael had got rid of the Kreeler.

"The Mad Witch put you into the No-place," said Gemant, and explained how they had toiled for her so that she would help Gemael. Gemael didn't seem grateful, only rather annoyed she hadn't been able to whirl through on her own. Gemant also told her of Ysome's part in the story–Gemael glared and clenched her small fists at the very mention of Ysome's name–and spoke of the Grey Magic.

"Yes. She would. No wonder *It* broke through."

"Just what is Grey Magic?" asked the Prince.

"You really *don't* know anything, do you?" said Gemael rudely. "All of us who learn spells know *how* to work Grey Magic. It's the magic you call up when you stop wanting ever to do anything for anyone else–because you care only for yourself and what you can get for yourself, and it helps you. But in its way Grey Magic is a part of—of—the thing that came into the Waste, and so no one with any sense would ever *dream* of using it. But, of course, Ysome would. And, as *Nulgrave* was near and wanting to come into the world, Grey Magic turned the key and opened the door to it."

"And what *is* Nulgrave?" asked the Prince, feeling he was asking for the nine-hundredth time.

"I don't know," said Gemael simply.

The Prince would have liked to be sarcastic, but he felt altogether too anxious and scared. He got up and paced about.

"If you ask me, it's all ridiculous," he said angrily. "After all, look at it. I arrive here–not knowing who I am or where I come from. Gemael appears and tells me to go to the Castle of Bone and gives me a sword to fight the Dragon of Brass. Why? Because she wants to upset Ysome. I destroy the Dragon with Gemael's sword, the castle falls, and Ysome goes off and gets captured by the Purple Knight and then makes friends with him and lives in his tower. Then Gemant wants to rescue her, and we arrive, and because of us–of me–the Honnerdrin wood comes and stamps until the tower falls. Ysome is furious, and works Grey Magic to get even with me. Because of Grey Magic, Nul—well, the *Thing* gets into the world. Now, I'm supposed to be the Looked-for Deliverer who's going to deliver everybody from the *Thing*. And it's *because* of me, in a way, that *It's* come."

There was a miserable silence, which was abruptly broken by a most terrifying bang in the distance.

Everyone jumped up in alarm.

"What is it? Where was it?" they cried.

And then, up over the line of cliffs, sprang a lurid yellow glare, as if a huge unhealthy fire were burning there. Other explosions followed the first, and a weird metallic grinding like rusty wheels.

The mermaids and sea-horses and fish dived into the water and swam down deep to hide.

Gradually the light and the noises faded.

But as they stared into the dark where they had been, a fourth moon rose into the sky.

"Horse," said the Prince, "you said there were only three moons, and none of them was round."

"There are," said the horse-lion, "and none of them is."

"Now," said the Prince, "there's a fourth moon, and it *is* round."

It hung in the sky, distant but troubling. And the Prince's heart throbbed heavily because he knew—as he had known about the Castle of Bone, the mountains, the Knight's tower and the sea—he *had* to go on towards that frightful new moon and the place under it where the light and the bangs had been. He didn't want to go, would do anything not to have to. . . . And yet he did have to go. And that was that.

They spent an uneasy night. In the grey dawn, the Prince rose and started to walk up the shore alone, though rather noisily. After a minute there was a yell, and Gemant came running after him.

"Where are you going?"

"I've got to go—up there, where there was all that noise last night. I don't think you ought to come. You've got Gemael to worry about now."

"Oh, Gemael's very brave. I'd never forgive myself if I didn't go with you. After all, you are the Looked-fo—"

"Yes, yes. But—oh, well," said the Prince, who was glad they were going to come because it seemed less scaring if you didn't have to face danger on your own. The horse also appeared, looking like a horse.

"You have to take me, anyway," it said. "You're supposed to ride on me. Get up."

Then Gemael came and began to arrange everyone.

She said a spell for two coal-black horses for Gemant and herself–they had trappings of scarlet and gold–and a magic sword for Gemant.

"Be careful," the Prince warned him. "It won't cut through a thing."

"Oh, you don't cut with them," said Gemant, "you throw them."

"And then you're left with no sword."

"Oh, no, if you need them again they come straight back."

Soon they were galloping bravely up the stony beach and riding along the cliff. The ground was bare and rocky, but the day was warmer than before, and below, the sea was bluish mauve and very bright.

It seemed to be a long journey. At noon they rested and Gemael said a spell for lunch. While they were eating a shadow fell over the table. They looked up and saw a huge bird wheeling high in the sky on silent wings.

"Is it watching us?" asked Gemant.

The bird circled and dropped lower. And lower still. It had a wicked hooked red beak and black cruel eyes. Gemael stood up and said some magic at it. The bird gave a ghastly cry, but, instead of vanishing or just flapping off, it dived suddenly at the Prince, seized a strand of his hair and pulled it out. It then flew off with its prize, making hideous, pleased noises.

The Prince was fed up–he'd only taken his helm off a moment before.

"Perhaps it wanted it for its nest," said Gemant, but the Prince was certain the bird had had other, nastier reasons.

On that particular evening, the sun decided to sink behind them–in the same place it had risen. They found themselves riding through a skeletal wood of dead trees, and beyond the wood, the land stretched downwards to a bay. The tide had drawn out from this bay, the water like blood in the sunset, and the wet sand stretched out to an island of rock thrust up from the sea. On the island was an incredible yet familiar sight.

"The Castle of Bone!" cried the Prince, but he was wrong.

It wasn't simply a castle, it was a whole city this time that seemed to be built entirely of the bones of colossal ancient monsters–bone towers and ribcage walls and vertebrae palisades, skull palaces and dinosaur-pelvis stairs. If the Prince had been in any doubt–which he wasn't–the saffron flags flapping over the roofs and the black things flapping round the flags would have told him that Ysome was here.

"How did she—?" he began.

"With Grey Magic, she could do almost anything," said Gemael. "Even put a new moon into the sky."

She pointed, and they gazed upwards. There, floating over the City of Bone was the round white moon they had seen the night before. And it was indeed the strangest moon of all the strange moons, because it was a big white clock face with gold numbers round it and a pair of ornate black hands.

"What time does it say?" whispered Gemant.

"Seven o'clock," said the horse. "Which is quite correct."

And as the hands touched seven, the clock moon struck seven times with a thin cold chime.

14

Clock Moon

There was nothing the Prince would have liked better than to say, "Let's wait until morning." Hadn't Gemael, after all, once said that Ysome's power was greater by night? And he knew perfectly well that Ysome–somehow understanding that he would come this way (or had she even magicked him into coming this way?)–was waiting for him and plotting revenge. Perhaps even the feeling he had that he *must* get into the city was Ysome's magic, but he felt it wasn't.

"We must go across now," he said. "The tide's bound to be as silly as everything else here, and so goodness knows when it'll go out far enough again for us to reach the island. I say 'us'," he added nervously, "but really–I don't want to–but I ought to go alone."

"Not without me to ride," said the horse. "It would look wrong."

"I'll fight beside you to the death!" said Gemant.

Gemael glanced at the Prince scornfully.

"On your own? Don't be stupid. You'd only make a mess of everything as usual."

The Prince got annoyed, and feeling less terrified because he was annoyed, he urged the horse out across the sand.

He reached the rock first, and rode up it. He came to a huge gate that seemed to be made out of pointed teeth, and realised he already didn't know what to do.

Gemael rode past him and pointed at the door.

"Jewelstar! Fly open bars!" she cried.

The Prince started. He suddenly remembered how the armies had cried "Jewelstar!" in the cup-picture the Theel had shown him.

"What's Jewelstar?" he asked her.

"Never mind," said Gemael. She obviously didn't know either.

The doors shuddered, and slid open a yard or so.

"Now!" cried Gemael.

They rode through, and the doors struggled out of the spell, closed again and relocked themselves, shutting the Prince and his companions into the city.

The streets of the city seemed deserted, and none of the palaces had any lamps in them. Thick darkness was falling, and soon the only light came from the great clock moon hanging overhead. They dismounted.

"Where now?" asked Gemant.

"I don't know. I—" the Prince broke off, listening. "Quick!"

They fled into a shadowy doormouth, and only just in time. Twenty large figures in iron armour and brass helmets came marching up the street, and turned out to be Beezles. They looked neither left nor right, but they carried burning torches, and axes. The Prince had an unpleasant feeling that they might be looking for something. However, they went past without stopping, and round a corner. When the heavy footfalls had died away they ventured out again.

"I think," said the Prince, "I have to go this way."

He set off up the street, the others close behind.

They moved on for a long while, once or twice seeing bands of marching Beezles, but always managing to hide in time. The Prince wished he knew where he was going. Finally they went up some steps, through a door, and he knew they were there. It was a circular room with many windows that looked out over the city. The Prince peered from each, and stared all round. Thunder sounded in the distance.

"I know it's here–but where is it, whatever it is?"

"Look up," said the horse.

They all did. Instead of a roof, the room was open to the sky, except where it was crossed over by four metal chains joined together in the middle. And from the middle a fifth chain of brass, each link as large as a cartwheel, started up into the night towards the spot where the clock moon hovered.

"The moon is anchored to the city by that chain," said the horse.

"Really?" said the Prince. "But why is that—"

There was an interruption, a distant noise that seemed to be coming closer and sounded like the baying of Skolks.

"Outside," cried the Prince, "or we'll be trapped in here."

They ran out, and down the steps. Overhead the clock moon struck eight, and suddenly a thousand lights appeared in the city, burning out of every palace window, every arch and doorway, blinding them. From each end of the street came pouring a horde of armoured Beezles with torches, and over the roofs and walls came packs of snuffling slavering Skolks, and a flapping fog of Oggrings.

"Surprise! Surprise!' screamed countless spiteful voices.

Before he could even draw his sword the Prince was grabbed by strong relentless arms, and saw Gemant and Gemael also grabbed. They were then borne away up the brightly-lit streets.

The Prince didn't remember much of that journey. It was all a horrible blur of being dragged and prodded, of Skolks nipping at him whenever they got the chance–which was often–and Oggrings beating round his head.

Eventually he was pulled up an ornate staircase and through doors of gold and brass into an enormous hall with bone pillars, and blazing with fierce yellow light. Golden cobweb draperies hung from the walls and the chandeliers were set with golden glow-worms. At the far end of the hall on a golden throne sat Ysome the Saffron in yellow silk and ermine, with a tall crown on her fair hair, guarded by twenty skeletons in gold armour leaning on brass axes.

Ysome waved a gracious hand.

"Welcome to my City of Clock Moon, sir Prince. I've been expecting you. One of my watch birds brought me this," she held up the piece of hair the bird had pulled out earlier in the day, "so I knew you were on your way. Do make yourself comfortable. You may throw him down here," she added.

And the Prince found himself thrown at her feet. He was bound hand and foot and hadn't even noticed before. Of Gemael and Gemant there was no sign.

"Where are my friends?" croaked the Prince, "and my horse?"

"In one of my nicest dungeons," said Ysome, sweetly. "And now, dear Prince, I expect you'd like to know what's in store for you."

"No," said the Prince.

"I'm really very grateful to you." said Ysome. "You gave me the idea of working Grey Magic. I can't think why I never did before. And so, as a reward, I'm going to let you meet an old friend."

The skeletons chuckled and the Prince's blood ran cold.

Ysome rose, came down the steps and, once the Beezles had hauled the Prince to his feet and unbound him, took his arm in a friendly way. The Prince shuddered.

"Dear me, are you cold? Never mind, a little exercise is very warming."

In this manner they went out of the hall and up more stairs, the guards giving the Prince an occasional prod and punch to help him on his way. He wondered wildly if he could seize Ysome and hold his sword to her throat and so escape while the skeletons and Beezles were too afraid for her safety to attack him. But his sword seemed to have gone, and, anyway, he had a feeling that if he did she would say some sort of spell at him that would turn him into stone or something like that.

Then they emerged into the open on to a bone walk lit by flaring torches. The walk surrounded a huge courtyard below that somehow looked familiar.

"You may choose a weapon," said Ysome.

"Why?"

"I like to see things done fairly. Now. Sword, axe or spear?"

"I'd like my own sword back," said the Prince, trying not to panic.

"Ah, no," Ysome tinkled. "That was the sword Vultikan the Hoiler made you, and we all know *that* can cut through anything. It will have to be an ordinary sword, I'm afraid. And remember, the foolish Lady of the Waste won't be able to help you now."

A Skolk ran up with a sword in its mouth. Ysome patted it, took the sword and held it out to the Prince. Even in his terror, he could see it was very blunt.

"I've changed my mind, I'd like an axe—"

"Oh, much too late. Only one choice, my dear. Down to the courtyard!"

About fifty Oggrings whizzed at the Prince, seized various bits of his clothing and of him in their teeth, and flew him down to the court, where they dropped him with a bump.

The Prince picked himself up. Thunder sounded very near, and a bright grey lightning flared overhead. His visor fell down over his face.

And then came a sound the Prince remembered only too well.

"It can't be. I shorted it," he wailed to himself, staring at the great widening black crack in the far wall. "And Vultikan wouldn't mend it, so it *can't* be—" but he remembered Ysome had worked Grey Magic, and with this power could do almost anything. Rusty smoke filled the court, and there came again the grinding of metal cogs. The wall opened wide, and through it, the light spilling on its brazen flanks, empty eyes burning, nostrils steaming, came the Dragon of Brass. It was just as terrible as he recalled, only now it seemed bigger, stronger, and, as it opened its appalling hinged jaws, he saw the metal mesh across its throat. No one would be able to throw a sword down into it this time.

The Prince backed away, and the Dragon came plodding after him, its joints screeching.

The Prince ran at the Dragon and hit it with the sword, which immediately snapped off at the hilt. Cheers came from the wall.

The Prince ran back.

"Perhaps if I could hit one of its eyes—?" He judged, balanced the hilt and threw it. It missed, glanced off the Dragon's crest and fell out of sight in the shadows. "It's useless," thought the Prince, near to tears of fright, anger and despair. "Oh, I'm sorry, Gemant and Gemael and horse and everyone. But it'll all be over in a few minutes, and there's nothing I can do."

And he stopped running away and stood quite still, and stared at the Dragon defiantly.

"Go on, then, do your worst. And I hope I choke you.

The Dragon, however, instead of coming on at him, suddenly stopped, and reared up its head at the sky. In the silence the Prince heard for the first time a horrible, thin, high-pitched hum. It seemed to come from above, and yet he felt it all around him. Confusion broke out on the wall. Skolks howled mournfully and Oggrings sank down in heaps. Ysome began to call out spells that apparently didn't work.

And then there was a noise–a sound like tearing paper except that it was much louder–and the sky was as bright as day.

"*Nulgrave!*" whispered the Prince.

For a moment he stood still, not knowing what to do. Then he realised that the Dragon seemed to be frozen to the spot, its head still craning at the sky, and that in the confusion on the wall no one was taking any notice of him. A shuddering ran through the ground, and he heard a tower fall somewhere in the City of Bone. He thought of Gemael and Gemant and the horse in the dungeons, and he ran past the Dragon, through the open wall and down a dark corridor.

Turning a corner he found a frightened skeleton.

"Which way to the dungeons?" cried the Prince.

The skeleton pointed with a trembling fingerbone.

Down and down ran the Prince until he found himself in a gloomy hall. At the hall's centre was an open well in the floor. As he peered into it, a voice said, "We're all here." It was the horse. "We're in a net," it went on, "and there's a rope attached to a pulley in the corner. If you turn the handle it will wind up the rope and lift us out."

The Prince ran to look for the pulley and collided with it. He got up again, turned the handle frantically, and panted, because it was hard work. Finally the heads of three horses and Gemael and Gemant appeared over the top of the well. They scrambled out.

"I would have thought you could have said a spell or something," puffed the Prince to Gemael.

"No magic would work now," said Gemael. "*It*'s here."

The ground shook under their feet. Thunder sounded, and again the tearing noise came, louder than at first.

"What next?" asked the Prince.

A silence fell. There seemed to be nowhere else to run to.

"I suggest—" said the horse.

"Yes? Yes?"

"We climb the brass chain to the clock moon."

Immediately they flew from the dungeon hall, up stairs, through doors, out into the streets, following the horse, who seemed to remember the way back. As they ran it occurred to the Prince what a silly idea it was that they climb the brass chain of the clock. In any case, where could it lead to apart from the open sky? But any idea was as good as another in this dreadful mess of a world.

"Here we are!" cried Gemant.

They had managed to get on to the edge of the open roof where the five chains were joined together. The Prince stared back over the city. Many palaces had fallen, but the sky was dark again overhead. A sort of fog seemed to be creeping towards them, and the Prince didn't like the look of it.

"Well, for a start," said the Prince, "how are the horses going to climb the chain?"

"They're magic horses," said Gemael. "They can do all sorts of things."

"I'll go first," said Gemant, "in case there's–anything–at the top."

He began to scale the chain as if it were a ladder, and the two black horses followed him, managing amazingly well with their hooves.

"You go next," said the Prince to Gemael, who looked pale and terrified.

"Oh, I'm not afraid," said she, scurrying after the horses.

The white horse turned into a lion and leaped after her, and the Prince went last. He wasn't sure how this had happened, nor that he really wanted to go last. Looking back as they climbed he saw a black swirling smoke coiling round tower after tower, and wondered if something were on fire.

It was very silent then except for the scrape of hooves and feet and claws on the brass chain of the clock.

15

The Palace in the Clouds

To the Prince it seemed they had been climbing for hours. The ground, which was now a long way below, was completely in darkness; not a light showed. They, on the other hand, were climbing up into the bright white glare of the clock moon which loomed enormously above them. The Prince squinted at it, and suddenly saw to his horror that the hands were just about to touch nine o'clock. The chime had sounded loud from the ground. Now they were so close to it, they would be deafened.

He looked wildly around him for escape. There wasn't one.

"Horse!" he cried, but in that moment the first stroke came. The Prince felt sure it was striking in his head, it was so loud and awful. He lost all sense of where he was, clapped his hands over his ears, and next second was falling downwards into the darkness.

"Help!" he tried to scream.

Then the next stroke sounded and blotted out even fear with its noise.

All around was soft stuff that felt rather like several furry quilts piled on top of each other. The Prince sat up and stared about him. It was dark, but with tufts of pale-blue light everywhere that the Prince didn't understand.

"Help?" he asked.

Had he fallen into Clock Moon and been killed? He

only remembered hearing two strokes of the frightful clock, and then—

A heaving and ruffing began to happen in the tufts in front of him. Suddenly something shoved its way through. Thinking it might be a monster of some sort–it usually had been up to now–the Prince jumped up and tried to draw his sword. While he was remembering he no longer had one he discovered that the thing in the hole was a pale face with black hair round it.

"Gemael!" he cried. "Wherever are we? What happened?"

Gemael floundered the rest of the way through the fluffy stuff which separated them.

"We all fell off the clock chain," she said unhappily. "The noise was so awful and the chain shook so. And now–I think we fell into a cloud."

"What? All of us?"

"No," Gemael wailed. "I don't know where Gemant is, or the horses. I couldn't find you for ages." And she burst into tears.

The Prince wasn't certain if she were crying over not being able to find him or because she *had* found him. Deciding it was the first, he put his arm round her.

"There, there," he said, and became quite fond of her, since comforting her took his mind off his own worries.

As they sat on the fluffy stuff, however, he had a feeling that the cloud, if it *was* a cloud, was moving. And then, not long after he had felt this, the cloud seemed to stop still.

"I wonder where we are now?" he asked.

Gemael dried her eyes and began to comb her hair.

"You should go out and see," she said sternly. "Here's a magic sword," and she produced one from the air.

The Prince took the sword and, filled with misgivings, tugged away at the wall of the cloud until he had made a sizeable gap. He peered out and saw only limitless blackness.

"I think, wherever we are, we ought to wait until it gets light," he told Gemael. But Gemael had fallen fast asleep. The Prince, very relieved, pulled the cloud together again, and lay down to do the same. The last thing he heard as the cloud-warmth lulled him into dreams was a distant tinkling sound.

He woke up because it was dawn, and somehow he seemed to be in the centre of it. Opening his eyes he saw that the cloud was no longer dark, but amber, pink and gold. He pulled open the sides of it again, and what was outside was so lovely he couldn't possibly be afraid.

They were in the sky, and the sky was golden streaked with silver thread like a tapestry. In front and away stretched a floor of clouds that were bronze, lilac and emerald, with pools of rose-red fire in them that must have been reflections of the sun. In the far distance stood up cloud-shapes like mountains, all soft purple, and on these stood the sun itself. And of all the amazing things the sun was the most amazing, for it was simply enormous and must be very near. It blazed like a diamond doughnut, but was no more bright than it had seemed from the ground, and gave only a pleasant warmth. The Prince was astonished. This close, he thought, it should have scorched them all up. But then, this silly sun wasn't a bit like the sun where *he* came from–wherever that was. You couldn't get anywhere near *his* sun.

He found Gemael was standing beside him.

"We're in the Cloud Lands," she said, "where the Sky People come from."

"Is that good?" asked the Prince.

Gemael stepped past him and out of the cloud. Although her feet seemed to sink a little way into the coloured mist, she didn't fall through. The Prince joined her. It was like walking in feathers.

"Look!" cried Gemael.

The Prince swung round in fright, clutching the magic sword. Behind the cloud, which was now lifting and drifting away, was an empty silver chariot drawn by two silver horses. They nodded at the Prince, and the crystals chinked on their bridles.

"We're meant to get in," said Gemael, and did so.

The Prince followed her, rather more slowly, and next minute the horses were leap-flying along about six feet above the clouds, flapping their fiery wings.

"Where are they taking us?" worried the Prince.

Neither Gemael nor the silver horses answered. They seemed to be making towards the purple mountains. Then they went down over a little dip into a lagoon of soft flame, and in the near distance stood an incredible building that looked as if it were made of green ice. As they got nearer there was a break in the cloud below, and pale sky showed through. The Prince thought the sky was rather like a moat of water around the green building, which seemed to be a palace of some sort. Sure enough, just then, a rainbow appeared over the sky-moat–a drawbridge. As they crossed it, the Prince peered down, but could see nothing of the ground, only some cloudlets swimming about like fish. And then they were off the rainbow, through a sparkling green arch, and into a vast hall with an open roof. The horses stopped.

The Prince felt embarrassed, because the hall was full of people who all seemed to be looking at him. Every so often a cloud would drift through the hall and out of the open roof, and partly because of this the Prince found it hard to see these people properly. Another thing was that they were all rather transparent like the two he had found in the chariot on the heath, and they were all very beautiful. Their long cloudy hair was every colour the clouds could be, and their rainbow clothes confused him, and they were extremely quiet. He recalled that the horse had said they never talked, and wondered if they would all stand there for ever, gazing at him and not saying anything.

But just as he was starting to go hot and cold, a man and a woman came through the cloud drifts up to the chariot. His hair was red like a sunset, hers apple green. They smiled at the Prince.

"You are very welcome," they murmured as one.

"The horse said you never talked," blurted the Prince.

"The horse often tells lies," said the woman, laughing. "Hadn't you noticed?"

"Well, now you come to mention it," said the Prince.

Just then he caught sight of a lion nodding modest agreement behind the chariot. Gemant and the two black horses were embracing Gemael.

"We fell into *another* cloud," Gemant was explaining.

The Prince got down from the chariot, and the red-haired man and apple-haired woman each took one of his arms. This made the Prince feel very happy, he wasn't certain why.

"We have much to tell you," said the man gently, "and we must be swift, because there isn't much time. My name is Themon."

"But first you must be hungry and thirsty," added the woman. "And my name is Themistra."

"You don't happen to know *my* name?" said the Prince.

"You are the Looked-for Deliverer."

"I was afraid I was."

They took him to a beautiful green-ice balcony which overlooked the cloud mountains. The cloud colours were changing all the time as the sun rolled slowly by overhead, and now everything was gold and blue and peach. The Prince sipped something that looked like mist out of a crystal goblet. It tasted delicious and satisfied both hunger and thirst. He wasn't sure where Gemant, Gemael and the horses were, but he knew they would be all right with the Sky People.

"You see," Themon said to him after a while, as if continuing an earlier conversation, "the laws of our world are quite different from those of the world you come from. They probably seem to make no sense to you at all."

"They don't," admitted the Prince.

"And that is the very reason," said Themon, "why only someone from another world could save us from the threat of Nulgrave. Although many things seem baffling and silly to you, certain dangers which would overcome someone who didn't think them baffling cannot harm *you* in the end."

"They still frighten me," said the Prince.

"That's different, and doesn't matter at all."

"For many thousands of years," went on Themistra, pouring the Prince more mist, "Nulgrave has waited around the borders of our world, ready to pounce. As time went by, resistance to Nulgrave grew weaker, and finally it only needed Grey Magic to open the door. But we have always known One would come who could fight Nulgrave, and win, as none of our world could. You are that One. The way you have already got the better of the Bezzles, Ysome, the Dragon of Brass, the Honnerdrin, the Purple Knight, the Mad Witch, the chiming clock moon–show that you are He."

"But I didn't–I mean, half the time it was some crazy mistake or accident, or someone else did something—not me."

"That is not the point," said Themon. "It was your *influence*— because you were *there*– that things went the way they should."

"Oh," said the Prince. He thought a moment. "Where is Nulgrave now?" he asked in a small voice.

Themon led him to the rail of the balcony and they looked down into the sky-moat. Themon murmured some strange words, and there was a sort of swirling below. Suddenly the clear brightness was gone. The Prince found he was staring down at the earth far beneath. But he couldn't see it very well. Here and there the top of a tower or a tall tree poked out, but mostly everything was smothered by a dark coiling *something*– like a poisonous fog. The Prince turned away and Themon said the spell to shield the sky again.

"Is it all–covered by–*that?*" asked the Prince.

"Yes. And soon, unless it is stopped, Nulgrave will rise to the Cloud Lands and there will be darkness everywhere."

"But what can *I* do?" cried the Prince in familiar panic.

"You can lead us all against it. Teach us how to fight it."

"But I don't even know what it is–it looks like smoke to me, how do you fight that?"

"Ah," said Themon, "I'd forgotten that you don't understand yet what Nulgrave *is*."

"Do *you?*" gasped the Prince.

"Do you remember times," said Themistra, "when you were truly unhappy? When nothing you could think of to do, nowhere you could think of to go, were worth it: when nothing could cheer you, and everything seemed quite useless and pointless, when each day was miserable and the next day was the same? Then you would simply sit and be sad, and it seemed you could never be anything *but* sad. Well, that is what Nulgrave is–only worse, far worse. Nulgrave is Despair."

"And if anyone from our world is enclosed by Tarshish, they become despairing and their lives waste away until they die," added Themon.

"Then I don't see what I can do!" almost shouted the Prince.

"You don't belong to our world," said Themon, smiling. "To you Tarshish will be a black smoke, an unpleasant prickly cold. You will fear it, yes. But it won't make you *feel* any different from the way you have always felt. You *won't* despair. And because of that you can help others to fight, for that is the only way to drive Nulgrave out–to *fight* it with happiness, to *fight* it by not caring about it or what it can do."

Themon took the Prince's left hand, Themistra took his right. They led him from the balcony into another great hall, and here waited rank upon rank of shining men and women mounted on silver horses.

"We are the first part of your army," said Themon.

A thousand glittering swords flashed in the air, and multi-hued banners fluttered. Suddenly the Prince felt warm and relaxed. A lump came into his throat, but he cleared it and cried out, "Jewelstar forever!"

And the shout echoed back to him from the Sky people, strong and unafraid.

The Prince looked at Themistra and asked very low, "What's Jewelstar?"

"Joy," said Themistra, and laughed joyfully.

16

The Battle against Darkness

Down the sky they whirled!

It was exciting and strange. They passed a huge, dim, pale shape, which was the square moon without its night-light on, and several crystal castles floated by on apricot clouds. The Prince was delighted that they had somehow given his horse a pair of fiery wings so that it too could flap through the air like all the others.

But the delight soon faded. It got dull and dark, and there below lay the black smoke clouds which were Nulgrave.

The Prince swallowed nervously.

"Courage, horse!" he cried.

"I'm not bothered," said the horse. "I've been with you so long I doubt if I shall despair either."

Themon and Themistra rode to the Prince's side in their chariot, and the horse slowed.

"We can go no further for the present," said Themon.

"What? But I thought you were coming with me."

"We shall–but we can't face Nulgrave until you have gone down first and exerted your influence over it." The Prince scowled, but Themistra leaned out and handed him a beautiful silver trumpet. "Sound this, and we shall come to fight the battle with you."

"Thank you," said the Prince, feeling they had led him up the garden path rather. "Well . . . I'll see you later then. If I make it, that is."

Themon and Themistra beamed at him, and so did

Gemant and Gemael, who were also showing no signs of following. The Prince glared at them all, and told the horse to carry on down.

"Well, I like that." He grumbled, "They all said they'd stick by me to the end and all that, and then they just leave me to it."

"Oh," said the horse, "they'll come after you, but if they came now Nulgrave would overwhelm them."

"It may overwhelm me," muttered the Prince.

And then the darkness seemed to rise to meet them, black vapour swirled round them, and they were into the heart of the evil thing.

The Prince looked round in horror, but, before he could decide if he was despairing or not, some of the stuff went down the wrong way and he had a coughing fit, sneezed a couple of times, blew his nose and cursed energetically. After which he realised he wasn't despairing, and, although it was rather cold and foggy and he couldn't see very well, he was neither miserable nor scared. Just then they collided with the top branches of a dead tree. The horse's fiery wings set it alight, and the next moment they were bumping on to the ground.

The Prince picked himself up.

"Are you all right, horse?"

The horse turned into a lion and clawed twigs out of its mane.

"Yes," said the horse-lion. "I couldn't make out where we were going. And the tree did something to the wings and they vanished. However, the blazing wood gives quite enough light to see now, doesn't it?"

The horse didn't sound despairing either. Encouraged, the Prince peered ahead of him, and it seemed to him that the darkness was not so thick around them as it was everywhere else.

"Ho!!!" something roared through the fog.

The Prince yelled in fear, and realised he shouldn't have because the something bawled back, "I'm a-coming! Keep shouting, I'll find you."

"Help," said the Prince, "let's run!"

But it was too late. A large shape was striding towards them, howling out, "I see you!"

In the light of the burning tree the Prince discovered a tall, muscular giant with red, ragged hair, yellow eyes, and a bag of tools over his shoulder.

"Vultikan!"

"Who else?" bellowed Vultikan. He leaned down to the Prince and held out a gleaming sword with a dragon hilt. "Left this in the enchantress's bone city. Vultikan makes you a sword, and then you leave it behind," he added disgustedly.

"How did you know where it was?" asked the Prince. "And how did you know where *I* was?"

"Still asking his daft questions," Vultikan remarked to the horse-lion.

"He still doesn't properly understand," said the horse.

"I'd better tell him then. You can hold off Nulgrave," said Vultikan scathingly, "so everyone is going to sense where you are by the *feel* of the place. They'll all be here soon."

"Who will?" asked the Prince uneasily.

"Everyone." Vultikan sat on a boulder. "Hung on to your armour," he congratulated.

The tree-fire was dying down, and the Prince was now certain that the darkness was drawing off from him, though it was just as thick a few yards away.

Vultikan broke alarmingly into song.

"Haven't felt like singing since Nulgrave came," he said after the third verse of something about hoiling and boiling and the mountain life, "but now you're back, well—"

"Er," said the Prince, trying to stop him from breaking out again, "who did you say was coming?"

Vultikan, however, had begun once more and wouldn't stop. He accompanied himself by banging his hammer on the boulder, and altogether he made a lot of noise. At least he seemed quite happy.

Suddenly the Prince's visor fell down with a crash. This always seemed to happen before some sort of fight or disaster, and the Prince became worried. The lion turned into a horse and said, "Get up on me now. It will look better."

The Prince started to argue, but then he realised he might be able to get away faster on the horse if anything dreadful occurred, so he mounted. Vultikan stopped singing, and in the quiet the Prince heard an alarming babble that seemed to be coming from below and yet was apparently getting closer by the second. It sounded like people crying and people shouting, and horses neighing and dogs barking and wheels grinding and bits of metal clanking. After a time the Prince could make out torches, smudged together by the fog into a dirty orange mist, crawling across some sort of valley beneath, and then up a slope that ran towards him.

It took about twenty minutes for the first people in the procession to reach him, but after that they arrived thick and fast. They were all sorts and shapes and sizes, wearing all kinds of strange clothes and weird armour, or what they thought might do for armour, such as iron buckets on their heads and silver dinner plates strapped over their chests. Some rode in wagons, some on horses, some walked. Most of them looked dreadfully miserable and were complaining or crying. Despite what Vultikan had said, and also the fact that they seemed to be dressed up for some sort of battle, they didn't appear to know why they'd come. They stood around, and a droning, mournful noise rose up from them like a thick cloud of wasps. It got darker.

"What shall I do with them?" muttered the Prince.

The horse pretended not to hear.

The Prince rode forward, and up and down the front of the crowd.

"I'm—er—the Looked-for Deliverer," he ventured.

They stared at him listlessly, all very pale, and too sad even to cry now.

"Nulgrave isn't so bad here," said the Prince jollily.

Some of them were almost transparent, like ghosts. The torches were fluttering out in their limp hands. He saw a woman in a green kirtle, and she looked like the one on the marsh who had thrown stones at him.

"Hallo again!" he cried cheerfully.

She gazed at him and heaved a melancholy sigh.

Just then there was an awful noise behind them. It was actually Vultikan sighing too. As if at a signal, the horse reared up in fright and the Prince rolled off its back. Falling with the usual crash and clatter, he didn't hear at first the titter which ran among the crowd. But as he struggled up he could see people at the front passing the word back about what had happened.

"I'm glad you think it's funny," said the Prince. "Well, I'm not doing it again just to make *you* laugh." At which he fell over a root. Roars of laughter. Scowling, the Prince got up once more. However, he was glad they looked more normal, and the darkness had drawn off again.

"Right!" he cried, "well, there's only one way to fight Nulgrave–and that's to be happy and occupied, so—er—Horse—?"

This time the horse had something to say.

"Party games," it said.

It really wasn't how the Prince had seen it at all. He'd thought it might be noble and dignified when you delivered people, but it wasn't. It meant groups yowling out songs and dancing ring-a-ring-a-roses, running races, having quizzes and asking each other totally silly-sounding questions (the Prince thought), and telling jokes. He considered it was all quite awful, but it certainly cheered them up, and it got lighter. In fact he could now see they were on some bunched-up hills, though the fog still circled round them about half a mile away on every side. They also built a bonfire, which kept everyone busy finding sticks, although Vultikan had done something to it so it couldn't go out unless he said so. Luckily there were some witches among the crowd who provided regular meals.

Three days passed in the hills, and all the while more people poured in. The Prince recognised the Purple Knight, looking sheepish with a group of Beezles riding on

Drumbils, who all swore to follow the Prince to the death, which he didn't believe, and other things he didn't believe either. There were knights too he hadn't met, but who looked as if they'd have behaved just like the Purple Knight. Buzzles arrived and Bezzles–squeaking and looking spiteful but scared–and even some things with eight legs which the horse said were Bizzles. As each band of travellers came in they told of others they'd passed on the road, and the Prince heard with some alarm that they had seen a great oak wood marching in the distance.

"Perhaps they won't get here," he consoled himself. And they didn't.

On the fourth day it seemed as if everyone who was going to arrive had done so. There were tents everywhere, and lots of mad games and noise.

"What happens now?" the Prince asked the horse.

"Post a look-out in that tree over there," said the horse.

"Why?"

"Because," said the horse.

The Prince did not want to send someone up the tree to be look-out because they would want to know what they were looking out for and he couldn't tell them, so he climbed up himself. It was a tall tree, and from the top he could see right out across the camp, over the hills, into the black fog that was Nulgrave. And something very odd was happening to Nulgrave. It was jetting up in great gusts, and cold little fires were jumping about in it. Soon he began to hear a thin, high-pitched hum. Down below, the people in the camp were making too much row with their quizzes and races to hear it. The Prince craned forward and almost fell out of the tree. Suddenly all the black smoke ran together and upwards into a towering, pitch-coloured pillar several miles high. Then it seemed to coil round and round itself like a furious snake, gushed over the backs of the hills–and was gone.

"Jewelstar!" screamed the Prince, half scrambling, half falling down the tree trunk. "It's gone, it's run away–I never knew it would be so easy–all this talk about fighting, and this silly armour—"

He slid the last foot or so and landed on the horse's back.

"You don't understand," said the horse.

The Prince looked round, and saw that all the games and noise had stopped. Everyone looked very stern and purposeful, and they were buckling on extra dinner plates.

"Nulgrave hasn't run off," said the horse. "It's drawn all its strength together in one place. There's a large valley over there, and that's where it will be. Waiting for us."

"But can't we just–er–leave it there?"

"No," said the horse. "This is the last fight. Either It or we will perish."

"I see," said the Prince.

"So blow the silver trumpet Themistra gave you."

At first the Prince couldn't find it. Then he couldn't blow it. It felt like trying to blow up a balloon, which he had never been any good at either. In the end, Vultikan blew it, and the Prince went deaf in the left ear for ten minutes.

There was a sound of wings overhead, and out of the pale blue sky came flying the army of the Cloud Lands and Themon and Themistra in their chariot. The horses landed in a rainbow fire-blaze on the hills, and up galloped two black stallions with Gemael and Gemant. Gemant clasped the Prince's hand.

"I say, so good to see you again."

"What?" asked the Prince.

Gemant spoke in his right ear.

"This is it, then."

"Apparently," said the Prince, as if it were nothing to do with him.

"Now a witch must cast the runes."

"What? What have prunes got to do with it?"

Gemael leaned over and tapped the Prince's ear in an irritated way, after which the Prince found he could hear again.

"It's always done before a battle," said Gemant, "to make sure of victory."

The Prince didn't understand–he still thought Gemant

had said something about prunes. But Gemael went up on to a little hillock where everyone could see her. She raised her arms and looked very impressive in all her scarlet, with her long black hair blowing in the wind.

"By Earth, by Air—" she began, and was promptly interrupted by a flash of green light. Out of the light jumped a thin figure with long thin arms, a wasp dress, a tide of fierce grey hair and a malicious grin.

"I am the Mad Witch!" it cried with glee, waving its staff which had a jade-green skull for a knob. "I've come to cast the runes! Ha! Nonsense!"

"I was here first," said Gemael with dignity.

"Rubbish," said the Witch, and obviously meant it.

"I—" began Gemael haughtily.

The Witch spun round on one foot in a gesture the Prince remembered too well. "Zellezor-in-Parrapax!" she yelled.

Poor Gemael made no further interruption as the Witch screamed her way through a lot of chants, pointing East, West, North and South, occasionally crying "Nonsense!" and jumping in the air. When she finally stopped there was some polite applause.

"You'd better go and thank her," said Gemant. "And ask her to turn Gemael back, would you?" he added in a troubled voice.

Uneasily the Prince dismounted and walked up on to the hillock.

"Oh, it's you!" cried the Witch.

"Thanks for casting the prunes," said the Prince vaguely, looking round to see just where she'd cast them in case he trod on one, "and will you undo the spell on Gemael?'

"No. Stuck-up baggage! Do her good. Bah!" The Witch approached unpleasantly near and poked the Prince in the chest with a skinny finger. "I've got some news for you."

"What?"

"That Egg of yours I took—"

"The Egg—My secret—" cried the Prince, thinking she might be going to return it to him.

"Gone!" screamed the Witch delightedly.

"Gone where?"

"The Honnerdrin," said the witch, and hugged herself and grinned as if this explained everything.

"What do you mean?"

Themon came up beside the Prince.

"I'm afraid," he said, "the Witch has given the Egg to a marsh-snake to play with. Didn't you, Mad Witch?"

The Witch screamed with laughter and nodded violently several times.

"Only it wasn't a snake—it was a Honnerdrin in disguise."

"So now the Honnerdrin have got my secret—and they're my sworn enemies!"

Themon looked very serious.

"Not only that, I'm sorry to say. We watched all these things from the sky, and the last we saw of the Honnerdrin was the great oak wood marching into the very maw of Nulgrave, offering your Egg as a token of friendship if Nulgrave would spare them. It won't, of course, but it may use the Honnerdrin while it needs them. And the Egg."

The Prince felt frightened, and then furious. Despite her magic, he turned and glared at the Witch and took a menacing step towards her. At which the Witch shrieked, "Myself begone!" There was a green flash again, and no Witch.

"What am I going to *do?*" wailed the Prince. Then he folded his arms and said sternly, "I shall pretend it didn't happen. Horse!" The horse came up and the Prince remounted. The Prince raised his arm. "Jewelstar!" he roared.

At once the army roared back, "Jewelstar!"

The Prince felt better.

"Form up behind me," he cried, "and I shall lead you all into battle."

Everyone began to rush around and shout and get jumbled up. While they were doing this, the Prince leaned over and kissed the frozen Gemael gently on her cheek.

He wasn't sure why he did. It just seemed the right thing to do.

"Don't worry, Gemael," he said. "The worst's happened, so things can only get better now. If I come back from the battle I'll release you from the spell somehow or other, I promise. If I don't come back and we lose–well. It won't really matter for very long if you're under a spell or not."

He looked away and blew his nose, and then noticed that the army was in place behind him.

"Forward!" cried the Prince. "And godspeed!"

"Jewelstar forever! Jewelstar undaunted!" shouted the armies.

"Right," said the Prince. "Come on, then, horse."

And the next second they were galloping, galloping, galloping over the hunch-backed hills, across the narrow ravines, towards the Valley of the Shadow where Nulgrave lay in wait.

In the bowl of the valley the dark thing rolled like ink.

It was like jumping forward down the steps into an old cellar–dark, cold, with no light anywhere except from the door behind you, and then the door slams shut, and there is no light at all. Thick, black, icy horror all around. A cry of terror went up from the army as they were flung down into it.

"Jewelstar!!!!" yelled the Prince, and the word seemed to give him unexpected strength.

He stared down at the horse and its eyes and nostrils were wide and red with fury as it dashed on. The Prince drew his sword and slashed left and right, not knowing if it did any good.

And then abruptly there was a kind of dim glow ahead, and in the glow stood up a mile-high solid wall that seemed to be made of stone. The army broke up in panic, veering left and right. But the Prince heard a faint, far-off rustling, like leaves, and he guessed.

"It's not real!" he cried out, "it's the Honnerdrin. Traitors!" he yelled and rode straight at the wall, wheeling his sword round and round his head, and stabbing into the stone, which groaned and fell apart and for a moment looked like trees, and then vanished. "Death to the traitors!" yelled the Prince. A battle-madness came on him so that he felt happy and strong and saw very little except a red mist in front of his eyes. Things loomed out of the mist and the blackness–giants, ogres, monsters with wings and teeth and lashing tails–and he cut them all down one after the other, not knowing if they were real, or the Honnerdrin, or part of Nulgrave itself. And the army, given great courage by the Prince's cries and brave actions, rushed after him and did as well as he did. Gemant slew seven fiends with live coals for eyes, who crashed down under his sword and became fallen oaks. The Purple Knight put paid to a dragon of flame which went out like a candle under his blade. Beezles and Bezzles and Buzzles lashed around them, Bizzles stamped, Drumbils reared and tore with their teeth, and Vultikan wielded his great hammer like an axe and felled twenty monsters in a neat row. There were even Skolks leaping on things, and Oggrings flapping at things, but there were no Theels, who were, as the horse had once remarked, "incapable of harming another".

The noise was incredible and frightful, and the blackness seemed all broken up in pieces.

And then the joy and anger faded out of the Prince, and he realised it was very quiet.

"That's odd," he said aloud, wondering if he had gone deaf again, but he hadn't. He found he was standing quite on his own–the horse had disappeared–and there wasn't a sound to be heard, not even a distant neigh or shout. The Prince felt nervous. He looked around him, and he was in a ghastly, ghostly oak wood, where all the trees were half transparent. It wasn't black, there was a sort of murky, iron-coloured light, shot through with lightning flickers. The Prince shivered. "I musn't be afraid," he said to himself. "That's what it wants." So he started to whistle, but the whistling sounded eerie in the silence so he stopped. "Anyone in?" enquired the Prince, managing not to sound too scared. He started to saunter up an avenue of trees, hoping he might find a way out and back to the others. And then a voice came into his head, a sickening, dull, inhuman voice, and, although it didn't speak words, the Prince understood exactly what it said.

"You are finished. Despair. Despair and weep."

"No thank you," said the Prince, gritting his teeth.

"Despair and weep. Weep and die."

"Hasn't anyone told you," said the Prince, shaking from head to foot, "that I come from another world? You don't upset *me* out here in the back of beyond."

"You are afraid."

"Not really. I often tremble like this–it means I'm bored."

"You are afraid."

"Well, even if I were–which I'm not–I'm not in despair." And this was very true. He felt the dark thing recoil slightly, as if it understood. And then a small figure came running between the trees holding up something in one hand. The Prince felt relieved for a moment, and then he saw what it was. It was a thin, brown child with long, acorn-coloured hair and greenish-yellow eyes, regarding the Prince with an amused sneer, and grasping an egg.

The child halted a few feet away, and casually tossed the egg–which was *the* Egg–from hand to hand.

"Destroy the Egg."

The Prince jumped. He was horrified. If the Egg were destroyed he would never know who he really was—

"More than that," whispered the voice in his mind, *"if the Egg is destroyed before it hatches out–you will cease to exist."*

The Prince jumped again.

"A mere Honnerdrin couldn't break the shell," he muttered. "The Theel said it couldn't be broken until it was ready to hatch."

"It is about to hatch. It will be easy to crack and ruin."

The Prince stared at the Honnerdrin child, and the child said slowly, "I warned you Nulgrave was coming."

He realised it was the same child he and Gemant had seen by the ditch when the oak wood chased them on the heath.

In its hands the Egg seemed to move.

"*Destroy the Egg. Destroy it.*"

The Honnerdrin child suddenly grinned.

"Honnerdrin," it said, "don't like obeying *anyone*. *Catch*!" And then it flung the Egg to the Prince.

With a yell the Prince leaped forward, grabbed at the Egg, dropped it, caught it again, and ended up on the ground clutching it in both hands. A great black wave came sweeping across the trees and the child vanished into it, but a bright crackling was coming from the Egg. Bits of shell burst out in all directions. A blue light glowed in the Prince's hands, took on for a moment the shape of a bird, and flew straight up at the Prince, and through his helm into his brain. The Prince gave a cry of pure joy. He leapt up and laughed.

"Well, that fixes *you*," he yelled at the darkness, "because now I know who I am, where I came from and what I'm doing here. And I know that I'll win. There isn't any reason why I should. I just *shall*!"

Then came an explosion the like of which the Prince hoped he would never hear again. A thousand colours flared around him, the earth shook, rocks cracked to pieces and a gale-force wind swept everything away.

When the Prince opened his eyes again, the valley was being washed with warm clear afternoon light, and every blade of grass was edged with gold. Not a trace of anything dark remained, but then he'd known it would be gone, gone far away, back to the no-place it had come from. All around, people and animals were milling and laughing, throwing bucket helmets in the air. Many oak trees lay toppled on the ground, the rest had apparently fled. Only one sapling stood a few feet away, the sapling that had belonged to the Honnerdrin child. The Prince looked up at it, and it was lifeless and withered, killed as the child had been when it had rebelled against Nulgrave. Even so, there was a curious look about it–as if it had had the last laugh against them all, and was still somehow laughing.

The Prince put his hand on the thin trunk, and swore a promise, occasionally wiping his eyes.

17

The Secret

It was twilight before the Prince could get away from the Victory Feast.

Eventually he slipped out in the middle of the one hundred and third toast, mounted the horse, and rode away up the hills to the place where Vultikan's bonfire still burned. It was a fine clear night, and stars were coming out, and every so often a silver flower-chariot would gallop by overhead, full of people singing sweet, strange, joyful songs.

Up on the hillock stood Gemael the Red, just as they had had to leave her. Her eyes darted at the Prince.

"We won," said he. "Didn't we, horse?"

"Naturally," said the horse.

The Prince got down and went up the hillock. When he was in front of Gemael he spun round the other way on his foot and said, "Pellepor-in-Zarrazax."

Gemael gave a small scream, waved her arms and ran up and hugged him.

"However did you do it? I thought only the Witch could make it work."

"I expect it's because I'm the Looked-for Deliverer," said the Prince. "Or there may be some even sillier reason. You know what it's like here."

The three moons rose together over the hills.

"They don't usually come all at once," said the horse.

"Perhaps they're celebrating too," said the Prince.

He sat himself and Gemael on the hillside while the

horse changed into a lion and went to roll in some ferns.

"I know who I am now," said the Prince.

"Yes. I guessed you did. So I suppose you'll be going back to–wherever it is. Where is it, actually?"

"It's a place with one moon and a very hot sun, with lots of buildings, and roads with things that run up and down on them and are called cars and buses. Everything there makes sense, and it's rather boring."

"How did you get here?" asked Gemael. "And *who* are you?"

"No one special," he said. "Certainly not a prince. I was very poor and very old, and had nothing and no one. As to how I got here. Well." The Prince smiled. "I remember the first thing I thought of in the Waste was an acorn."

"An *acorn*?"

"Yes. And no wonder. I was sheltering from the rain under an oak tree–not a Honnerdrin tree, there's nothing like that where *I* come from–and an acorn fell on my head from a great height. I expect you know that if something small falls a long way it becomes very dangerous when it hits you. And it was *very* dangerous. I'm afraid that that acorn finished me off in my world, so I *can't* go back, even if I wanted to. Which I don't," he added. "Something pushed me right out of one world into another. And this world is a challenge. Look at all the bare ground and the dead trees and the wastes. Someone needs to plant things and build things–besides, I promised a friend I'd do my best. We'll have to give it a name. How about Threemoon?"

"Threemoon," echoed Gemael disapprovingly.

"And it really is the back of beyond," smiled the Prince wistfully, "and in a way we *are* on its back, aren't we? Its stone bones show through a lot, and it hasn't much fur, though the horse is rolling in some now–fern fur."

Gemael clicked her tongue, so the Prince said quickly, "Tell me, Gemael, if I built you a palace, would you come and live with me in it, and be Lady of that instead of Lady of the Waste?"

Gemael had never been one for not speaking her mind.

"Yes," she said promptly. "A very good idea."

They stared up at the daisy-white stars and down at the horse-lion rolling on its back below them.

"Tell us a story, horse," said the Prince dreamily.

"Once upon a time—" began the horse.

The Prince interrupted, "Sorry. I forgot. You can't talk, can you?"

In the middle of the night Gemant the Red felt a terrible urge to ride off over the hills of Threemoon. He buckled on his magic sword, jumped on his coal-black horse, and did so.

As dawn was breaking he came to a barren rocky place. On a rock a large, evil-looking bird, with black eyes, was preening itself with a hooked red beak.

"Oh, er—" said Gemant, feeling he'd seen the bird somewhere before.

"She's in there," said the bird, jerking one wing at a small cave nearby. "If you want her."

Gemant got off the horse and went into the cave.

A beautiful girl, with long fair hair and a ragged yellow dress, was sitting in one corner. At her feet crouched a black furry thing with a tail, which Gemant recognised as a Bozzle, and a grey snaky thing with two heads, which was a Bazzle.

"Sir Knight," whispered the beautiful girl, "I throw myself on your mercy."

The Bozzle and the Bazzle leered at each other.

Gemant squared his shoulders.

"I'll look after you, Ysome," he said firmly, "as long as you do as you're told."

"Yes, Gemant," said Ysome the Saffron meekly, and put her hand in his.

"Out!" roared Gemant to the Bozzle and the Bazzle, and they fled. "Off with you!" shouted Gemant at the evil-looking bird, which flapped up into the sky along with three or four Oggrings that had been hanging around hopefully on the rocks.

Gemant mounted Ysome before him on his horse, and

rode with her back towards the Victory Camp. They only stopped once, shortly after Ysome had started to practise spells and mutter about bone castles and dragons, and then it wasn't for long. Just long enough, in fact, for Gemant to bellow her into astonished total silence.